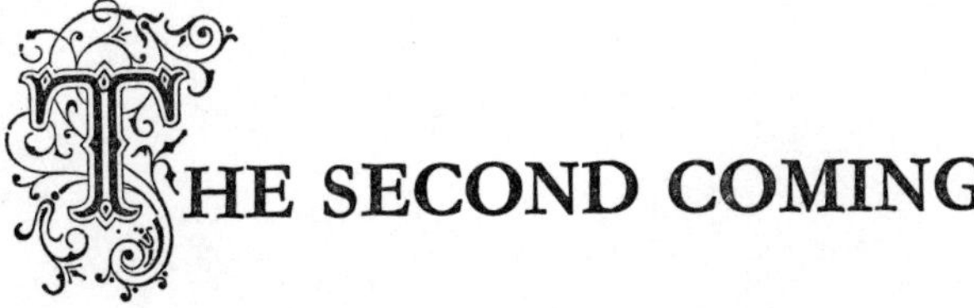THE SECOND COMING

The Second Coming is about revelation and revolution. It shows in marvellous detail, through Yesha—the hero of this novel—the complex and intrigue-filled life of Jesus. Transfigured from the legendary Christ of ecclesiastical piety into a living man, an evolutionary mystic, Jesus is caught up in a powerful wave of religious politics which eventually pushes him to sacrifice himself on the cross . . . the reality of a new myth. It is this reality as the myth-making structure that is the real substance of this book.

W. H. ALLEN . LONDON & NEW YORK

A division of Howard & Wyndham Ltd

1972

Printed in Great Britain by
The Anchor Press, Ltd., Tiptree, Essex,
for the publishers W. H. Allen & Co. Ltd,
43 Essex Street, London WC2R 3JG

Bound at Tiptree by
Wm. Brendon & Son Ltd

ISBN 0 491 00693 4

The Second Coming

Reginae Coelesti

Turning and turning in the widening gyre
The falcon cannot hear the falconer;
Things fall apart; the centre cannot hold;
Mere anarchy is loosed upon the world,
The blood-dimmed tide is loosed, and everywhere
The ceremony of innocence is drowned;
The best lack all conviction, while the worst
Are full of passionate intensity.

Surely some revelation is at hand;
Surely the Second Coming is at hand.
The Second Coming! Hardly are those words out
When a vast image out of *Spiritus Mundi*
Troubles my sight: somewhere in sands of the desert
A shape with lion body and the head of a man,
A gaze blank and pitiless as the sun,
Is moving its slow thighs, while all about it
Reel shadows of the indignant desert birds.
The darkness drops again; but now I know
That twenty centuries of stony sleep
Were vexed to nightmare by a rocking cradle,
And what rough beast, its hour come round at last,
Slouches towards Bethlehem to be born?

The Second Coming,
W. B. Yeats.

*Reprinted by kind permissoon of M. B, Yeats, Macmillan & Co.
Ltd, and Macmillan of Canada*

PROLOGUE

High in the wilderness, in the hills of white dust and sheer black ravines, was the place Yesha chose for the battle. From a distance his naked body, covered in the fine powder of millions of years, appeared to shine like a crystal monolith, radiating a light of its own, as though focussing the meridian sun into its own refractions, reflecting itself to itself, containing its radiations from spreading through the heavy hot waves of shimmering air.

Yesha had been away from the camp for a long time. Too many days for the others not to worry that he had been eaten by wild beasts, or led by the hyena with one eye who enchanted men to leave their secret vigils and follow him to the circle of scavengers who would pick apart his bones. However, the day was too hot; and the hyenas were elsewhere, sleeping in shady chasms, biting fleas and bickering with each other. They would be hunting again when the evening was cool and light was fading.

A battle. Yesha's eyes are wild and frightening but they do not see the days passing, the nights passing. The crags and colours of the desert are invisible. The brightness comes when God is in him and around him. Then Yesha falls to the ground on his mountain table altar. Then he is humbled; and the mountains themselves, the plains are gone. He is seared in the funeral pyre of light. He melts. He has no body. He is the body and the glory, and the sheer glory is too much. There is nothing very pleasant about too much glory; there is nothing more painful. This is not the scented gardens of eternity. No ripe fruits in orchards or green meadows just so or terraced vineyards are in this heaven. That is the heaven of the land . . . the land . . . the land . . .

Points of dark fray the edges around him. There is relief in this since the light does not flee but implodes, swallows itself into his body. He breathes the light in through his nose and mouth. He breathes; it breathes him. Then the demons come. Shapes in the spirit of himself and his life confound him, parade in armies, array themselves in purples and golds. They have distilled the splendour of terror and dropped it into his soul. There are countless ranks of them, numbers beyond numbers; they speak in him and he speaks to them though his lips do not move and there are no words. Glorious demons, glorious pain.

'What you feel,' says one voice, a very old voice, 'is to our glory as a drop of water to the great sea.'

The body of Yesha vomits.

'Why try to impress me?' asks the body's spirit. 'Here I am. Take me. Kill me. You can do as you please. I know this.'

'You are already dead,' they say.

'I am me, and that's that!' Yesha declares.

The laughter of all demons, a deep chuckle echoes through spirals of centuries.

'Take your life and join us.'

'If you want me—take me. I cannot take my life.'

'Give it—of your own free will.'

'It is not mine to give. I am helpless, as you see. Cut me from the body if you will.'

'Why not give?'

'Me is sacred.'

'Come, come.'

'Me is sacred.'

'You are mere vomit on the face of the earth.'

'I cannot disagree.'

'What is so important, then?'

'Me is sacred.'

The Baptist, for all the roughness of his appearance, his wild grizzly hair, his blustery beard, his massive head on a squat brown body clothed in animal skins and bits of rags, was a quiet man. Certainly he could roar when he wanted to be heard by large numbers of people, or when he wanted to let his whole encampment know that some order should be carried out immediately, or when the voices were upon him, or when he was casting out demons. His roar was enough to make the Lion of Judah tremble. He was, all the same, a quiet man, a learned man who could recite the Torah by heart and had studied as a young man with the communities of healers in Alexandria.

In those days he was a refined disputant always eager to enter the lists with the pagan philosophers in public discussions before crowds who, though indifferent to the matter being debated, would applaud every point with contemptuous impartiality, enjoying the wrangle, quite sceptically, for its own sake. He had argued about that which was better than the Good and purer than the One and more ancient than the Monad.

He had travelled far and was fully acquainted with all but the most obscure of pagan mysteries. He had been initiated into the Chaldæan, Orphic and Eleusinian Mysteries and the secrets of Seth and Osiris, and had some knowledge of the good Devas from the far places to the East. Pythagoras he regarded merely as the enunciator of old truths and had more of a preference for whatever he could find of the teachings of Pherecydes, Anaximander and Thales before him. If there was anything to be *known* in pagan religions, secrets or mysteries, then the Baptist knew it. He was the Master of the great truths of 'Things-that-Are'.

Some could recall the time when the Baptist's main obsession was cleanliness, inner and outer; and, though that was now a practice completly abandoned by him, he still held fast to peculiar eating habits. He abstained entirely from meat of any kind (though somewhat partial to grasshoppers), preferring grains, meals, wild honey and other vegetarian food.

He had finally returned to his own land at a time when the Chaldæan astronomers were coming to the certain conclusion that it was the end of the Age of the Ram and the beginning of the New Age—the Age of the Fish. Confusion was anticipated throughout the world. The transition would give rise to disharmony and disaffection. Among his own people it was called 'The End of the Days' and he saw more plentiful than ever the familiar prophets-of-doom, declaring that the world was about to be destroyed, and such things, which had a great effect among the poor. The mood was one of rampant apathy and with it came men who preyed on the situation. Bandits roamed the hills and plundered the valleys. The Priesthood in Jerusalem was more and more falling under the sway of the Eagle ensigns of Rome. The power of the old Herod was broken; the provinces of the land were divided. Superstition, idolatry and paganism were breaking the spirit of the people. In short, the Baptist was called to do something about it.

He told the peasants that the world was not coming to an end, but to a new beginning. He announced that a New Age was coming. He called attention to the Holy Writings which forecast the coming of a saviour. He saw hope in the future where others saw none, and he tried to communicate his hope to anyone who would listen. He came to see himself, through the first years, as a voice crying out in protest. As long as there was a voice. As long as there was one voice raised in protest, then there was a point to it.

He began to get angry. The angrier he got, it seemed, the more his reputation grew and the more he was called the incarnation of this or that prophet.

At the age of fifty-five he struck a spark that was to become a blaze. In the countryside around Galilee was a new store of kindling: sons who had lost fathers after insurrections against the barbarian hordes of Rome. There was scarcely a family in the whole northern province which had not lost their men. Two thousand, he discovered, had been crucified when 'rebels' had attacked the arsenal and treasury at Sepphoris, many of them innocent men seized at random. Centre after centre of rebellion was put down with the cruelty customary to the barbarian. Sepphoris was burned to the ground and all its inhabitants sold into slavery. The Baptist had been in Alexandria at that time. Now he was finding that he had been so busy crying out his own protests that he did not know the feelings of the young Galileans. Only when he had learned how to listen did he find out about Judah of Galilee, who had led the rebellion and who had survived to form a most secret alliance with Zaddok and certain other important disciples of the school of Shammai among the Pharisees. These were men whose zeal for God and hatred for anything heathen had been smouldering quietly, needing only a wind to set the embers glowing. The humour was not lost on the Baptist when he realised that, as ever, he was there to provide the wind.

To the south, in desert communes, were healers, so inbred and busy with their own mysteries that they ventured out to heal no-one. They were the centres of other lay orders, non-initiates to the ways of God. People were clamouring for some speck of truth, some reassurance, and it was being withheld by these ascetic so-called Lovers-of-Wisdom.

Then one night, while studying the dog-star and making certain calculations having to do with the weighing and measuring of things, a revelation came to the Baptist. It was something he had known for a long time, though he did not know he knew (as is the way with revelations). He wept at the simplicity of the Gematria. He saw the changes in the stars and the confusion in his people, and he saw the bridge of Mysteries. The Baptist then did what had been undreamed of in two thousand years. In the Name of God and in the name of the New Age he revealed the Mysteries to the common man.

or several hours the Baptist walked through the desert. He started before dawn and took the most direct and most difficult path to where Yesha had chosen to stay. From the top of a ridge the Baptist could see the twists and turns of the river. He imagined it as a snake biting through the rock. He took time to breathe in and out regularly and deeply, feeling the air burning in his nose but suffering it for its beneficial effects.

Over the next ridge he found Yesha, not quite where he had expected him to be, but on the correct hill. Yesha stood rigid and unmoving. The Baptist smiled, though he never doubted that Yesha had the endurance for this ultimate test. Still, others had died, good men all of them, and there were that handful of others who had lived but had their minds taken.

Yesha had picked a ledge on the side of the hill, a small ledge with a sharp drop. It looked an impossible place to reach, but the Baptist scrambled and scraped his way to the top of the hill, and then inch by inch, using every finger and toehold, he lowered himself onto the ledge behind Yesha.

The Baptist sat down in Yesha's shadow, unnoticed by the glaze-eyed body. Then he heaved himself up and decided to enact the ritual before bringing the spirit back to the body. The Baptist looked right into Yesha's face and stared hard and searchingly at him. Yesha saw nothing. Perhaps, the Baptist wondered, he saw everything.

'Yesha?'

No reply.

'Yesha?' said the Baptist carefully.

Yesha's mouth began to move, but could form no words. His throat was parched. The Baptist took off his little goatskin bag of water and forced it between Yesha's moving lips. The natural reaction of the body was to swallow, though some poured from the corners of his mouth.

'Yesha . . . what do you see?'

Yesha saw visions of sacrifices, images of Abraham and Isaac which fluttered into a great brightness, a new light. His eyes fluttered open. Somewhere in another world he heard a small voice calling his name. His name, all names, all existence.

'Have you seen him?' asked the Baptist.

There was no reply, and more urgently he asked the question again.

A low rumble came from Yesha's throat. It was something like a sigh.

'Speak up!'

Yesha saw shapes. He could feel his body, numb and burning. He could hear a voice that was calling to him, asking questions, questions. Slowly he turned and looked at where the voices seemed to come from. He saw a great shaggy bear. He was not frightened. It was another demon to deal with . . . just another demon.

'Can you see Him?' someone asked.

'Can you see the Light?' questioned another. Was it the voice of the demon that faced him?

A third said, 'Can you see His Light?'

The demon was not going to trick him. Yesha knew he had swallowed the Light and it was in him, it *was* him. He spoke softly to himself. The sound of his own voice was to him just a murmur; to the Baptist it was loud and direct, though spaced out with long pauses.

'I . . . I am the . . . light . . .'

'Yesha . . .'

'I am the . . .'

'You are with God.'

'I am . . . I . . . I . . . I *am*.'

The Baptist smiled with satisfaction.

'You are with God and He is the Light,' he said.

'I am.'

'Yesha. You are Yesha. You are a man. You are the son of a man. Do you understand?'

It was hard for him, but Yesha knew it was good to look the demon manfully in the face and do battle with him if need be.

'You have been chosen, Yesha.'

'Chosen . . .'

The fiery ball, Yesha knew, was trying to tell him that he was God. That was what he was trying to say. Yesha was afraid. They told him he was dead. Were they right? Had he now ascended into some other existence? Was he being proclaimed? Had he finally come to his own?

'I am God,' he said to the demon, intending to display his oneness with the Lord.

'You are a man with the Lord!' roared the demon.

Yesha was forced to sweep up into the sky. The demon pursued him.

'So . . .' said the Baptist, 'you are God. Are we not *all*?'

'We are all . . . I . . . am . . .'

Slowly, after talking to the Baptist for hours and when it was almost dark, Yesha began to revive. Perhaps it was the cooler night air blowing in, or the Baptist's continual talking in circles, or perhaps it was the Baptist tricking Yesha that brought him back. The Baptist had tucked his chin into his neck, and in some amazing way deformed his body into a grotesque crooked shape. The Baptist changed his voice into the most unctuous, sweet and devilish tones that his normally strident speech could utter.

'Master . . .' said the Baptist, 'these are not visions. Look out over the valley . . . you see all the lands of the earth. Yes, you *see* . . ` Look and they appear. Do you see them?'

'All the Universe,' said Yesha.

'They are yours.'

'Yes.'

'Master . . .' the Baptist went on sweetly, 'you see the temples of gold and the marble cities of the world, and palaces of Kings and Emperors. You *see*?'

'Yes.'

'They are yours! You have power over them.'

'Yes.'

'Do you see the people of the world reaching out to you? Bowing to you? They are your slaves.'

'Yes.'

'The Emperors and Kings are your slaves.'

Yesha made no reply to this. The Baptist pressed on.

'The palaces are yours. The temples are yours. The fields and the trees . . .'

'Yes.'

'Take them!' the Baptist hissed.

Yesha's voice was small and distant.

'They're just . . . a moment . . . in time,' he said unsurely.

'Take them. Take them!' urged the Baptist.

Yesha looked at the Baptist a long time. His eyes were fierce and frightened. Then he howled out in alarm,

'Who are you?'

'Take them. Use them. Enjoy them!'

'WHO ARE YOU?'

'You know me, Yesha.'

'I think . . . I . . . don't know.'

'I'm Yohanan.'

Yesha started to shake. Yohanan. Yohanan. He knew Yohanan. Yohanan was his teacher. This wasn't Yohanan. It was some creature that was unfurling from a woolly ball of sparks and lightening into something that *looked* like Yohanan. And the land around him . . . it was almost a perfect re-creation of the world he had lived in.

'No!' Yesha cried out. 'You're different!'

The Baptist moved towards Yesha but the young man stumbled away from him. He looked from the ledge to the long drop down the ravine.

'Stay back! I'll jump,' he said desperately. His eyes filled with tears and confusion. The Baptist took a sharp and sarcastic tone.

'Jump?' he said bitterly. 'What do you mean "jump"? You're God, aren't you? You can *fly*. Why don't you just float up and fly. You can do anything you want.'

'I . . . I . . .' said Yesha and stamped his foot.

He felt the earth under his feet. He stooped jerkily and picked
up a rock with some difficulty. He held the rock up threateningly.
The Baptist did not move.

'Fly, Lord,' the Baptist taunted. 'You know better than I that a
thousand angels will rescue you. Hands from Heaven will lift you
up. Why do you stumble on these poor stones?'

'Get back. Get away!'

'Rise up, little king, and shed your light on my darkness.'

'You're the *Devil*! I know you. I know you. I know your name!'

'I am Yohanan,' said the Baptist evenly.

Yesha raised his head and howled a piercing and prolonged cry.
It was the shriek of a man whose mind was tearing into him. It
was a scream as ancient as the birth-pangs of the earth. Madly
Yesha hurled his stone at the Baptist. It was far wide of its target.

The Baptist did not move.

The echoes of Yesha's scream bounded from stone to stone.
Every grain threw his scream back at him. Yesha's arms fell limp
at his sides. The Baptist moved close and Yesha made no protest.

'I am Yohanan. You are Yesha. We are together again.'

Yesha tried to catch his breath. It was Yohanan. It really was
Yohanan who had come to save him! He had driven the demons
out, and the king of the demons was gone. It was Yohanan
standing in front of him. His fear dropped away and he fell into
the Baptist's arms, crying with all his heart and soul.

'It's all right . . . You're back,' said the Baptist.

His lungs bursting, Yesha pushed out from under water.
The Baptist was beside him, up to his waist in the river,
with his head tossed back and roaring with laughter.
Yesha was just spluttering and trying to get his soaked hair out
of his eyes when the Baptist lunged forward and with both hands
pushed down on Yesha's head and held him under the water
again. Yesha pushed up, but the Baptist had now taken a grip on
his shoulders and seemed determined to drown him. Yesha

pushed up with all his might and broke surface. Deftly he grabbed the Baptist's arm and pulled him closer. He grabbed the Baptist's beard and then more or less jumped on him. This time a very surprised Baptist went under the water, and this time Yesha struggled to hold him under. After a few moments he let go, at the same time wading back out of the Baptist's reach.

'Now if anybody tells you that you've never been clean higher than the waist, you can deny it in good conscience,' laughed Yesha.

'I'll break your neck, God forbid,' shouted the Baptist.

Yesha kept moving backwards, in case the Baptist should make a miraculous lunge at him. They stood suitably apart, facing each other, both of them panting and brushing the water from their faces.

Those who had come down to the river from the camp were surprised at the incident. Certainly Yesha was like a son to the Baptist; and it was said that they were cousins, but then who wasn't somebody's cousin in this land? From the shore it looked like more than playful romping. It looked as though Yesha had just baptised the Baptist!

Yesha splashed and tried to float on his back, though he could hardly swim. When he felt himself sinking, he dropped a leg to the riverbed and pushed himself along. He could hear that the Baptist was shouting something at him, but the solemnity of the ritual had come back into his mind. He was trying to feel the water all around him. He wanted the magical currents to run around him, over him, through him. His purification was more than a quaint rite or a symbol as it was to many of the simpler of the Baptist's converts. He was aware of the elements in all their degrees, aware of the blue canopy of the sky above him, of the fire and desert earth that surrounded him, the air he breathed, and now the water. It was the full turn of the water to possess him. Droplets in his eyes broke the sky into bleary blue haze, removed the heat of the land and prevented him from breathing deeply— unless he wanted to drown. It was the water, and all that went with water: all the teachings and spirits in this sacred river, the regenerations and ablutions, sources and springs for body and mind in inseparable fluidity. Yesha wallowed in the thoughts.

The Baptist had stopped shouting after Yesha. Watching him trying to float on his back and kicking his feet was a ridiculous sight, and the Baptist laughed.

Still, he saw that his teachings had not been lost on his pupil. He understood that Yesha was making friends with water and understanding its ways. He forgot about the impertinence of being ducked and realised that Yesha's action had been correct. In this Yesha had shown himself to be the Baptist's equal; no longer his pupil. He waited till Yesha had finished his communion with the river and waded over to him. Yesha stood and smiled at the Baptist, and the Baptist laughed with a good deep roar from his belly and slapped Yesha on the back.

'Now,' grinned the Baptist, 'there are no more secrets. It is done. We can begin!'

The Baptist's camp was hidden in the shelter of a small valley in the hills several miles from the river. Once a village had stood in the valley, but had left behind only ruined walls and a few roofless houses when its inhabitants, whoever they may have been, had moved on.

Now the tents of the Baptist's thirty-seven-strong followers, believers, new converts and hangers-on were woven into the crumbling brickwork. One scrap of remaining wall made a fourth sheltering wall for a tent whose goatskins had rotted away. Scraps of brush and wattle re-roofed the more solid structures. A central square had been cleared of rubble, and the women of the group attended to the fires and the cooking.

All meals were taken communally. The Sabbath meals were love feasts that went on from before the sunrise until it had set. To such meals only the elders and true initiates of the Healers had been privy. Here they were open to all; and the degree of a man's understanding of the poor community's sacred things was limited only by the Will of God.

The followers and friends of the Baptist, scouting the forests in the late summer shortly after the first rains, brought the secret flesh of God to the encampment at the favourable times. Sometimes the Baptist himself would make long treks to the caravan routes for prearranged meetings with old friends, wise calm men from the great land far far to the east, who were knowledgeable of the secret plants, sometimes knowing as many as sixty varieties and the names of the Gods or demiurges residing in them. These hosts of God were always seen by the Baptist and his flock not as the heathens saw them—in terms of individual forces—but as many-faceted reflections of the one crystal, the flawless, the perfect unhewn stone from which all things were hewn. Man was the dust breathing on the great stone.

It was of such things that the Baptist spoke in the evenings around the fire, and his symbols and metaphors were interpreted by each of his listeners. The Baptist used stones as his favourite demonstrations of Things-that-Are. He often proclaimed (though it scandalised new listeners) that the people of Israel had never been 'in bondage' in Egypt. He held that Moses and Aaron and Yusef were *Princes* in Egypt not by some Divine whim, but because of their knowledge of the hewing and shaping of stones, their order, measurement and mass, the relation of one to the other and to the many. This had been a great power handed down through their people from the knowing to the knowing by ancient tradition. Their forbears, he maintained, had not been made to build the pyramids by forced labour but were the Master Masons. They had the ability to make bricks without straw and build eternal edifices, though secretly they were the final statements of the previous Age. They were the repositories of souls, millions and millions of souls. These masterpieces of spiritual engineering constellating all science and all Truth were not held together by what he called 'mortal mortar'.

'Sorcery!' an indignant Pharisee had once shouted, and the Baptist railed at him for a full hour with citations, chapter and verse, from the Torah. Had not Moses and Aaron, their task accomplished, tried to leave Egypt with their kinsmen? Had they not been hindered in this by the priests of Seth, whose knowledge was degenerate, misused and misunderstood? Had

Moses and Aaron not been challenged to a contest of sorcery by the High Priests? Had they not squarely beaten them when Aaron, faced with the power of the snake, changed it at once into a measuring stick? (The Baptist often thought that it was the humour of this magical statement—the breezy insolence of the visual pun that had so angered the High Priests that they prevailed on their Pharaoh to pursue the departing magicians.) And then had not the attack of the Egyptian soldiers been held back at the sea by a great fire seen in the form of 'pillars'? Was it sorcery to talk so about stones? Finally the Baptist was moved to go up to the Pharisee, jut his beard out almost into the now timorous face of the poor man and roar 'What do you live by, Pharisee?'

'By the Law,' replied the Pharisee, rallying his righteousness but not his voice.

'By *whose* Law?' demanded the Baptist.

'By the Law of Moses.'

'No, Pharisee,' said the Baptist contemptuously, 'by the Law of God!'

'The Law of God, given to Moses,' retorted the Pharisee, thinking to save face at the last moment.

The Baptist nodded and walked away. The crowd was utterly silent. The Baptist looked around the firelit faces of his audience, breathing calmly, and then fixed his eyes on the Pharisee.

'And by what means did the Almighty Lord give Moses these Laws which you so uprightly live by?'

'On the tablets of stone,' said the Pharisee, and even before he had spoken these words his heart dropped to his stomach and the bottom from his argument.

'SORCERER!' shouted the Baptist and emphatically sat down to the cheers and laughter of his audience.

The reason for the Baptist's long perorations on the subject of stones was to slowly lead his listeners to the subject of the Altar Stone. He denounced the spilling of blood on a sacrificial stone as being the crudest and most blasphemous of idolatries. God had guided Abraham and his people wisely against the practice of human sacrifice. Was the blood of animals required in Isaac's place?

The High Priests in Jerusalem were ignorant of their own idolatry.

The Baptist called out for reform. He called for the Priesthood to break tradition, the strangler of the Spirit, and recognise their heritage fallen into corruption. To spill blood on a stone sacred as an intercessor to God was to worship the stone itself!

(None who followed the whole of the Baptist's argument failed to be convinced by it.)

From his poor ruined village the Baptist would, with a few followers, strike into the countryside, spreading his ideas of a reformed new priesthood. There was no set pattern to his teachings. One day he would talk about stones, the next about trees or soil or cloth, but always he would bring his subject into relation with God and end by calling for changes from the Sacerdotal authorities. He found he was more and more welcomed in Galilee, while in certain other parts of the country he knew his life was in danger.

As the Baptist spoke of the New Age that was at hand, of the re-establishment of a Priesthood of Holy men, who would not hide their knowledge from the people but give it freely to those who asked, and of a new kingdom of God stripped of ritual authoritarian fiddle-faddle, so did he find that he could less and less ignore the questions of young Galileans about the Romans. The Baptist saw plainly that they agreed with his every word. More came forward at every meeting to receive the Light, and sometimes there was simply not enough to go round. But the zeal of those converted to the Baptist's new philosophy was marked by a savage hatred of the Imperial Forces occupying their Holy City, garrisoning their land and levying men for menial labour on their estates and roads.

'Can the Kingdom of God ever come while the Heathen rules?'

'Will the New Age pass us by if the land is filled with idols?'

'Are you the Saviour promised in the Writings?'

'Are legions of angels going to drive them out, or are *we* the sword of the Lord?'

'Will you lead us? We'll follow!'

'You say the New Age is yet to come, but the Romans say that it has begun with Caesar Augustus, and that he is the Saviour and God on earth. Is this the end of the world as we know it?'

The Baptist became persuaded by their arguments as they were by his, but he could not condone killing, even in the Name of the Lord, for he could not contradict the writing on the stone and the certainty of his heart and soul that all life is sacred.

Nevertheless, groups of men came forward to the Baptist at certain times and explained to him forthrightly that his teachings and demonstration of the Light were true and, though murder was expressly forbidden by God, they were still prepared to offer their souls to eternal damnation in the belief that by driving the Romans from the land in time, they could save countless millions, their children's children's children's children for the reign of God on earth. These groups were always thirteen in number both because of the binding strength of that number for ancient reasons based on the Kb'Allah and because of the compactness and mobility of such units which intended to do their utmost to harass and, where possible, to destroy the Roman wherever he could be waylaid. Furthermore, the Baptist was made aware that other similar groups were forming and that his philosophy was their credo. He demurred, he protested, but he returned to his quiet encampment assured of their undying loyalty to his teachings and to himself as a prophet to be honoured.

After one such large meeting at Kana, approached by the leaders of two such groups and having answered personal questions while the crowd was dispersing, the Baptist came to the last of those seeking private audience. He was a young man in rich clothes with the lighter hair and beard that suggested Greek blood from Tyre or Sidon in the family. The young man had a graceful, almost studied carriage and the Baptist knew that he was not about to be questioned by a worried smallholder seeking some shred of assurance that the end of the world would not do something drastic to the grape market.

'Master . . .' said the young man—without the usual preamble of 'God forbid, Master, that I should waste your time with some insignificant troubles that are too foolish, really, to even mention, but . . .'—which usually had to do with family problems of the kind the Baptist loathed but tolerated, and which anyone can imagine for themselves.

'What is it?' the Baptist asked.

'I wish to be your servant, Master, and to learn your teachings for as long as you will have me.'

'Have you money?'

'Yes.'

'Give it away.'

'Yes.'

'A family?'

'Yes.'

'Who you will leave?'

'Yes.'

'What's your name?'

'Yesha bar Yusef . . . ben Panther.'

'Yusef "the Panther"?'

'Yes.'

'How old are you?'

'Twenty-eight.'

The Baptist looked at Yesha, grandson of 'the Panther', the general of Judah of Galilee. A family of respect and wealth and learning. The Baptist knew that the young man had a brother well placed in the Sanhedrin. It was possible he was a spy. No— the Baptist could see in Yesha's earnestness that he was a Galilean in all senses, the way the Baptist could see into all men.

'We're walking for two days south through Samaria. Carry the bag of provisions.'

And Yesha did that.

By the time Yesha joined the Baptist's camp it had grown to a sprawling citadel of 148 dedicated men and women.

The Baptist taught Yesha everything he knew, and how to speculate even beyond the limits of his teachings. Yesha learned and retained everything and was in all things guided by the Light. He accompanied the Baptist on all his travels through the country until one morning, after they had greeted the rising sun, the Baptist asked Yesha to come with him to talk. Yesha expected nothing more than some dream the Baptist had remembered and interpreted. The Baptist lived in a lean-to shanty, scarcely shelter enough for one person from the heat and none from the cold winds at night. The Baptist sat down outside his shelter, and Yesha faced him, crosslegged. He held his back still so that he no longer felt his body.

'Two messengers have come: one from Galilee and one from your brother in Jerusalem.'

'My brother?'

'First let me tell you that the troops of Herod have captured Josiah of Kana and a hundred with him at a meeting. They have interned them without trial.'

Yesha looked pained. 'He was a good man and not violent.'

'This has caused a lash of resentment among the Galileans, and you can be sure that this act will bring new leaders to the fore with less wisdom and more radical methods.'

'The other groups?' asked Yesha.

'They are divided. Some have taken to hiding-places to consider their future strategies. Other groups are continuing to teach as openly as always, and you can be sure that more persecution will follow.'

Yesha nodded his head.

'And my brother?' he asked.

'He asked me to beg you to keep out of these activities. To stay away from Anarchy.'

'What do *you* want me to do, Yohanan?'

The Baptist sighed. In the dust he doodled the sign of the fish.

'If Josiah of Kana is kept in prison, his brother Zachariah will try to lead the Kanaans. He'll count on support from his brother's followers and break away from the agreement I had come to with his brother. He may preach in my name but he won't be using the restraint. He'll be ranting for blood, and it will extinguish our work with the Light.'

The Baptist faltered, then spoke softly to Yesha, 'I have never sent a group from my followers to work with these Galilean movements. I know how much I am to blame for them, but I am not the leader they are looking for. I have never committed myself to sending anyone in my name. Look at the age of me! Who have I ever had to trust more than I trust myself? Who could do such things even after hearing his brother's warning to stay away from them?'

Yesha nodded and rocked back and forth, surprised at the Baptist's change of mind and the honour of being offered the chance to go to the zealous groups and work directly with them as the Baptist's spokesman . . . his named successor. This appeal contrasted so untimely with the message from his brother Yaacov not to indulge in this very thing. His brother was an important man, a fair man, who was well-considered in the priestly government with friends in its highest echelons.

'I know the urgency, Yohanan. You know yourself how late it is for you to get control of this affair. There are even more sects, cults and schisms now that have already split from your philosophy . . . the famous "fourth philosophy", that it is becoming a beast with a hundred horns.'

The Baptist frowned, but in agreement, though he had never heard such harsh criticism from Yesha. The Baptist recalled all their arguments and disputations, some that had even ended with the two men not speaking to each other for a week. Now, he realised that he had never once taken Yesha into his confidence about his own fears, never even asked his advice as a Galilean, though now the very word 'Galilean' was synonymous with dissidence and unrest, and descriptive of men who dared defy the authority of the priestly government, who were fast reviving the zealot fervour of Judah of Galilee and seeking to attack the invincible Mother Goddess Roma and her Divine consort, Caesar Tiberius. Never had the Baptist unfolded his deep doubt that this New Age was just another Age, and that Yahweh, living in Timelessness, was not bringing the Kingdom of his chosen people just at that moment. A 'moment' the Baptist defined as one minute of arc represented by the solar power of 666, each minute having thirty degrees in twelve houses of the zodiac, as the children of Israel were in twelve tribes. The Baptist saw that it was not impossible for the Age to have begun with the Apotheosis of Caesar Augustus, and that this Age, this twinkling in the eye of God, a mere 1999 years, was not to be the Golden Age for Jerusalem, but for Rome. Perhaps the next Age . . . Alexander the Great had meddled with years to fix the Zodion of the Fish to coincide with his own deification some 360 years earlier, on the twenty-fifth of December in the Libyan Temple of Jupiter Ammon. In that temple he found Aries regnant; he left it with Pisces triumphant. There was absolutely no doubt in the Baptist's mind that great conquerors chose flexible astrologers. His own calculations differed . . .

Yesha saw that his words caused a look of despair to flicker in the Baptist's eyes. He did not know of the calculations the Baptist was working and re-working in his head; chiselled words and shapes from stellar geometry, gematria that whirled in him as a vision.

The Baptist saw clearly the sign of the Fish, two of them, each pointing in different directions, swimming in separate streams. He saw the fish change their size and shape and watched one fish grow to giant proportions and the other become very small and in a flash the tiny fish devoured the giant fish.

'Something can be done!' he said, so sharply and strangely that Yesha thought that a Voice possessed him. Then the Baptist closed his eyes and breathed deeply.

'Yohanan . . .' Yesha said softly. 'This is a very heavy matter. You must take all my pupils, and I will take the youngest with me to where the forest meets the scrubland. I shall be with Yahweh for four days. On the fifth day I will come back and tell you what I have been instructed.'

The Baptist nodded his head in agreement. Yesha would consult the Light.

In a piney, sandy landscape, where the desert starts to melt into fertile cultivated ground, Zachariah, the brother of Josiah of Kana, thundered his message to a crowd of perhaps fifty. Zachariah's preaching was based loosely on that of his brother, who had been interned, together with his closest companions, by the soldiers of Herod Antipas, without any just cause. He was being kept in prison without any charges made against him and no hope of justice. Josiah was allowed no visitors, and there was no legal approach that had not been tried to free him or even make his conditions in prison more comfortable. It was certain that he was being brutalised in detention. Nonetheless, the ones who had been freed admitted that nothing more had happened to them than endless interrogations and a little kicking and arm-twisting.

Josiah would probably never get out alive. Zachariah had a good idea why his brother had been taken. Josiah had followed the Baptist's line of attack against 'moral turpitude' and at meeting after meeting he had denounced Antipas for having incestuous relations with his illegitimate daughter, Salome. Josiah denounced the Royal and Priestly families of the Sadducees, who so jealously maintained their hereditary privileges. They were a wealthy class with their power centred in Jerusalem and they were not ashamed of keeping their power by making all manner of unworthy and ungodly concessions to foreigners, and now to the heathen Romans.

Zachariah did not have his brother's hatred for Herod Antipas and the goings-on at the Herodian court. If Antipas had taken his brother prisoner, he had been forced to do so by the Sadducees, acting in their own interests. And their interests were the interests of Rome. There was no-one in the land who did not see in Antipas a feeble puppet-king whose every act was determined ultimately by the Procurator of Judaea and his masters in Rome.

'The world is coming to an end!' Zachariah preached. His thesis had hardly changed in any way since he had tried to collect together his brother's scattered followers. If the Baptist, whose following was huge throughout the people—even influencing the Healers, the Pharisees and one or two of the poorer Sadducees— was unwilling to save his people, then it was Zachariah's duty to his nation and his brother to do it.

'I have been chosen by the Lord to show his people their true oppressors!' Zachariah pealed. 'I have come to show you that there is only one way to serve God and save his chosen Kingdom. The Pharisees teach that man has a spirit that lives after death; the Sadducees say he has not—but those who have witnessed the Light of the Baptist know that there is Heaven and Hell in this world and, just as surely, in the next. I have come to show you the way to save your spirits from infernal damnation! Woe to the oppressed and polluted sanctuaries of Jerusalem! Her priests do nothing against the heathens of Rome, whose idols fill the cities and are carried at the head of their armies. Does this not offend God? Is he not angry that his people are so weak in their faith that they will not defend his holy land? The tenth part of our goods and more we gladly give to the Temple of God, but the Romans set themselves above his authority. They worship their Caesar Tiberius as God on earth! The taxes we pay to Rome are tribute to Caesar as a God above our God, and there is no Lord but Yahweh!'

Zachariah's audience loved to hear his harangues. And if they were few, they knew it was because the larger crowds were frightened away by the capture of Zachariah's brother, who had preached more against loose morals and wicked ways, speaking of the need for the nation to spiritually rearm. Zachariah however stirred them more deeply. He condemned Roman taxes and idols, and they agreed wholeheartedly to resistance . . . especially of the taxes.

Zachariah stirred them further with his call for rearmament not of the spirit, as his brother had, but with whatever weapons they could lay hands on. He fired them with the story of the heroic resistance to Rome by Judah of Galilee, who, within living memory, had raised the whole of Galilee against the heathens. He recalled to them the glorious deeds of Judah, 'the Hammer', who had driven the forces of Greece from the land when the Romans were just a horde of robbers on the edge of the civilised world. He reminded them that the Empire of the Greeks had been far greater than that of Rome. In those days, too, the Temple had been defiled and robbed. A golden idol had been placed in the Holy of Holies, but Judah 'the Hammer' had raised the spirit of God in his people and driven the Greeks from the whole land. The Temple was purified. The pagan altars and idols were broken up.

The small crowd swelled with fierce pride at Zachariah's account. Did not every man there commemorate Judah's cleansing of the Temple in the ceremony of the kindling of lights at Hanukah?

In the distance a small cloud of dust rose like a lazy storm. Twelve horsemen galloped along a road. Advance knowledge of the meeting had been passed on to certain Sadducees. Pressure had been applied, and Antipas was pitiably susceptible to pressure of any kind. A patrol had been put on alert from the Herodian Guard's garrison at Capernaum. The exact location of the meeting had reached Intelligence only a few hours before. After a few moments the little cloud of dust disappeared behind a hill.

Zachariah was carried away by his own speech. He was just concluding the preliminaries and beginning to get to the warm-up with quotations from the Prophets.

'And I swear to you that this time will end! This time, times and a half, when they finish breaking up this power in you ... this power of the holy people, and this time is NOW! We shall take up arms as a mighty force. You ... *You* shall take up weapons, and march on Jerusalem and we shall capture it and return it to the rule of God!'

The crowd cheered him on.

'We shall throw out of the Temple anyone who has profaned it in any way. Our judges are doing violence to the Law. They are evening wolves and we are the bones picked white by morning! Our Kings are Kings in name only and dance when they are tied to Roman strings—purse strings!'

Zachariah's audience murmured its approval. The Saviour raised his hand to God ...

'I shall lead you! I shall punish the oppressors! Let me see the might of the nation gather around me! I have come to tell you that it is no crime to defend yourself with a sword, no, but it is an honour to defend our God and His holy nation. We can get ready now! The Temple shall be purified and the New Age shall come!' Zachariah raised both hands to God and looked up in prayer to the Lord. 'Take up arms! Follow me! I am the Saviour!' he cried.

The dust storm rounded the hill and fell upon the crowd without warning. The stamp of the hoofbeats had been lost in the soft sand and the muffling shrubs on the other side of the hill. The patrol drew its swords. The crowd scattered in a chaos of dust and falling bodies and the cries of men and horses.

Bodies were hacked. Sword-slashes cut into the necks of farmers, a fig-planter's head, two running children. The patrol spread out to pick off the escapers and probe hiding-places. The Captain and three officers specially chosen for the mission reined up. The dust was settling.

On a rocky ledge that served as a rostrum stood Zachariah and three of his men who had held close to him.

Zachariah had drawn a sword; his companions had only short daggers hidden in the folds of their robes.

The Captain looked at his officers. A fair match—four to four. He spurred his horse and his lieutenants cantered alongside. Zachariah in his fierce defensive stand was cut down on the first run. His remaining two loyal believers were killed on the return gallop. One officer stayed to make sure that they were dead and, with several thrusts, dismembered them.

The patrol re-formed and reported back to their garrison. A despatch was sent by a fast messenger without change of horse to the commander at the Herodian fortress at Machaerus, and then by diverse Sadducean messengers to a certain pious courtier close to the Tetrarch.

'It is reported that the bandits have been killed in a fierce fight,' Antipas was told, by way of conversation, during dinner several weeks later.

'Oh,' said Antipas. He had not heard.

esha had to walk for a day and half a night to reach the place chosen to consult with the Spirit. He took his youngest pupil with him, a strong self-reliant boy of twelve called Eleazar, the son of Eleazar of Bethany, an old friend and supporter of the Baptist.

Yesha had often stayed with Eleazar's family. The boy had two aunts, both of them beautiful girls of fifteen and sixteen. Miriamne, the youngest, was a little plumper than her sister but she had fairer skin and large innocently sensuous eyes. Martha was more outrageously handsome, with fine high cheekbones and a proud way of holding herself that alone was enough to captivate a man's attention without touching on any of her other virtues. Local women, who thought that they had an eye for such things, held that Miriamne, when she lost her puppy-fat, would far outshine her sister and that Martha would be well advised to find a man before the little flower blossomed and hid the dark rose's refined comeliness. Yesha had seen the promise of their loveliness when he had first met them on a visit two years before. The girls had always treated Yesha as they had behaved all their lives toward the Baptist: with a mixture of awe and fear and love that was due, with reverence, to wild Holy Men from the desert.

Young Eleazar, who had lost his mother in childbirth, had been sent by his father for apprenticeship in hallowed learning. The boy had been promised to the Baptist since he was four years old. He had been at the encampment for hardly two weeks. He had been welcomed as a favourite by the Baptist, but his elementary teaching was handed over to Yesha. For the first week he was left to wander around the camp as he pleased, getting to know the rest of the community and speaking to the other boys, all older, displaying neither shyness, no too much braggadocio. This was his first trip with Yesha.

It was dark and cold when Yesha and the boy stopped, and they had no warm robes to protect them. The moon, which would be full in another two days, gave them enough light to avoid rocks, bushes and dangerous holes in the ground.

Yesha started to gather brittle brushwood for a fire and the boy followed his example. In no time there was a leaping bonfire to take the chill from the marrow. Yesha gazed for a time into the canopy of the night, but the brilliance of the moon and the nearer flame from the fire obscured many stars. He was grateful that the boy did not speak, so that for a few moments he was able to meditate on the Abyss of Profundity—the Great Silence. He fell into the hierarchy of Deeps, of Silence unspeakably beyond Silence, where the mind is mute, the spirit is at rest in union with the inward world, the Within-of-Things.

It appeared to Yesha as but a few moments of silence, though it was more than an hour, and Eleazar got up two or three times to pick up more kindling for the fire while his master contemplated the passing from the world of men, soared through the visible and invisible spaces below the moon, passed the moon's vault into the regions of the star-worlds to the Great Boundary to everywhere and—no 'where'. This was the boundary between the 'real' and phenomenal universes which was barricaded by the Ring called 'Pass Not'. At this point Yesha expelled all the air from his lungs, rubbed his eyes, and, seeing how far on the moon had moved, he got to his feet. Sunrise would be only a few hours away.

'Follow me and attend closely to what I do,' he said to the boy.

Young Eleazar nodded. His heart pounded with fear of the unknown and anticipation.

'Before we start,' said Yesha, 'you must vow to me that you will be a true witness . . . that you will not swear falsely, not swear at all for that matter. I know there are no such thoughts in your head, Eleazar, but I must tell you never to fornicate or commit adultery. You have renounced the material pleasures of this world, and you will never steal and never desire other men's property. You must keep God's commandments in all things. I must command you never to invoke the names of the seventy-two evil Rulers for any purpose.'

'I don't know about the seventy-two evil Rulers,' the boy demurred.

'These are commands that I must give you, and which you will have to give before you reveal the Light-Treasure. You will see the first mystery and in time it will be explained to you.'

'By you?'

'By yourself.'

The boy looked perplexed and Yesha tried to put him at ease.

'There are things that can't be explained to you yet in words, so it may seem to you that I'm talking in riddles. There is no way to describe these Mysteries; but ask questions if you must, and I will do my best to give language to my replies. If what I say to you is nonsense, try to understand that there is "no-sense" in the way you have learned in this world.'

'How many Mysteries are there, Master?'

'Thirteen. That is to say twelve Mysteries of different types and the one Mystery that is the combination of all twelve.'

'What is the greatest Mystery?' the boy asked.

Yesha rocked with laughter and slapped his thigh.

'It's . . . *Nothing*!' he exclaimed and, laughing louder at the dear thought of it, he took a plain flint knife from his pouch.

'We'll follow the straight track and will not move away from it,' Yesha ordered and set off at a careful pace to the east.

The boy followed Yesha away from the light of the fire. He could make out nothing in the black and white landscape, but walked as closely as he could in the Master's footprints and did not stumble once.

From time to time Yesha stopped; and, muttering a sacred name under his breath, he would cut something with his knife, put it carefully in one hand and with the other take a pinch of something and follow some ritual. Then he would put the object into a small pouch around his neck.

The boy could see nothing of what Yesha was doing in the darkness. It looked as though he were collecting stones. Perhaps the knife was to make sacred marks on the earth? He did not understand how Yesha could see what he was doing or what he was looking for. As Yesha stooped to the ground for the fifth time, the boy spoke up.

'Can I look, Master?'

Yesha motioned the boy to come to his side and stoop down with him. Now Eleazar could see a small plant that looked to him like the night sky. It was like the blackness of space with white stars, and it had a white stem.

'How can you see, Master?'

'They glow,' said Yesha. 'I can see them stretching ahead like little lamps.'

The boy watched intently as Yesha cut the stalk with his knife and said some name to himself—he did not dare ask what. Yesha make a further incision before holding the star-plant out to him. A black trickle of ooze came from the scar on the plant.

'It bleeds,' said Yesha.

As before he took a pinch of powder and sprinkled it over the cut.

'What's that?'

'Sulphur,' Yesha answered, slipping the plant into his special pouch. 'To heal the wound,' he explained.

Yesha's pouch was filled quite quickly and they were soon back at the fire. Eleazar quickly gathered as many twigs as he could find and heaped them onto the embers.

Yesha sized up the boy's weight carefully, noting his strong bones and exactly recalling his height. He opened his pouch and took out a star-plant, broke it in two and gave half to Eleazar. He ate the other half and three more whole plants besides.

'Go ahead,' said Yesha. 'Don't worry.'

Eleazar ate what had been given to him by the Master. It tasted nutty, not at all as unpleasant as he had expected.

'Nothing's happening,' said the boy concerned.

'Wait.'

Yesha bowed his head and started to pray aloud, then prayed raising his arms and looking to Heaven, 'All-giving Yahweh, and the One and Ineffable, who reads my thoughts and sees my soul and feels my heart . . . you know what has been asked of me by the friend and teacher I love, and my brother whom I honour and love. Please help me, Lord. Please help me, for it is beyond my understanding. Help me, Lord. Help me to understand. Help me to remember. In your hands I place my spirit. Lord . . . guard my spirit and give me your guidance.'

Yesha turned to the boy and continued his prayer, 'Lord, be with Eleazar. Be gentle with him and show him the Light. Help him as you help all who commune with you, for we are frail and helpless spirits without your love and protection.'

Yesha fell silent. The fire began to die down but the light before dawn was painting the eastern horizon with the palest rose, so sweet you could smell the coming sunrise. He turned with a little difficulty to young Eleazar, who was sitting bolt upright facing the dawn and breathing shallowly.

'You can pray before your spirit is taken,' Yesha said slowly.

There was no reply for some moments.

'I . . . feel . . . sick,' said Eleazar ben Eleazar.

'Good,' said Yesha. As he left his body he heard the boy retching and he heard the world coughing out its poisons and impurities as the sun rose.

On the fourth day Yesha and Eleazar made their way back to the settlement. Both were physically weary and made many stops to rest, but Eleazar could not restrain himself from asking Yesha question after question. Yesha himself was no calmer from his experience. He had a great deal to examine and things of terrible importance to discuss with the Baptist, but he tirelessly answered the boy's questions where he could. The boy became more and more confused with the terminology of the Light as explained by his Master.

'Everything is the "Great" this and the "Great" that . . . the "Ineffable", the "Boundaries" and "Paths" and . . . and . . . I don't know . . . You make it so much more difficult than it really is.'

Yesha knew that it was impossible to explain all things to the boy. It took so much more than this gentle first Baptism of Fire. If he could not give young Eleazar, who had heard such talk from his earliest years, a better understanding of the true things, the Eternity of the Soul, the nature and destiny of man, how could he possibly explain them to poor people, the labourers and farmers and peasants? These folk were the mass of their audience. They listened raptly enough, but were they hearing just the magnificent phrases and the fervour of it all? Those who had come forward and received the Light would never forget it. They would always know that there was something they could experience that was beyond their dreams; perhaps it was equally beyond their grasp. No amount of words could tell them anything about the experience. It would affirm the belief they had always had that there was one God and that his Laws were true.

Yesha tried to answer the boy in the most simple terms.

'There is no easy way,' he said, 'but I'll try.'

'Why do you call the plants "Hosts"?'

'Because Yahweh is a guest in them.'

'But Yahweh is everywhere, isn't he?'

'Yes, but he has chosen a humble little plant so that men can come to him and see his Light.'

'Can't they see his Light by long fasting and prayer and meditation?'

'These are important. They clear the way, and they can take you through the narrow gate beyond death. Imagine that this narrow gate is the death of the body, and that when the soul is freed you can go through. You find you are in the City of God. Contemplation and fasting can take you to the market-place of this city. You can find peace and truth inside these walls and there is knowledge and inspiration there. You have seen this.'

'Yes,' said the boy.

'You know,' said Yesha, 'but have you fasted and prayed and meditated?'

'A little,' said Eleazar humbly.

'Have *you* been through the narrow gate?'

'No. Not until . . .' the boy stopped. 'It takes years to get . . . to get . . . there.'

'But you have been there now, so you know what I'm talking about.'

'Then why have we not always come to God by the straightest way?'

'Because when the spirit has left your body and you come to the gates, the gate-keepers may see that your spirit is soiled. It may have lied or cheated or killed or done things in the body that were not right, and it may have tried to conquer the wrong the body has done and failed. At the gates the spirit is naked and it can be plainly seen that the spirit is not clean. In life, keeping the body clean may seem to be what is right. The Pharisee may become obsessed with his cleanliness and purity and may become proud of his cleanliness, prouder perhaps than his pride in God, who he thinks he serves perfectly. At the gate to the City of God it is the spirit that stands there, and the spirit has black smears on it, for it has spent so much piety on worshipping its own body. Then other gates are open, and the spirit is taken into the lightless void of She'ol and the inner city of Gehenna.'

'You never go there in meditation,' said the boy. He knew the stories of the valley of Ge'Hinnon where piles of bodies had been burnt in flames of sacrifice to the idol-god Moloch. There were three gates to Gehenna: one at the bottom of the sea, one in the desert and one right in Jerusalem 'for so many spirits go to Gehenna from Jerusalem that it needs its own gate', his father had often joked.

'Meditation,' Yesha agreed, 'is a straight and good way to the City of God, and by it there is peace for the body on earth. But if it is *only* for the body's perfect silence, then its spirit will show its troubled scars to the Guardians. Do you understand so far?'

'But . . .' said the boy, still wanting to know why their people had not always gone to Yahweh by the direct path he had just taken. Yesha did not let him interrupt because he knew that he could now explain to Eleazar the answer to his question.

'With the "host" a man has no choice where he goes. When his spirit leaves him it goes where it deserves to go. It can go to Heaven, as yours did, or it could go to the void, just as it would after the real death of your body. You might just as easily have gone to Gehenna as to Heaven. There you would have been taken to the parts set aside for your spirit's misdeeds. As many demons as there are people in the world would have tormented you and then taken you to the flames of the seven fire-places. After any of the fires, when your spirit is seen to be clean again, it is returned to your body.'

The boy was worried.

'Then I might not have seen the Light! I might have gone to Gehenna!' he exclaimed.

'And you would have come back to your body with a spirit purified by the fire. You would have seen the errors for which your spirit was tortured. You could then and there make a new beginning. In the communion with Hell your spirit is given the chance to save itself. In communion with Heaven its grace is confirmed.'

'I could have gone to Gehenna . . .' said the boy again, with a look of great amazement at his Master.

'You could have gone to both places,' laughed Yesha. 'If your sins were so very very small you might have been whirled around a few times by the torturers of the void and then whisked through the first fire straight into the City of God. Paradise and Hell are situated side by side and from Heaven's windows you can see the two of them.'

'The straight path to Yahweh has its disadvantages,' the boy decided.

'None that cannot be learned from.'

'All this is known by our priests?'

'Not all. So many are absorbed in the Law and its interpretations that they will always be blind. Others know it but regard it as a danger for men to know such things.'

'Why?'

'They fear that it will drive those without learning to madness.'

'Could it?'

'What is madness?'

'Like screaming and shouting about their visions.'

'Like the prophets?' Yesha said archly.

The boy stopped talking and thought about that. The riddles

of the prophets were understood by priests and scribes who went on endlessly about the definition of this or that phrase in the Books, but he could not understand how they could ignore the straight path to Yahweh that the Baptist and his ministers taught.

'We could all be prophets!' the boy exclaimed.

'And in a country of prophets who would work the fields? Who would work at all if they could live in Paradise? Man is made to live and work and return his spirit undefiled to the glory of God. The glory is too great for the body of man. He could not live with it for any time . . . he would kill himself to join his Creator. If he did that, he would fail the Lord and be born into a new body to work out the riddle all over again. The Baptist wants a New Priesthood who will teach Yahweh's mysteries to every man and woman, who will show them how to live and work in the Light . . . in the New Age and forever.'

The boy had heard the Baptist's views about a Priesthood of Holy Men for many years. He walked along for a while asking no more questions, but understanding many new things. He wondered how the New Priesthood would be chosen. He knew from his father and the Baptist that such men were capable of understanding things far far higher and deeper than his own novice's experience which, shattering and vivid and indescribable to him, would be nothing at all to the Baptist and Yesha and his father. He knew that there were thirteen layers or Mysteries higher than the common market-place inside the gates of the City of God. What were they? Was each as unimaginable as his own first visit to the gates had been in comparison to his previous ignorance, his darkness? The Baptist was right. The Kingdom of God could come to his people on earth! A new beginning was here, was coming, as he had heard so often but never understood until now. How long before the good news could reach everyone? There was nothing to stop them!

Then he remembered his father using the very same words, pacing up and down the room, slapping his fist into the palm of his hand, furrowing his brow in contained anger and frustration. The Baptist and three friends had just left the farm. As ever the Baptist's speeches and arguments had worked his father up to a fever of enthusiasm. 'Nothing can stop us! Nothing can stop us!' his father had said over and over again, until he was saying it in anger. The girls were in the field and his father did not seem to notice him as he stamped the floor.

When they arrived back, Yesha told the boy to go to bed, or, if he was still too alert, to talk to the other more experienced novices. He told the boy that he had done very well and was a good pupil. Eleazar glowed as the Master walked away. A thousand things were going through his mind. He wanted to talk to the older novices but his legs were sore and his back was hot and aching. He found his way to his bed and lay there, dreaming and trying to interpret the things he had seen.

Yesha went straight to the Baptist's shelter. The Baptist jumped to his feet and clasped Yesha's shoulders.

'I will do whatever you tell me,' said Yesha at once. 'I must explain what I have seen.'

'Sleep now,' said the Baptist gruffly. 'We'll talk when you wake up. Sleep first, I insist, Yesha. Talk to me with a clear head.'

Young Eleazar lay still, just before falling asleep. He kept thinking about his Master. How frail he seemed and how strong he was. He saw him in the shadow of the Baptist's thunder. His Master was so close but so much more distant. He could hardly picture him now. It was as if he had never been there. Eleazar fell asleep wondering whether his Master really existed, or whether he was a fragrant essence left over from his dream.

For twenty-one hours Yesha slept. Some of the women found furs and goatskins to put around him since he slept feverishly through the night. Apart from that he was left alone, and the Baptist ordered that no-one should disturb his sleep. When he woke up, he washed his face in water from a skin and then went immediately to the Baptist.

The Baptist sat down with Yesha and opened the conversation in a formal manner.

'I asked you if you would go to my followers and unite them. You believe that there are too many rival groups, and that their interpretation of my teachings has become corrupt, that they quarrel with each other and that it is an impossible task. You have asked Yahweh for instruction, and you have told me that you accept the mission. Are you still certain?'

'Yes.'

'Tell me what you saw.'

'So many things,' sighed Yesha.

'Yes . . . but how did the decision come to you?'

'In an image and at the same time in a voice. The voice said "Gather together the people!" '

The Baptist nodded, 'Just that?'

'Just that.'

'At the same time as the image?'

'The same time. The duration of both was equal but the image was long and detailed and complex, and yet the voice and image began and finished together.'

The Baptist understood at once that this was the highest order of Thalatth, the voice of awakening.

'And the image?' he asked.

'I do not know if I can tell you,' said Yesha worriedly.

'Me?' said the Baptist. 'You can't tell *me*? What's this that cannot be told? Don't you remember?'

The Baptist looked surprised and hurt, but he saw that Yesha had closed his eyes in despair. 'Tell me why,' he pleaded.

'I saw something that I know from the Writings and that you have told me yourself that no eye has ever seen.'

'Ahhh!' gibed the Baptist, 'they all say that!'

Yesha hesitated and then, stung by the jeer, began.

'I was in the garden that was above even the seventh heaven. From it I could see the seven halls in the Temple, beyond the thirteen spheres, past the gates of the City of God. I knew that I was in a place that had been set apart and above. I could see Paradise directly opposite the place and situated on earth.

'I saw before me a great tree but at first I thought it was a bird's nest. The sky behind the tree was like night but the place was in day. It was a pomegranate tree, but its fruit were the stars from the sky. At the foot of the tree there was a pool of water gushing from a spring like a fountain. I walked to the water and drank from it because I knew I had to. I climbed the tree as though I were a small child. I climbed to the very top and I was not at all afraid. I picked the highest star-fruit and immediately found that I was standing in front of the tree again with a pomegranate in my hands. I split open the fruit and 18,000 worlds fell out and turned to dust. A raven and a dove swooped down from the tree and each snatched a half of the husk of the empty pomegranate and flew away.

'I looked down at my hands. In the palm of my right hand was a grain of mustard seed. I looked at it more closely and saw that there was a drop of dew on it. I brought it even nearer to my eyes and saw the 18,000 worlds which had flown from the pomegranate inside the drop of dew. I put the grain of mustard and the dew on the tip of my tongue. Then I looked up and saw that the tree had spread its limbs and revealed a snake tied to its trunk. It struggled free from its bonds and wound itself once around the tree and bit its own tail. Again it appeared bound to the tree and it looked to me for help. Then *I* was tied to the tree and the snake was standing upright before me and I begged it to help *me*.

'Suddenly the tree turned into a bird's nest and I was standing by it as I had when I came to the place. In the nest was the snake. It crawled into a large egg and the hole it crawled into was sealed up. The nest vanished. The tree was gone. This was the end of the vision and the end of the voice.'

The Baptist stared at Yesha. He said nothing, but put his head in his hands. The Baptist thought about it for a long time. Usually the two men discussed the interpretation of such things with each other, but neither man spoke. Eventually the Baptist lifted his head from his hands and looked at Yesha in a strange way.

'Do you know all the meaning of this?' he asked Yesha.

'Not everything.'

The Baptist's face grew black as though a thunder-cloud was passing over the rough landscape of his features.

'You were right,' he said. 'You should not have told me.'

'I thought it meant that I should go, as you asked . . .'

'Yes,' said the Baptist, dully.

'How soon?'

'Now.'

Yesha was perturbed by the Baptist's mood.

'Are you angry with me?' he asked.

'With myself,' the Baptist replied.

'Why?'

'Why? Because I could not till now see something right in front of my eyes. I'm angry because I was wrong, and it's so late. Peace, peace, peace, I've been saying like a parrot. Now I open my eyes and I see a great big mistake, like a camel sitting on my head. Have you ever walked around for years with a camel on your head? It makes you angry!' he roared.

'Do you still want me to go?'

'You have to go! You should have gone thirty years ago. *I* should have gone thirty years ago!' He stared intently into Yesha's eyes.

'If your answer was "yes", you said you would go in my name.'

'Yes.'

'You will go as though it were me going? You will be me?'

'I will be guided by you in all things. I'll act in your name, but I am me. I can't be you. Look who you are in this country, Yohanan!'

'You will be better than me,' the Baptist said incisively. He would make sure of that. He had letters to write—many, many letters, to the highest places and the poorest. He had more messages to send than his campful of messengers could carry. Many people had sworn allegiance to him and now he had to call on their alliance. A letter must go immediately to Yesha's brother to warn him and to tell him who to contact. Letters to Kana, letters to Samaria, Jericho, Caesarea, many to Jerusalem, more to Galilee. His plan of operations would keep him busy for a long time. Yesha would be in his place. Could he do it? The Baptist already knew the answer, had known it from his parentage, from his horoscope, from his strange immediate fatherly affection for the boy. Yesha had travelled faster and further than some men, considered sages, had done in seventy years of study. Now he had seen a vision, far keener than his own, that showed him the terrible truth: the total destruction of the Light—the swallowing up of Yahweh's whole nation, who alone could spread the true word and the treasury of the mastery of the Light. Not the Greeks, not the Egyptians, not the far people of the East, capable as they were, could save the Light in the darkness to come. That was the deepest duty of his race. If the children of Israel were a 'chosen' people, they were chosen for this sacred duty and not for some kind of divine favouritism. If there was paternalism in God's beneficence, it was in exchange for the arduous duty of taking the Light to the quarters of the world. Yesha . . . Yesha . . .

'What do you want me to do?' said Yesha for the third time.

'Go to Galilee. The lake. A town next to Capernaum on the Lake of Gennesaret. Find two brothers who are fishermen— Andros and Shimon. You will assemble a group of twelve. Tell this to Shimon and he will arrange it.'

'Then?'

'You will go to Samaria and call on a friend. We studied together at two centres of knowledge before he left for a far pagan place. Don't trust him an inch. His name is Simon of Gidda, but he goes by the nickname of "Magus". He prefers living in a Greek style. He is tolerated in the town as an eccentric. Be careful of him, he's full of tricks and jokes and illusions, but he's very necessary to us.'

Yesha had no belongings apart from his pouch for basic supplies, writing materials, a phylactery and other charms to ward off the evil eye and demonic spirits which lurked in shrubs and ruins, ever ready to pounce on the solitary traveller. No Jew, however strong his belief in the one God, could ignore these spirits. What house was there in the land without its mezuzah? The Baptist watched over Yesha's final preparations. He told Yesha to say good-bye to no-one, friend or pupil, not even

46

young Eleazar. With regret Yesha complied. The Baptist then gave Yesha a number of small gifts: a forked root of mandrake and another root which was extremely precious to the Baptist, which he called 'Yin Shem' and which had healing powers for all kinds of ailments. Yesha had been taught how and when to use it but was reluctant to take it since he knew that the Baptist had got it from a fabled healer who had plucked it from the cliff at the end of the world. The Baptist moodily insisted, cautioning only that it be used sparingly. For his last gift the Baptist gave him something surrounded by fleece and sealed in calfskin. It was very small and Yesha asked what it was. The Baptist told him that it was not to be opened but to be given to Simon of Gidda, the mischievous Samarian, for it would put him in Yesha's debt forever, though it was worthless to any other man.

Yesha tucked the gifts carefully into his pouch and then the Baptist pulled Yesha to him and hugged him. There were tears in the old man's eyes when he pulled away. The Baptist turned quickly and walked back to his shelter across the camp without saying farewell. Yesha stood for a moment looking at the teacher he loved so dearly, then hitched up his robe and started the walk to the Lake of Gennesaret.

The two eldest sons of Zebedee, Chaim and Yohanan, had pulled their boat out of the water onto the beach, and were sitting in its shade, watching their sisters repair the nets. The catch during the week had been so heavy that they would be able to live a little better than they had for months past. On the other hand, Chaim doubted that theirs was the only successful catch and there was likely to be a glut in the markets. They might have to be more industrious still and travel to farther markets, but then the fish didn't travel that well and what they made in higher prices only compensated for the stock that was spoiled. What could they expect with one boat? There were men in Capernaum and Magdala with ten or twenty boats. In Tiberias there were twenty-two boats reserved solely for Herod Antipas, who handed the catches to the local Roman posts and garrisons in exchange for a fixed amount of silver. Then there were the deep ocean fleets which fished out of Caesarea-on-the-sea and Sidon and Tyre, not to mention the giant merchantmen, carriers of corn from Galilee, and the ships he had never seen, legendary Leviathans—triremes and quinquiremes. The best he could do, Chaim decided, was to get the big catches to Tarichae, where they could be dried, cured and packed for export.

'We could get another boat,' said Yohanan, dreamily propped up against the beached prow, happy in the shade.

Chaim was waiting for it. The subject came up every day about this time. He had his argument ready.

'Another boat you say . . . why not two?'

'Two?' exclaimed Yohanan. What an idea, eh? Two more boats!

'Why not three?'

'Three?' he queried, wondering if that were possible.

'Think of all that fish.'

'Ah! All that fish!'

'Ten boats!' said Chaim.

Yohanan shaded his eyes and looked at him.

'Ten?'

'Why not?'

'We'd need more men.'

'So we've got ten boats, haven't we? We can afford to pay them from ten boats bursting with fish,' said Chaim, straight-faced.

'Of course,' he went on carefully, 'we'd be businessmen then. We'd be buying out the little men . . . the four and five boaters. Then the real big fry—the ones with ten boats. Some owners with more.'

A couple of the girls who were listening giggled, but Yohanan heard nothing. 'What fish! What fish!' he muttered in amazement.

Chaim pressed on drily: 'The biggest fleet on the lake.'

'The whole lake!' said Yohanan in awe. His sisters giggled some more.

48

Chaim lolled back, letting the big beautiful dream take its own magnificent proportions in his brother's fancy. He glanced at Yohanan whose face was rapt, no doubt dreaming of whaling fleets and boatloads of sturgeon for the epicurean tables of the world! Chaim savoured the pause till just the right moment. Then he threw in the harpoon.

'You'd have to give up fishing, of course,' he said, as matter-of-factly as he could.

It took a few moments for the harpoon to sink in.

'Give up fishing?' said Yohanan with a look of horror.

'You'd have to.'

'Give up *fishing*?'

'You . . .' Chaim emphasised, 'the biggest boat owner in Galilee . . . out fishing? What kind of sinker-head thing would that be?'

'But . . .'

'You'd have all the accounts to work out. You could hire people but they'd be sure to cheat you. Then you'd have to see to the nets . . . hundreds of nets . . . just to make sure. You'd be so busy haggling with buyers that you'd never be able to work out the taxes . . .'

'Taxes? Taxes?'

'With your wealth you'd be robbed blind. How could you avoid paying at least half a talent . . . a week?'

'I'm ruined!' cried Yohanan. 'How can I pay? I'd have to sell everything and I'd still be in debt! I'd have to sell my last boat!'

'*Our* last boat,' said Chaim.

'And I wouldn't be able to fish any more!'

'Especially without a boat.'

Yohanan, very agitated, turned to his brother. 'We have our boat, don't we?'

'This rotting thing?' said Chaim, banging his fist against it. 'What good's this to anybody?'

'It sails, doesn't it? It catches fish, doesn't it? That's all I want to do.'

Chaim was diffident. 'After your third or fourth boat you'd think differently. You'd be ashamed of it.'

'Never!' Yohanan declared. 'I don't want more boats . . . what a headache! I just want to catch fish, not pay taxes! Nobody but an idiot would want all that trouble. God save us.'

Chaim stretched back, pleased with himself. He had tried a new tack with Yohanan and had utterly defeated him. What style! He had not needed to go through the ritual for the hundredth time of explaining the cost of another boat, or the difficulty the girls would have with twice the nets and twice the catch to carry. He sighed. Contentment fanned over him with the cool air from the lake.

'Chaim?'

'Yes?'

'You're right, you know.'

'Yes.'

'We'll get a big haul in later. I know just where. I have a feeling. We'll fill her till she's bursting. All the big stuff . . . we'll throw the tiddlers back.'

'Hmm,' Chaim grunted.

'A real big one.'

'Yes.'

'We could do with another boat!'

'. . .!' Chaim looked up incredulously. Yohanan tried to keep a straight face, tried to look dumb and simple-minded to keep the whole thing going, but he failed. He burst apart laughing. What a really smart one! What a cranky old stick-in-the-mud was his brother! He looked at Chaim's face frozen with that ridiculous incredulity and hooted and rolled in the sand with laughter. The old know-it-all! What a pillar of salt! What an old woman! What a fool to actually believe he was making a fool of him. Best of all Chaim didn't see what was funny. He never did. Yohanan smothered his laughter. Chaim would just treat it as another of his strange outbursts and carry on afterwards as if it had never happened.

Yohanan remembered how lively his brother had been a few years ago when they were with the Baptist—a different Chaim who laughed and played little pranks to everyone's delight. Then the Baptist told them both that they were no longer seekers but Children of God. He said that they could stay at the camp if they had nowhere to go, but their duty lay with their families. He asked them to honour their parents as Yahweh had commanded by caring for them. They knew the Light. It was right that they should return home. Since that time his brother had become more and more disagreeable and intolerant. There was no doubt, for instance, that they needed another boat. There was little money, but things had not been so bad. Better to invest it in a boat than save it for the hard times Chaim was expecting to come. No use sitting on money—give it to the poor-poor boat-builders especially. Their father listened only to what Chaim said. Well, he would persevere. Chaim must have his reasons for his scrupulous saving, but he would never explain them. It was as though Chaim was steadfastly waiting for some disaster to happen.

They talked about fish mostly. When they were working on the lake, they were real brothers; more than just brother fishermen.

The girls stopped chattering. Yohanan looked at Chaim who was shading his eyes and looking down the empty beach. Chaim pointed, and Yohanan saw a figure coming towards them. He was wearing white and could hardly be defined against the white beach at this blazing time of day. Yohanan sat up. What was a man doing walking this far up the sand in the hottest hour?

'Do you know him?' Yohanan asked softly as the man came nearer.

'No.'

The man came right up to them, not even glancing at the girls.

'I'm looking for the sons of Zebedee along this shore. Do you know them?'

Yohanan wondered if Chaim had been so wrong. Was this a tax-collector?

'Zebedee has many sons, and many of them live along here and have families, and some have moved away,' said Yohanan cagily. 'Who exactly would you be looking for?'

'Chaim or Yohanan.'

'Why?' asked Chaim.

'I was told that they are friends of a friend of mine, and might know where they are.'

'Maybe we can help you find these friends. We know people here. What's the name?'

'Shimon and Andros. Brothers.'

Chaim and Yohanan looked at each other. Andros and Shimon were good friends, and were fellow witnesses for Yahweh's Light. Shimon was spending a lot of his time talking to the various groups of illuminated hotheads around. Was this one of them? Had they got in some trouble?

'Is there a price for them?' Yohanan asked cunningly.

'I have no money.'

'Do they owe you any?' asked Chaim.

'No.'

'Do they know you're coming?' Chaim asked.

'No.'

'I could go and look. I might have to take the boat out on the lake,' said Yohanan. 'Who shall I say is looking for them?'

'They won't know my name. Tell them I've come from Yohanan in the south.'

'The Baptist!' Chaim exclaimed, jumping to his feet. Yohanan also got up.

'What's your name?'

'Yesha.'

'We're the sons of Zebedee you're looking for, and we can take you to Andros and Shimon,' said Yohanan.

'Are you the one who he promised would come in his name?'

'Yes.'

Chaim leapt into the air with a yell of delight. Yohanan was astounded. Then he understood everything.

Eagerly Chaim and Yohanan led Yesha another mile down the beach. There was a collection of fishermen's huts with a few women, children and dogs around. Yohanan apologised for the dogs that ran up and barked at them.

'We're all God's dogs,' said Yesha. 'We take the scraps and trust the provider.'

Chaim went up to one of the shanties and asked an old woman something. She said a few words and pointed out across the lake. Yesha saw a few scattered boats further down the beach, where the woman pointed. Chaim came back after checking his information with a few others. Heads nodded.

'Andros and Shimon are with two others in the second boat there,' he said, pointing.

The first boat was the nearest but out in deep water. The second boat had just put out from the strand and was only a few minutes further.

'Come on!' Yohanan urged, and slapped his brother's arm.

Chaim turned to Yesha. 'Pardon us a moment, Master,' he gabbled. Then the two raced off ahead of Yesha.

'We'll get 'em,' Chaim sang back.

The two fishermen ran along the sand until they had caught up to the boat, which was now in the shallows. They threw off some of their clothes and waded into the water. Yesha quickened his step to catch up, but he had come a long distance that day and found his legs too stiff to sprint along the soft sand. By the time he got level with the boat, it was in deeper water, about thirty yards out. Chaim and Yohanan were swimming out to the boat, unseen by the four men aboard who were throwing their weighted, rather than their trawling nets, from the other side of the boat. Chaim and Yohanan were three-fourths of the way to the bobbing craft. The men at the nets waited some minutes and then pulled in their catch, or rather their lack of catch, for though Yesha was a good reach distant, he could see that the nets were almost empty. By this time Chaim and Yohanan had arrived in the lee of the boat and their heads bobbed in the water as they paused to catch their breath.

'Other side!' Yesha bellowed.

His yell attracted the attention of one of the boatmen who pointed him out to the others.

'What?' one of them boomed back.

Yesha cupped his hands to his mouth. 'Try the other side!' he bawled.

'Fish there?' demanded the one doing the shouting.

'FISH!' cried Yesha with a flourish.

The men in the boat conferred for a moment. Chaim and Yohanan stayed hidden, for they had seen the little joke. Two of the fishers gathered up the small hābāk nets, wound them around their arms and flung them out.

Chaim and Yohanan grabbed the nets and pulled with all their might. One of the fishermen was jerked right out of the boat and fell into the water with a tidal wave of a bellyflop on top of Chaim, momentarily sinking him. The other net-throwers leaned over the side and looked down at the tangle of men and nets—one laughing, one blusteringly angry and the third nearly drowned. 'Hey! You two . . .' (words failed him)—'You two trouble . . .'—'makers' he would have cursed, but Yohanan grabbed his arm and pulled him into the wet tangle. There was great commotion and the other two men on the boat looked down, unable to do anything but laugh.

'Andros! Shimon! *He's here!*' Yohanan blurted out.

'Idiots! Our nets!'

'He's come! He's come!' Yohanan ranted.

'Wait till we're ashore . . .' threatened Andros.

'Who? Who's come?' Shimon spluttered.

'He's asking for you two!' Chaim gabbled.

'Who? *Who?*'

'The man from the Baptist!' cried Chaim and Yohanan in unison.

Shimon and Andros looked in amazement at the white figure on the beach . . . the one who'd lured them into this trap.

'Just some visitor using the Baptist's name,' Andros pronounced in irritation.

'No, you rotten cod! The one the Baptist promised would come!'

'The man!' Chaim declared.

Without another word the four men disentangled themselves and raced for the shore.

Shimon, the strongest of the four, a brawling big-boned seaman, about five years older than the others, was the first to scramble from the lake, followed closely by Andros, who was equally big but more round-backed, with a nose so prominently and grandly chiselled from the relief of his face that to blow it would have brought down the walls of Jericho. The brothers looked piercingly at Yesha but were tongue-tied. Yohanan and Chaim were soon together with them. Chaim broke straight in.

'Master . . .' he said to Yesha, 'this one is Shimon and this is Andros.'

'They call me the "Rock'," said Shimon bluntly.

There were many Shimons around the lake and more through the rest of the land, so that the most noteworthy were distinguished by a special name while the rest were just Shimon son of so-and-so. Andros, whose name was Galilean Greek, had nothing to say until he knew what was going on and left it all to his brother.

'Rock,' said Yesha, savouring the name. 'Rock . . . you will be my cornerstone,' he said with a wry grin.

It was the great delight of learned men to make puns in three or four languages. Yesha was an out-and-out punster. He spoke Greek, Aramaic and Hebrew as languages native to him, so that he was the master of each of their several dialects, syntax, pitch and stress. Moreover, he had acquired some basic Chaldæn and sufficient Egyptian to get by in his studies. He had nothing but rudimentary soldier-Latin. As with all good puns, they caused the ordinary man to wince, the sage to grin, the peasant not to notice and the deliverer alone to laugh, preferably inwardly.

Later, when Yesha was alone with the Rock he discovered that his had not been the first joke with Shimon's name. The 'Rock', indeed, had been so named directly by the Baptist. Yesha had presumed that it was a local name because of the fisherman's monolithic size and granite toughness but that was only part of the joke. The Baptist, as ever aware of the relativity of all things, had immediately discovered that Andros and Shimon were from one of the Greek settlements in Galilee and had equated Shimon, in one of his amazing discussions on stones, with the significant number 755, which was the numerical equivalent of the Greek for 'the Rock'. Yet again Yesha praised the thought of the Baptist and his God-sent ability to teach difficult things with amusing little games, coincidences and stories.

The Rock had not benefited much by the Baptist's sciences. He and Andros had been the most valuable men at a time when physical strength had been required at the camp, and they were willing and devoted listeners, though not so often understanders, of the Prophet's campfire tirades and discourses. They had gone to the mountain place not far from Bethabara with Chaim and Yohanan, their friends and fellow converts, and all four had received the three baptisms and more than a few times seen the Light in some of its manifestations. They regarded the Baptist as a true prophet reborn and treated him with the highest respect but spent a good deal of their time with the poorest and most radical members of the camp.

The Baptist had long been aware that his camp was divided between the spiritual and the 'practical', and saw it as the natural balance of things. Those who had told him they would die for him, he knew, probably would, and the Rock was one of them. He told the Rock to resist violence and live a simple life. This the Rock had done until recently when more and more radical groups, reviving the old fervours of Judah of Galilee's Zealot party, were adopting the Baptist's words. The Rock felt the urge to join a suitable group and had spent the last few months looking for one that would allow him to feel that he was doing something of use for the New Age. In his search he had approached many groups, but found that they were so at odds with each other that he could not make up his mind. The Baptist had promised that one would come 'after him' and the leaders of the most hard-line activists were vying with each other as self-professed saviours of the holy nation, but none of them had the blessing of the Baptist— until now.

Yesha was pleased that the Rock had detailed knowledge of the many groups in the area, and those that were sympathisers but not yet committed. How well the Baptist had chosen the man to send him to! Yesha said little of the Baptist's plans, except to explain that he was to choose, with the Rock's help, a group of twelve like those in the other groups.

'Not like any of the others,' boasted the Rock.

'How so?'

'None of the others have the Master chosen by the prophet.'

'It will take time,' said Yesha.

'You have four already, Master. Eight more will take two days —when I tell them who you . . .'

'No, don't spread it round yet. Choose carefully and discreetly who you're going to ask. Tell them.'

'What kind of men?'

'Men who've seen the Light. Men who can leave everything behind and follow me wherever I have to go.'

'There are some fine men in other Zealot groups who'd like a crack at joining us, Master. We need men with weapons.'

Yesha saw the Rock's blood rising. He rebuked him.

'Not "men with weapons" but men who can *use* weapons and *know* them. We'll have fighters, not hotheads!

'What can I possibly tell you, Rock? I'd like enlightened scholar-warriors who have given away everything and are planting the fields and spreading the Light and who are tireless, agreeable, hopefully orphaned, enjoy travel and who love people and get along well with them. Good speakers, good listeners. Men who know the Baptist's word and will do as I say. Preferably under the age of thirty,' Yesha proposed scornfully.

'I'm thirty-seven . . .' said the Rock.

'Under the age of thirty-seven,' said Yesha.

The Rock made a grimace like he was thinking very hard. Yesha thought for a moment of the smell he was breathing—the fragrance of the Valley of Flowers mingling with the warm tang of the lake.

'We'll get the best we can get, whoever they are,' the Rock stated. He looked to Yesha for approval.

'What else?'

'I think I know the very names.'

'Yes?'

'And I think I know that they'll come.' He paused. 'Though some have a wife and children . . . like myself.'

'Shimon . . .' Yesha said sadly.

'There's Philip just up the lake at Bethsaida. That's the last fisherman. He's twenty-eight. All these men are true to the Baptist.'

Yesha nodded. The Rock gave names, occupations, ages and family gossip concerning forbears. He even tried to recall their star signs to see if they would get along together. He delivered it all in his laconic, abbreviated way of speaking.

There was a sweetmaker called Toma, a farm labourer called Taddai; there was Hashimoni who made scrolls and rolls, Matthai who used a hoe or a sword with equal skill, a reformed gambling addict called Bar Talmai, and finally two musicians, totally inseparable, called Nathanael and Shimon. This Shimon was privately called 'the Zealot'. It would be wiser to call him Shimon. Those men were to be approached to join up with the five fishermen.

'They'll all come?' Yesha asked.

'Yes.'

Yesha tried to plan ahead. He would hear from the Baptist when he found this Simon who was in Samaria. Why had the Baptist warned him so insistently? How could he have a childhood friend, to whom he sent gifts, who could be made to sound so treacherous?

The Rock got up and shuffled his feet edgily in the sand.

'If it's all right with you, Master, we four will be gone for a day or two.'

'God bless you, Rock,' said Yesha.

aacov, the elder brother of Yesha by some twelve years, hurried down a dark street in Jerusalem. Lanterns and oil-lamps cast scant illumination that distorted the shapes of passers-by.

Yaacov was a member of the Sanhedrin and the news he had just received from Yohanan 'the Baptist' had put his position in jeopardy. For three days he thought and re-thought of the Baptist's message from the desert before he decided to act. He was not worried about his position in the priestly government, although that had been the first thing to come into his mind when he read the message. Yaacov was a man whose time was devoted to his priestly duties and the exact study of the written Law. He had only heard rumoured stories of the sparks of insurrection blowing through the people in the northern districts. He knew of the Baptist's teachings, for they were often the subject of discussion among his colleagues. Many priests considered the Baptist a man inspired and a man of peace, so he was thrown into dismay by this communication. Luckily he had written to his brother Yesha only a few weeks before, asking him to stay away from any groups of anarchists. But Yesha was a strange boy, apt to be carried away by odd new beliefs and impulsive whims. Yaacov had been glad to hear that Yesha had joined the following of the Baptist. He thought he understood his brother's attraction to Yohanan—the man's caustic manner, strange appearance and inspired teaching were exactly suited to Yesha. Then had come a sudden apprehension that Yesha would tire of the Baptist and be drawn to these anarchists . . . 'rumoured anarchists' he corrected himself. Now he found that the Baptist himself had done something drastic.

He hurried to an alley off the Straight Avenue to an address but no name, except that he was to ask for 'the bridegroom'. When he got to the house he thought he recognised it. He had the eerie sensation that he had walked like this before, by night, to that same door. The door was open. People were sitting on the stairs leading up to it.

'I've come to see . . . the bridegroom?' Yaacov asked a man on the steps.

'The bridegroom, Rabbe?'

'Yes. Yes. I believe that's right,' said Yaacov with deliberation. The man stood up.

'I'll see for you,' said the man and walked into the house where he spoke to another fellow leaning on a wall of the narrow hallway.

The respectful man came back and told Yaacov to go with his friend in the hallway. Yaacov blessed him and walked up into the hallway towards the man who was to direct him. Before he could greet and thank him the man turned away from Yaacov and started walking. Yaacov followed. Perhaps he was being led into a den of thieves? Twisted stairways sprang from bends in the wall. Passages rose and descended through many turns and angles. It was a hive of apartments, houses within houses. They passed many doorways. Still it seemed familiar to Yaacov. He thought he recognised little things, the carving on a doorway or a particularly acute bend on some stairs, and the way the cobbles were set there.

His guide stopped in front of a doorway and knocked. Yaacov caught up with him, out of breath from the long excursion through the tenement that lay concealed behind a single alleyway door.

'Enter,' called a voice inside.

The man opened the door for Yaacov. He turned to thank the man but he was gone. The passage was ill-lit here.

'Come in,' said the voice, before Yaacov had time to wonder at the guide's supernatural disappearance.

Yaacov walked into a simple room and closed the door. He looked up and was never before or ever after more surprised. There, facing him, was his friend and councillor on the Sanhedrin —Gur ben David! Of course, Yaacov realised: he had taken an evening meal here some seven years before. Of course the way was familiar! Yaacov stepped back in complete astonishment; more amazed than a falling leaf. There were six or seven men in the room all known to him, some better than others. They were all priests of the Sanhedrin! Mannasseh, Daniel . . . Elal! A veritable conspiracy of priests, Yaacov thought. And he was right.

s soon as the four fishermen had left, very excited, to collect themselves into a band of twelve, Yesha followed the Baptist's instructions and set off to Samaria. The Rock had been told that he was to see that the chosen men were housed as close together as possible, and wait for Yesha to return. Yesha could not tell them when this would be, since he did not know how long he would be in Samaria with this singularly curious, tricky and perhaps dangerous friend of the Baptist. The fishermen had gone to catch men, and now Yesha was to seek a queer fish—or red herring.

It was two, perhaps three days' walk to Gidda, and Yesha spent the hours debating with himself about the coming encounter. He tried to remember the exact words that the Baptist had used to describe the man. Simon, he called himself, and not Shimon, and he preferred living 'in a Greek style'. Style of what? Eating? Clothing? Stoic, Cynic, Epicurean? Yesha was familiar with the philosophies of Greece from his contacts with Greek colonists and wise men in Galilee and Phoenicia. He had read some of the writings of Plato, shown to him by a scholar in Sidon long before he had gone to the Baptist. Why had the Baptist never mentioned the name of this man before? If the man was so eccentric, why had he never heard a story or two about him? What was the 'pagan place' he had gone to? If the Baptist meant Rome, he would have said Rome. Where else then?

Samaria itself was quite pagan enough and its people were excluded from even the outer courts of the Temple in Jerusalem since the time when a band of them had entered Jerusalem at midnight, during the feast of the Passover, and made the sacred courts unclean by littering them with human bones. Yesha had remembered this incident as a boy, for he had been in Jerusalem at the time with all his family. It was said that to eat the food of the Samarians was worse than eating pig's flesh, and they were loathed by the Galileans north of them and by the people of Judaea to the south. Yesha had no particular dislike for the Samarians. They worshipped Yahweh in their own grand temple at Sebaste, and whatever the resentments between them and neighbouring districts, they were Israelites in all things.

Only in Samaria could a man be called 'the Magus' and not be challenged by the priestly authorities and stoned as a blasphemer. In ancient times a Magus was a philosopher of the Persians, a priest of the secrets of nature. Now the title had fallen into disrespect, especially among the so-called Pietists, thirsty for the blood of sorcerers and evil demoniacs.

Yesha was aware that he was not beyond being called a sorcerer himself, nor had the Baptist been beyond criticism. The idea of the New Age and the revelation of the ancient mysteries caused confusion and fear in people. The Baptist had withstood assaults that were meant to show that his knowledge was based on pagan devilry aided by demons in league with fallen angels. Always the Baptist had claimed that he had the inspiration of Yahweh, the One, the Almighty, and that there was no God on earth but the One God, the God of Israel and Moses and Abraham. This reputation was quite strong enough to keep the crazy demon-hunters away.

Did Simon 'the magician' of Gidda call Yahweh to witness in the same way? Whatever his trickeries, the selling of potions or amulets, conjuring hoaxes or wily spoofs, he was still (halevai) in good health. This led Yesha to think that perhaps the man had earned the name as a teasingly droll title for a man who was an entertainer at weddings, or whose sleight-of-hand delighted children under the age of six. No. Of course not. The Baptist had said that he was full of tricks and jokes and illusions but had warned Yesha in such a meaningful way as to indicate that 'the magician' was a man to be reckoned with. In that case, Yesha reasoned, even the 'Magus' must have been careful with what he did and said, and must always have maintained at least a show of belief in the absolute supremacy of the One God.

'One God?' the Magus queried, very vaguely. 'Of course, if that's what you believe—of course.'

'Yahweh,' affirmed Yesha.

'Who else?' said the Magus with a little shrug of the shoulders.

'The Lord of Israel,' Yesha emphasised.

'Especially,' said the Magus seriously and then laughed.

Yesha saw nothing to laugh at. The Magus was infuriatingly obscure. It was not that Yesha disliked the Magus, it was just that he could get no sense out of him. He did not deliberately evade questions, or use the manner of teaching where a question is answered by a question; on the contrary, he was always direct in his answers. But he always talked in such a way that Yesha was never sure whether the answers were sincere or not. The Magus laughed so much in their conversations where Yesha saw nothing to laugh at. He wondered whether this was a house for madmen only.

In spite of entreaties, the Magus would not give Yesha any message from the Baptist. He admitted that a message had been received but would not say what it was, always saying 'in time' or 'We'll deal with that later', as if Yesha had all the time in the world. Yesha further did not appreciate the Magus' condescending manner, as though Yesha was his pupil and not a Master in his own right and chosen above others by the very best teacher and prophet in the world. What was even worse was that the Magus now and again made some extremely irreverent remarks abou the Baptist and his teachings.

'Ah! So the old bore is still going on about the stones,' said the Magus when Yesha made a remark about the significance of Moses' tablets with the New Jerusalem and Heaven, all valued at 961. 'Give him an inch,' the Magus went on, 'and he'll take a cubit.'

Later, when Yesha was quoting the Baptist on the necessity of remaining chaste in mind and body and that both Seeker and Master should refrain from the temptations of a woman's body, the Magus said, 'Ah, so that's the old goat's excuse these days'— a remark that Yesha found so slanderous, profane and disturbing that he was about to get up and leave the room to show his displeasure when the Magus shouted 'Helene!' and a fairly buxom woman floated into the room as though she were a cloud and greeted Yesha, pouting and rolling her eyes.

'This is my little Moon-Goddess,' said the Magus. 'She is my human soul fallen into matter . . . my power of thought . . . the Mother of All, who the Powers wished to keep for themselves, though she escaped, Age after Age moving from body to body, suffering indignity upon indignity till I discovered her in a brothel in Tyre and my soul was returned to me.'

The 'soul' of the Magus wriggled her middle-aged body in pleasure, and, wiping her hands on her apron, floated back to the kitchen.

The Magus paused for a moment to let her get out of earshot and then said, 'As day has night, though they only mingle for a few moments in harmony, so man has woman.' He leaned over to Yesha more confidentially. 'The trouble is,' he said, 'she thinks she's Helen of Troy!'

This so amused Yesha that he forgave the Magus' insult to the Baptist, deciding that his words were the rather hasty and thoughtless remarks of an old man. After all, the Magus was nearly seventy.

In fact, the Magus had been most generous to Yesha, and welcomed him as though expecting his arrival. That had been Yesha's first hint that the Baptist had already contacted his friend. Indeed the Magus had been so overjoyed by the gift handed him by Yesha on the Baptist's behalf that he swore to entertain Yesha nobly 'during his visit' and even promised to leave off his work, the writing of a treatise he had provisionally entitled 'The Four Quarters of the World', for a number of hours every day to discuss or dispute any topic that Yesha cared to name. Yesha, who knew he was knowledgeable in matters far above the scope of many Masters, considered this a presumptuous warranty.

The gift, from the brief glimpse Yesha got of it, was a ring of carved green stone and sapphire set in silver and gold, in an unfamiliar snake-like design. The Magus excused himself and hurried from the room, excited as a small boy. He returned almost instantly, rubbing his hands together. He was most hospitable to Yesha thereafter, except as regards to the Baptist's message. Of that, not a word.

'Do you realise,' said the Magus one afternoon, 'what confusion you are going to cause?'

'No,' Yesha replied. 'How?'

'You think it is right to spread the Light?'

'Of course, Magus, the truth is not to be hidden.'

'Ah, the truth, the truth . . .' the Magus sighed. 'What will happen when everyone has the Light?'

'The Powers of darkness will be driven from the earth,' Yesha vowed.

'So the Light seeks out darkness?'

'As I said,' Yesha rejoined crisply.

'Does it find it?'

'Everywhere.'

'How can that be?' asked the Magus, adding abstractly, 'How can the Light find darkness?'

'As I have just said, Magus . . . by searching it out,' said Yesha, annoyed that the Magus should be driving him in circles.

The Magus paused for a minute to let Yesha, who knew he was irritated, remember his twice-repeated affirmation. Then he struck.

'How can the Light find darkness, when no darkness can be found wherever the Light is?' he probed. 'Can the searcher ever find what has vanished? The only thing he can "find" is the understanding that it can't be found.'

Yesha answered a shade too hastily, 'The Light is knowledge.'

'What use is knowledge?' the Magus appealed. It was not for Yesha to get wound up in the Magus' nonsense. As a Master he would reach the root of this argument and dispose of it.

'The use of knowledge,' said Yesha, trying to remain calm, 'is to dispel ignorance.'

'Can knowledge dispel ignorance when there is no ignorance where knowledge is? Isn't ignorance the absence of Knowledge?'

Yesha now took some moments to reflect on this. The Magus having initiated this discussion must already be several steps ahead, and Yesha searched for a reply that would conclude this intellectual nonsense. To accuse the Magus of making pointless paradoxes would be an admission of defeat. Yesha moved the dispute away from the Magus' academic position.

'If I find a man who is lost in ignorance and darkness, I can show him the Light.'

'You carry the Light to this man in ignorance and darkness, so you are the Light?'

'In that way, yes,' said Yesha warily.

'You are the Light, seeking the darkness?'

'Yes,' said Yesha more firmly. He felt he was getting the upper hand.

'Tell me then,' said the Magus, 'why are you, the bearer of Light, so determined to destroy the darkness? Were not darkness and Light both the creations of God?'

'I am talking about the Light that shines inside a man, Magus, not that thing in the sky.'

'I see,' conceded the Magus, 'that you are confirmed in your belief.'

'I do not believe—I *know*.'

'So do I,' said the Magus seriously. Then he started laughing.

During the following days several people called at the Magus' house. To some townspeople he gave remedies for cattle or crying babies. One or two, seeking stronger spells, never got past the door. A young student came to ask the Magus to be his Master, but the Magus said, not unkindly, that he never instructed pupils, gave public performances or made speeches. He explained that he was writing a book and expected to be occupied on it for at least another ten years. The student left, after opining that the Magus was not 'committed' and that he ought to 'get out and see what's going on'.

On the night that Helene stayed with friends in Shechem on some errand, the Magus let in a younger and slightly more comely woman than his day-to-day enchantress and was not seen all night. He appeared much later than usual the next morning, looking many years younger, and was in very exceptionally high spirits. He winked at Yesha and gabbled something about 'a little luminary angel' that the All-Knowing had 'placed in his fate-sphere'. Yesha made no comment. The Magus, taking advantage of his exuberance, started a dialogue with Yesha, or rather, launched an attack on him.

66

'Do you think the Light grows dimmer or brighter when mixed with the pleasures of a woman's love?'

'The Baptist . . .' Yesha started, but was interrupted.

'Is the union a great surge of energy?' The Magus asked, 'Or do you think, as Pythagoras did, that it makes a man weaker than himself?'

'I can't say,' Yesha replied.

'Can't or won't?—Never mind . . . your business, though you are welcome to my opinion.'

'I can see your opinion in your manner . . .'

'Ah—Helene!' laughed the Magus. 'Our souls are mated—and our relationship is as heavenly bodies, sometimes in conjunction, sometimes in opposition, and whirling moments in exaltation.'

Yesha laughed. The Magus peered at him earnestly.

'You have complaints about her cooking, maybe?' he demanded.

'No, no, no,' Yesha protested.

The Magus fell into a convulsive fit of laughter. When he calmed down, he spoke seriously to Yesha.

'You are the Master of many mysteries, but there is a mystery that the poorest peasant could explain in simpler terms than I. It is the uniting of Boundless Power and Mind, ordering all things male, and the Great Conception from below which is female. And each, coming from the One, has the other hidden in it. Nature is the connection in both heads. Consider it, Master.'

Their conversation was interrupted by a knock at the door. The Magus tried to compose himself, thinking that Helene had returned, but it was another kind of visitor—one of those who the Magus ushered in quickly and guided into his library. These men were never introduced to Yesha, nor was anything said about them when they had gone. Yesha had once asked, but he had been put off by the Magus in the same way that the Magus dismissed any enquiry about a message from the Baptist.

After a week with the Magus, Yesha, itching as he was to return to Galilee and see how the Rock had done, restrained himself for a further indefinite period of waiting. He knew that something was happening.

*　　*　　*

During those hours when the Magus was writing at his treatise, Yesha would leave the house and go to the highest spot above Gidda. There he would go over all the things that the Magus said to him, hoping to extract from his words some indication, one little thread in the carpet of conversation, that would give him a clue to the Baptist's reason for sending him here. There was no doubt in Yesha's mind that more than one message had been exchanged with the Baptist, and he was just as certain that the Magus' three other visitors had come from Jerusalem. He knew that all the activity concerned him and was inter-related, but he could not understand why the Magus was withholding inform-ation from him.

Yesha had now come to like the Magus. He was charmed by him. One moment Yesha would work himself up to have a pitched battle with the old man and would storm into the house only to find himself laughing at some enchantingly winsome idea that the Magus would come up with and embellish. Only hours later would he realize that his purpose had been diverted. He could never remember precisely what kind of charm, what power of entrancement could so parry his assaults before he made them and keep him in captivation. Day by day his restlessness increased. He was constantly hoping that he would get word from the Baptist and he was worried that the twelve men chosen by the Rock had not been assembled. If they were already together it would be a test for them to still be there when he returned . . . whenever he returned.

After a restless night, Yesha heard the Magus get up and go into his library. He addressed a prayer of longing and a plea for guidance to the Lord at the sun's rising and then paced up and down between the confining walls, searching for some way to tell the Magus that his patience was at an end and that either there was a message for him or there was not. Two weeks had passed and Yesha felt impelled to beard the lion in his den. He resolved that he would not be put off this time, and decided not to be aggressive, nor too persistent. He would try a new tack.

Outside the library Yesha politely announced his arrival and walked in. The Magus was not at his writing-desk but at a table piled with scripts and scrolls, some held open by paperweights, such as smooth oval grey stones with red designs, an old chipped jar containing writing implements or a worn-out sandal.

'Ah!' said the Magus, 'I was expecting you.'

This surprised and alarmed Yesha. The Magus had expected him?

'I hope I'm not disturbing you, Master?'

'No, no. Exactly the opposite. I have taken out something here that I'm sure will interest you.'

'Look, Magus, I . . .'

'See!' exclaimed the old man, pointing to a map. 'It is a copy of the best map ever made by man, done by a scribe I trust absolutely. It's the frontpiece to my treatise. Here, if you can imagine it, is the whole world on one plane!' the Magus glowed with bright enthusiasm. 'Look! Here is Jerusalem, the centre. There's Alexandria. Up here is Rome . . . Athens.'

'It is a beautiful design,' said Yesha. He found the map a great curiosity. 'There seems to be no order in it,' he said.

'Order? Do you mean that there is no symmetry in it? Surely you don't expect the earth to have the perfect order of the heavens?'

'I said "seems",' Yesha explained. 'I didn't think it would be ordered in a manner immediately visible at first glance. The geometry must be laid out in the most sacred configurations.'

'Bah!' the Magus jeered lightly. 'You sound like the Baptist, expecting to find hidden ratios and pyramidal equations. This is not geometry, it is *geography*.'

'Since you mention the Baptist, that's a subject I wanted to . . .'

The Magus did not appear to be listening. He was poring over the map as though trying to climb into it.

'Here!' he said, pointing to the farthest and highest point on the earth. 'That's where I studied certain things when I was a younger man.'

Yesha recalled that the Baptist had told him about the Magus' departure for a pagan place. What place could be so far from the centre and God's holy Temple?

'What is that place?' Yesha asked. It looked like an island.

'It has many names. The bright land, or white land . . . many names.'

'What was it like?'

'Oh, you wouldn't like it. Half the year it rains and the other half the whole land is turned into snow and ice like a mountain top. The people are blue and they set great store by stones, like the Baptist. No doubt he'd find some equations to link their great circles with his Egyptian measurements. Their priests have academies attended by the wisest monks from all the Four Quarters spread out here.' The Magus laughed. 'When I learned to speak to them they laughed and laughed at our customs and accused us of Divine arrogance, for they believe in the One God and that he is God of all the Quarters you see here and not one people.'

'And you stayed with them?'

'For three years.'

Before he realized it Yesha was talking with the Magus about stories of distant lands and foul customs and pagan habits that made Rome sound almost civilised. The Magus never seemed at all worried about anything, and even delighted in recounting the more nauseous details of these practices, as though he considered them natural and not abominable to the sight of Yahweh. Swept off again into the Magus' stories and fantasies, Yesha found that he had lost his readiness for a confrontation about the message from the Baptist. It was a surprise when the Magus himself brought the subject up.

'What a trial it is, waiting,' said the Magus.

'A trial?'

'Thinking that I am hindering your progress and keeping from you a message that will send you on your way.'

'You are,' said Yesha, fiercely.

The Magus gave a little smile. 'What do you think I am keeping you from, exactly?' he asked.

For a moment Yesha was at a loss to answer; and when words were at the tip of his tongue, the Magus, still smiling, shook his head and declared: 'What an innocent you are!'

Yesha took instant offence and bristled at this remark. 'What do you mean?'

'I will soon be able to tell you everything,' the Magus went on.

70

'What do you mean by "innocent"?' Yesha questioned again.

'Have I insulted you . . . Master?' the Magus queried.

'I want to know what you meant.'

'You are going blindly into a situation which you know little of,' said the Magus. 'When desires and ideas are astir, things do not often go as one would wish. Heaven and earth are out of balance. It is your innocence, if I may use that word without being assaulted, that confirms in my mind that you are suited to your task. I mean by this that I see that you are without ulterior designs and in harmony with your Divine fate. That is primal innocence. If you did not have that redeeming grace, where could you go? What good would you be able to do? If you are not protected by the will of Yahweh, what can you do at all?'

Yesha was silent. He could find no reply to the old Master's words. True, it was a trial to stay here, without knowing why, but perhaps this was as the Baptist had meant it to be. He could not say for himself, as the Magus had done, that he was in harmony within himself, since he thought he was troubled and full of anxiety. Then he saw that it was the people, the whole nation that was troubled and disquieted, and that it was among the people that desires and ideas were astir. He was, in his being, a reflection of the people, but he knew no more than was revealed to him in his vision, and the fact that he was chosen to do something. What exactly? He did not know. Everything depended on the Baptist. Without word from him Yesha had no resources, had dreamed of no initiatives, had nothing but the knowledge that he had been chosen for a task to sustain him. The Magus was right; waiting was a great trial. He was sure now that all this time the magician had been summing him up for himself, without paying attention to anything the Baptist may have said to recommend him.

'Let me conclude for the moment,' the Magus said. 'I have this work to get on with, and I am expecting one more visitor before the night. Later I will explain everything I can to you.'

As predicted, the Magus did have a caller that afternoon. He talked in private to the Magus for some time and left after dark.

Helene served dinner to the two Masters and afterwards cleared the table and left them to talk.

'What,' the Magus asked, 'do you know about politics?'

'The organisation of authority?'

'That is one definition.'

'Nothing beyond what the Baptist has told me.'

'Ah—nothing,' the Magus emphasised.

'What kind of politics?'

'Any kind,' said the Magus. 'Parochial, communal, municipal, domestic, national or Imperial. The principles, convictions and sympathies of any party. Acts determined by policy and men skilled in the making of policy rather than the personal decision.'

'I know the Law of the Lord,' said Yesha.

'There is more to the Law of the Lord than the Law of the Lord, if I may say. Isn't there a body of scribes and Priests who add to the Law? Who interpret it in any number of ways? Is there, or not, a body of Laws of God and a Sanhedrin to keep council over them?'

'The Law is the Law,' said Yesha firmly. The Magus laughed.

'The Baptist sent you to me because there are some things beyond his resources. Please do not protest. This is the reason that the Baptist has sent you to me.'

Yesha merely nodded, showing his concern at what the Magus was leading up to, for it was not at all clear to him.

'Let me explain,' the Magus went on. 'The Baptist knows that you have embarked on a dangerous course. The currents are fast-flowing and the under-currents are deep and treacherous. Rapids and rocks appear from nowhere. In the normal course of events you would be a dead man in a few months. The reason for this has very little to do with the Law of God but the laws of the Romans, imposed upon our Priesthood. What the Romans decree for the city of Zion is done by way of their politics, and as one wise old man of Israel has said of these politics, they are the art of governing a nation by deceiving them.'

Yesha remained puzzled. 'I can see what you mean, but I can't see how it has to do with me.'

'You are spreading the Light.'

'Yes.'

'This is the root of Yahweh and it is considered dangerous to the policies of Rome, for they fear that the Light foments revolution.'

'The vision of God . . .' Yesha began.

'Revelation leads to revolution,' the Magus asserted. 'This is known to the Roman authorites. They would see the Light stamped out forever, leaving only black smoke over a scorched land.'

'I don't understand.'

'Never mind, little Master,' the Magus chuckled. 'The Realm of politics is one of the lowest domains of the Kingdom of God. I know you are used to higher things.'

'Please . . .'

'In brief, then. The Baptist has sent you to me because he believes that your visionary powers and your knowledge and love of God are a sign that you have been chosen by Yahweh. This you also believe.'

'Yes.'

'To survive and keep the truth is easier than to broadcast it. The Baptist has friends in Jerusalem who will help him see that you are well advised and come to no harm, but they are not enough. He needs to know of the possibility of support from the Jewish communities in Babylon and even in Rome. These are contacts that I have. I have had to observe you, Yesha, and make reports to agents in Jerusalem and receive answers. Questions are asked. How far will you go? Is Zion to be free? Are weapons required? Will there be a war?'

'A Holy war.'

'A Holy war that may be of speculative interest to merchants, exiled in luxury, with dreams of a liberated people. You see, we have our own politics between Jerusalem and our fellow Jews in every great city.'

'In *brief*, I believe, was . . .'

'Initial reaction is, I may tell you, highly favourable, but there's a high risk. You are an outsider, you see. If you already had a popular following, there would be no questions. They must get to hear more of you.'

'They will.'

'Then you can be sure of support on a large scale. Meanwhile, everything will be done, as the Baptist requests, to see that you come to no harm.'

'I thank you for the help of your invisible forces, Master,' rapped out Yesha, 'but now I would like to know the Baptist's message to me.'

The Magus got up from the table and walked towards his room. Yesha could not see the displeasure on his face but he could feel it falling in waves from the old man. Yesha got to his feet quickly and put down his own pride and anger. The Magus, in his mysterious way, had offered him help. Some kind of help that he did not understand, but had been asked of the Magus by the Baptist.

'Master, I'm sorry,' Yesha called after the Magus.

The old man turned round. Yesha had never seen such a dark expression on the Magus' face. His figure grew large over Yesha, as though the Magus was standing on the air for a fleeting moment. Then the formidable figure seemed to recede to the other end of the room, almost instantaneously, and the Magus stood, looking stooped and old and tired, wearing his familiar facetious grin. The concentrated force that had built up in the room vanished. The Magus dismissed the matter with a wave of his hand. 'Later. Later,' he muttered.

Yesha did not argue further. The Magus went to join his waning moon-goddess.

It was the cool part of the later afternoon when the villagers came out of their sunbaked houses to take the fragrant breeze from the lake, using the beach as a promenade, to gossip about their neighbours and talk of fish and the future.

Yesha had divided his group into three, being careful that a larger mass than the other groups of fishermen would not call too much attention to them. They were all, except for the four fishermen, strangers to the town. The Rock and the other brothers had done their best to spread it around that the others were relatives and cousins who had come to settle a disputed estate, and this gave little pretext for gossip to the villagers, who could wonder only as to the amount of money or goods that was under discussion.

No word had got about yet that Yesha was the emissary of Yohanan the Baptist—the Rock had seen to that. All the men he had gathered together knew the importance of this being kept a secret until the time was right. If people in the district were to know, there would be large crowds coming to hear the fiery rabble-rousing they so much enjoyed. Yesha needed the time to get to know his followers and to instruct them in the way they were to carry out their various missions.

All the men that the Rock had named had come as he promised, leaving their work, their wives, families and possessions in order to follow the man chosen by the Baptist. Since the murder of Zachariah and the subsequent disposal of his imprisoned brother Josiah, there had been other incidents. Two more demonstrations had been broken up by the forces of Antipas in Galilee; and the procurator of the other provinces, Pontius Pilate, had dispersed other gatherings with troops from the fortresses of Caesarea and Antonia in Jerusalem. In these latest forays the troops of both forces had been warned against indiscriminate bloodshed. The crowd themselves had been freed after reprimands, while the leaders and organisers, when they could be found, were made an example to the public and crucified as bandits outside the walls of towns and cities. More than ever the people were seeing successive executions of uncondemned persons and were constantly reminded by these barbarities and excessive cruelties that the Chosen race of God were the slaves of an alien and repressive rule that cared nothing for the sacred worship of a subject people. It was even becoming difficult for priests and holy men to preach in towns and villages without fear of being crucified in this new wave of tyranny. Thus, Yesha and his followers were most circumspect in their movements and behaviour.

'Whoever comes with me,' Yesha told them, 'is in danger of being nailed up by the authorities. By following me you are carrying your own crosses to the places of execution.'

All of them considered the warning in their hearts and were prepared for their actions to lead them to their deaths.

'We have our eyes open,' said Matthai, who spent all his time sharpening a fish-knife into a razor.

'The time has gone when we could trust and wait. Peace has failed. Waiting has failed. Trust has failed. If I must, I will have the matter argued out and resolved in every household in the land. I will set son against father and brother against brother.'

'Not in *our* house,' grinned Chaim at his brother.

'Our innocence is lost,' said Yesha, seriously.

'Then we are forced to purify ourselves in blood,' said Matthai.

Yesha said no more. He retreated into himself as the others threw out their warlike threats and bloody oaths. He fired them with rage only to hold them back. In the same way he said there was no more time, while playing and praying for time. He had decried their lost innocence, knowing that it was not lost. There was so much that they did not know. He could give them the Light and teachings of righteousness but they could never know him. There was no point in thinking of the matter. A dark mood came down on him. He could have dispersed it and the demons of the mood with it but he let it come. It was as though he had to wrestle with his doubts and let them hurt him before he conquered them. He could have sidestepped into the blissful void of meditation but he chose to be hurt.

Some few yards away the Rock was sitting with the two ardent musicians, Nathaniel and Shimon, who were trying in concert to impress a fact on Toma, the sweetmaker, without success. Toma would only believe it when he saw it, which was the way with ambitious and over-imaginative confectioners. Too much had been sticky where it should have been creamy and too many more had new tastes that were unpopular for the man's temperament to have been other than sceptical. He had no doubts about the Light; he had seen it and believed it, and it had stolen him away. It was so powerful in its effect on him that now the thought of sweetmeats made him shudder that he had devoted so many years to making pretty rubbish.

'In the same way,' said Nathaniel, bringing in an example to prove his argument, 'that you have to destroy in order to build.'

'That's not so, necessarily,' said Toma.

'You have to knock down an old house to put up a new one.'

'You can build elsewhere,' Toma replied.

'But if you want that particular space, and the house is falling down . . .'

'It's not beyond repair.'

'Let's *say* it's beyond repair. Then you build on top? No! You pull it all down, foundations and all, and then you build just what you want. That's exactly what we're saying.'

The argument continued. The Rock looked over to the Master and was distressed to see him suddenly so melancholy. He put the Master's brooding down to deep thought, the working out of details in the future that would carry them all into the Kingdom of God. It would not do at all to disturb him. The Master's withdrawn and heavy gloom of concentration had caused his group to begin to fall silent. Perhaps they too had caught the same feeling as the Rock—that the Master's body was there but the Master was not. If that was the case, then he had left his body frozen in an attitude that would frighten the most fearful demon from entering it to take possession.

Nathaniel noticed that the Rock had lost interest in the dispute and turned to see what he was looking at. Shimon looked too, and Toma. They fell silent, like those in the Master's group. None of them had seen the Master like this. It was undoubtedly a sign.

Yaacov's house in Jerusalem was a simple one. He did not have the acquired or inherited wealth of many of his colleagues on the council, nor did he want them. His asceticism was a private thing, uninfluenced by the vaunted righteousness of pharasaic thought. His main room was bare except for some worn and carefully folded bedding and a small table with candlesticks.

Yaacov was disturbed. His friend Gur ben David had arrived. For the first time he expressed the doubts that had assailed him since he had been aware of his brother's activities.

'I do not know that he is strong enough,' said Yaacov, anguished.

'The Baptist thinks he is. That must be accepted.'

'Yesha's joining the Baptist was all to the good when he was learning to heal and studying the writings and rituals of possessing spirits. What he is doing now . . .'

'All the same, Yaacov, listen to me. He had been chosen and has been carrying out his task with a clever astuteness and wisdom rarely seen in anyone of his age. The time has come that he should let the people know that he is the one chosen by Yohanan, their prophet.'

'In my bones I do not feel it,' Yaacov sighed.

'Yesha will be proclaimed a holy man.'

'Could he . . .?'

'Not by himself, perhaps, but our own agents will carry the news ahead of him and after him wherever he goes. I understand your fears. Only in his own family is a prophet considered unworthy of praise.'

'I know the aphorism.'

'But you dismiss it and continue with your fears,' snapped ben David.

'If I could see some other course . . .'

'You,' rapped Gur ben David severely, 'can do more harm to the confidence of the movement and the faith of those within our own circle by speaking just as you are doing. We are trying to unite and gain strength within the Council so that we can help your brother,' Gur ben David emphasised. 'You understand if the resistance is not to fail its planning must be in the hands of responsible men.'

'Responsible to whom?'

'To Yesha who is responsible to the Baptist and to God and his people. Yahweh has promised us that he shall alone rule the world and his people shall rule it with him! We believe that the Romans can be driven out!' Gur ben David swore passionately. 'Yahweh is calling his people to action and they must be made to hear and rise up!'

Yaacov had heard the words expressed passionately all his life, but he had never had them forced so close to home; to his own family. His young brother was to be the forceful arm of a group who were willing to kill and be killed for their ideals. Once blood began to be spilled by their own people, then it would soon turn to internal argument. Fighting would be murder; terror would become the only bond uniting the people. It would be the young and the poor that would be hurt, whatever the outcome. Roman reprisals would be quick and merciless. Yaacov thought how little there was that could be done to save Yesha. He was as good as dead already. Gur ben David offered hope at the same time as he preached death . . . even his own death. Hope was enough.

'There are others and many of them have failed,' Yaacov muttered.

'There has been no leadership until the Baptist committed Yesha.'

'How long do you think it will be before you . . . succeed?'

'We cannot be unrealistic. It will need time. Perhaps two years or more. He will see it done.'

'I want a good man to be with him,' Yaacov declared. 'Someone who can be at his side to protect him and can be trusted to run a link between the core of resistance in the country and your organisation here.'

'That has already been decided,' ben David replied. 'There was no better man than the one we have approached. He has some of the leanings of the healers and has lived with the Baptist in the desert. Naturally such a man is invaluable . . . to him and to us.'

'If Yesha is killed . . . I do not want to think about it.'

'Our choice is the best dagger-man known.'

'Will he go?'

'As I said—he is being approached. We have no doubt whatsoever that he will go to Yesha,' ben David said meaningfully. He

hinted that there was more to his certainty than he could say.
Yaacov was exhausted with worries. He could say nothing more
to Gur ben David.

'If it must be.'

'It must.'

Yesha had been on the road, moving from village to village
for weeks. With him he took only Shimon, who, in
spite of constant reminders, could not shake people
from calling him Shimon the Zealot. Even Yesha's own followers
could not prevent them from calling him simply 'the Zealot' in
a familiar and half-mocking way. In so many ways he was a
Zealot of the old and almost sentimental early Galilean revolt.
So much of his talk was of the traditional Zealot ideals knocked
into him by his father that it showed by making him a mimic
of himself. The others, who might equally have been called
Zealots, did not use this name. They called themselves by such a
variety of names that the invention of a new appellation was like
a gem of poetry in itself. They were 'the Children of God' and 'the
light-bringers' and 'the Brotherhood' and 'the Sons of Man' and
'the scourge of Israel'. They called themselves 'the Word' or 'the
Word in flesh' and 'the Baptised', 'the Inheritors' and code-names
such as 'the Kanaans' or 'the roots'. Jokingly they even called
themselves 'the lepers', 'the fishermen' and 'the Damned'. Shimon,
however, knew that whatever they called themselves, and whatever
caused God's Light to be revealed to them, they were still, by
all the standards he knew, Zealots. He bore their teasing with
a smug satisfaction. At least he was known and acknowledged as
what he was.

At the chosen hill, a high and renowned sacred place, he met
up with the brothers. Chaim came first with Taddai and Bar
Talmai. They were joined by the Rock with Nathaniel and Toma.
Matthai and Philip came with Yohanan. Andros arrived by
himself.

They had been in the villages and visited the small farms spreading the good news that the 'Chosen' promised by the Baptist had come and would speak to them on the hill at a certain time. Not all were visited, there were characters that they were warned to stay clear of.

A good number had promised to come to hear the Master and even more appeared. There were sick and ailing people, brought by families looking for cures. There were young men keen to see the Light. There were the merely curious and the fanatical misfits, all wishing to hear what the Master chosen by the Baptist had to say for them personally. Some came early and were the first to see the new Master.

Yesha, flanked by the Rock and Matthai, greeted the arrivals and analysed the sick as they came to him. He had to tell them that he could not heal everyone since his healing power, which was strong when it came on him, could heal many, but the period it lasted was short and drained him of energy. It had to be saved until he had spoken to them and healed hearts before he healed bodies.

Yesha's other helpers went through the gathering crowd to talk to the people and feel out their opinions and concerns, and to encourage them to sit down and relax themselves until the Master was ready. They noticed members of other dissident groups in the audience and greeted them as brothers, expressing the wish for a new solidarity between all the factions that opposed Rome and sought a reformed priesthood in Jerusalem. Andros was able to discover by talking to these men whether there were any spies or suspected informants among the crowd.

Gradually the assembly quietened down and people settled as comfortably as possible on the ground. Yesha came to the front and his helpers gathered around him and sat down at his feet. Yesha stood still until there was absolute silence and then spoke out clearly and firmly so that even those furthest away could hear every word.

'I am here to tell you about a new heaven and a new earth. I have come to tell you about a new creation and a new age. The Kingdom of God is here, and I want to tell you that it is *yours*!

I know that you are oppressed—this Kingdom of God is for the oppressed. It is for the meek and the humble who expect nothing from this life. It will be the reign of Yahweh's Light on earth and in this land. The new age is for the hungry and the thirsty—for those who hunger for the love of their Lord and for those who thirst after the redeeming waters of his purification. It is coming for those of you whose spirits are weak and troubled. You, whose spirits mourn for Israel, who fear for this holy nation and can see no way to embrace the salvation that is to come. For those who have pure and shining spirits and who have hope of the days that are to come, I can assure you that you shall see God and he will live in you forever. His Light will shine in all hearts. The Kingdom of Light is here! You can *take* it! It is the Kingdom to be sought out with Love for each other and uniting as the legions of God! It can be won if you can stop quarrelling with your neighbours and listen to the voice, the Word, the Light inside that will lead us into a great new Creation. We can do this with our common love and with our *strength* . . . our strength of purpose. Together we can bring peace to this land forever! We shall be blessed for making this peace for it is making peace with Yahweh. Happy we will then be to show mercy and forgive those who have persecuted and robbed and taxed our spirits beyond endurance. We have learned to endure, but now is the time that we can unite our spirits and rid ourselves of all afflictions and all misfortunes. Those who carry the Light will be the light of the world, and this Light cannot be hidden any more than you can hide a city built on the top of a hill. *We* are the city that will be built as a beacon. Look around you and you will see in your fellows the foundation-stones of this city—it is the City of God!

'I have not come here to mock and destroy the Law and the prophets. If you think that, you are wrong. I have come to fulfil the prophecies and to see that the law of this land is the Law of God and Moses and no other!

'We turn for knowledge of the Light of God to the Holy Temple and we see that our High Priests are chosen by the Romans and under them our elders are puppets and collaborators, who would destroy the Light if ever they could! Come forward and

I will show you the Light that will heal your minds and your bodies. Come forward those who are strong and resolved to prepare themselves for the coming of the Kingdom. Come forward! Come to me! I will show you things hidden since the beginning of the world!'

After a month Yesha's reputation had grown so strong that it was known throughout Galilee that the man promised by the Baptist had come and was speaking to crowds in the countryside. He had spoken only a few times, but to ever-increasing numbers. Twice he had gone into towns and spoken in the temples. On these occasions he wore the white robe of the healers. He stayed with the Rock and Andros and their sisters, parents and grandmother. At one point the Rock's mother was unwell with some minor complaint and Yesha was able to make her well again. When the Rock's mother had a minor complaint, it meant that the ailment was minor but the complaint of the woman was almost unbearable. Her main topic of conversation was her health and fond memories of former maladies. Just as loud and long as her complainings was her praise for Yesha when she was well again. She told her friends of her pain and discomfort and how it had vanished in minutes. 'I've never known such healing!' she would exclaim, or 'I tell you it's a miracle I'm here to see you at all and not dead and buried—a miracle!' These sentiments were echoed by anyone he had been able to help or soothe after his speeches.

It was not long before so many visitors were coming to see Yesha that all local houses had filled their rooms and barns, and small encampments were beginning to form. So many aches and wheezes and little pains here and there and big pains shooting from here to there seemed to exist that it was like a battleground where the demons of disease paraded their ranks. Yesha used this time to instruct his followers how to deal with a great number of illnesses. He taught them how to distinguish a real disease from an imagined one, or rather real enough but having causes that needed no herbs for treatment since they sprang from burdens on the spirit or soul. How often they were able to relieve a pain that came from some wrong act or groundless worry. How easily Yesha taught them the manner to reach the heart of the question and then become a sympathetic listener to a mass of confessions of guilt and despair. What large numbers of pains fled away when the reassurance of God's everlasting love was given to them. For serious defects they learned how to use herbs and berries and grasses to actually cure in many cases, and always to soothe the incurable. Using only a few tiny grains of the mandrake, Yesha was able to do wonders with warts.

The greater the number of people coming to the gatherings by lake, the further spread the news. Andros, always on the watch, pointed out to Yesha two men he thought had come to spy, and the next day there were two more. Even Yesha could see that these last two were from the court of Antipas by the foolish ways they attempted to disguise themselves. Their clothes, ill-chosen and almost funny, could not cover up their bearing, gait and mannerisms. Eventually one of these men came to Yesha on the pretext of having something wrong with his wrist. The man bared his arm for Yesha to examine it.

'They say you are a better healer than the Baptist,' said the man.

'No-one is better,' said Yesha. There was nothing wrong with the man's wrist but Yesha continued to examine it to see what else this man had to say.

'When will you speak again? They say you have not made a speech to these people.'

'Why should I make a speech to sick people?' said Yesha and twisted the man's wrist a tiny bit so that he gave a little yelp.

'There,' said Yesha, releasing the informant's hand. 'That should do the trick. Is that better?'

'It feels much the same as I described it,' said the informer.

'If there is discomfort, it will go away.'

'Thank you. Thank you, Master,' the man replied, with the slightest hint of sourness.

'I won't be speaking here,' Yesha told him.

'I am sorry not to get the chance to hear you,' said the man. He was moved on by Shimon and Nathaniel to let another person receive Yesha's attention.

'They want to report on what you are saying,' Andros said quietly to Yesha. 'I'm sure they won't stay now, Master. You're wise not to make a speech here.'

'But I will,' said Yesha, and told a mother what to do for the rash on her young son's back.

Both pairs of spies left two days later, and Yesha knew that it was time to move on. The chances were that these men were taking back all kinds of gossip about his words. It was not un- likely that there might be an attack by Antipas' soldiers. The best way to get well clear of any sudden vicious reaction was to cross the lake.

The Rock got some friends to help Chaim and Yohanan to bring the boats back. There was only just room enough to carry everybody across the lake right out of Antipas' province. Yesha told them it would be best for the fishermen's families and friends, and the scores of sick people, if they wasted no time in getting away. The boats were ready. There was some leavetaking to be done. Yesha got up into the prow of the Rock's boat.

Word was sent through the people of Yesha's departure. Immediately the crowd surged to the shore. The last of Yesha's followers waded out to Zebedee's boat and were hauled aboard. Many of those that Yesha had not yet had a chance to help waded out into the water, pleading that the Master stay and cure them. Some of the more able got to the boats and tried to clamber aboard but they were held off by the nearest of Yesha's followers. One more person in the boat and it would have slipped slowly under the water. Fully loaded there were only a few inches of topboard and the boat was old and already taking water.

Yesha held up his arms to call for silence. He bawled out his message.

'It is no longer safe for us to stay here. Your own lives and not just your health are in peril here. Please listen to me and go quickly from this place. You all know the measures of the authorities. I will return again to cure your ills. Pray for our mission and bear witness to what good has been done here. Spread the good news wherever you go to those you trust. I have been told by the Lord God who dwells in me . . . and by his servant Yohanan the Baptist who is possessed by Elohim's spirit. I have been told to take a city—even Jerusalem. I am told to lay siege against it and set camps against it. The time is coming. You will be called. It is up to you to understand and be ready.'

The crowd gathered in tighter to hear Yesha's words. The Rock tried to indicate to Yesha that all was ready for them to set sail, but the Master did not seem to see anything around him. Yesha was rapt in his exhortation.

'I prophesy this!—that there will be dark days when smoke shall cover the sun and the moon will be turned to blood! The sounds in the city will be weeping and screaming, but those who hear the new will of Yahweh shall be spared for the rule of Heaven on earth! The Law is corrupt! The Temple is defiled! It is the End of the Days and those who love the Lord will follow me and purify this holy nation!'

The sails unfurled and the fishermen in the two boats pulled on the oars until the wind carried them away from the shore and into the deeps of the lake.

As evening drew on, the winds started to gust and blow up white spray across the water. The waves became stronger and those who were not seamen feared a storm. The fishermen were themselves concerned at the appearance of even small waves since the boats were so low in the water that there was a danger of them swamping.

The boats drifted apart, tacking as best they could to avoid the increasing surge of the waves. Chaim looked across to the boat carrying Yesha. In the dim light it was almost impossible to make out any details. The boat itself was hidden by rolling waves. He could only see the white figure of Yesha, standing high in the prow. It was as though the ghostly figure of the Master was alone, suspended above the water. Chaim pointed the apparition to Matthai and Toma. They looked at the weird sight for a few moments and then, nodding their heads, ducked back down and carried on bailing.

Only three of Yesha's party went into the town. It was dangerous to go into this town since it was situated near a Roman post on the road from the south of the lake to Damascus. It was necessary to hold the meeting in a known clearing in the rugged land, about two hours' walk through rocky ravines. It was arranged that the meeting would be held late enough in the day for darkness to come down just as the returning groups got back to the town and surrounding villages. It was a great advantage if those who came to hear Yesha were able to slip back to their homes hidden by the night.

Hundreds came. Hundreds more than the recruiting group had estimated. Men, women and children had crossed the rough terrain.

'There's thousands!' said Bar Talmai.

'Speak to them, Master,' Yohanan urged in a panicky whisper.

Yesha sent his band through the crowd to act as marshals, ordering everybody to sit down, to spread out, so that all might see. The flock gradually sat down and fell silent. Everyone stared at Yesha. He sensed an air of uneasiness in the people. They were hot, dusty and sore-footed after the walk to get to this place. He felt that they were tense and in no mood to be receptive to what he had to say. The crowd's nervousness was mirrored in Yohanan. He begged Yesha once more to begin.

'Please, Master—they're waiting,' said Yohanan in agitation.

'But they've walked hard to get here. I cannot speak to them until we have eaten and drunk together,' Yesha replied.

Yohanan looked incredulously at Yesha. 'There is no food, Master. There is nothing!'

Yesha smiled at Yohanan and spoke with the slightest tinge of sarcasm. 'How well you know these people, Yohanan,' he said, then called to Andros who hurried to the Master's side. 'How much food do we have, Andros?'

'For us?'

'Yes. What have we got?'

'Some fish, Master. Some bread.'

'How much?'

'Scarcely enough to go around the thirteen of us, Master.'

'Bring me a small loaf.'

Andros went to their bag of provisions. Those around looked on in dismay as Yesha took a loaf of bread from Andros. He held the loaf up to the crowd. Then he laughed and broke the loaf in two halves. With a big grin on his face Yesha addressed his audience.

'We're all a little tired. We can't listen without refreshment,' he said. 'Let's eat!'

There was a murmur from the crowd. Neighbour looked suspiciously at neighbour. Then a gasp of delight from part of the multitude spread as a sigh of relief and then a ripple of laughter.

Yesha watched as the poor but not stupid congregation reached under their garments and into their travelling pouches, packets, bags, and brought out their personal food and drink. A very few had not come prepared with food and drink across the hot rugged land and these were handed things to eat and drink by those around them. In what seemed the blink of an eye everybody in the crowd was laughing with food and drink in their hands.

The Rock roared with laughter. Andros looked in amazement from the people to Yesha. Yohanan blushed with embarrassment but Yesha just grinned and threw half a loaf of bread across to him. Their own food was divided and they joined in the meal. Everyone felt good. The whole mood of the gathering had changed.

'They're eating out of my hands,' Yesha said jokingly to the Rock.

Yesha did not join in the meal. He turned to the gathering and shouted out to them at the top of his voice. 'Brothers! Sisters! I have been sent to you by Yohanan the Baptist, the living

Elijah, to tell you of what is to come! I have come to tell you of a new heaven and a new earth! I have come to tell you about a new creation and a new age! The Kingdom of God is here! . . .'

erod Antipas, the son of Herod the Great by Malthace, a Samarian woman, was made tetrarch of Galilee and Peraea in his father's will. He had held the position safely under the Romans for thirty-five years and looked to be keeping it for some years to come. He achieved this by doing exactly what everybody wanted him to do. He was a pious Jew, who gave all priestly parties an ear, and he was unquestionably answerable to the Emperor in Rome. He managed both powers by losing himself in his open-natured vagueness and perceptive forgetfulness. He cultivated a nature totally opposite to that of his father, a man remembered as diseased, despotic and unpopular but who built the great Temple in Jerusalem and many other great buildings and had held the sacred nation through diplomacy and battled against any foreign overlord. He had played against Octavius Caesar and Antony and Cleopatra, eight wives and a diabolical plotting sister. He had won by tyranny and had paid for his victory in raging madness. He was a barbarian, and an Arab. He had murdered his own family, and many others. He had little regard for the Jews. But for all that, he was Herod called 'The Great'.

Antipas, thus, removed himself as far as was possible from the shadow of his despotic father's image.

In all things Antipas was compliant with Roman wishes. He simply remained as far aloof from matters as he could, appearing unaware of any of the manœuvring that went on around him.

With Antipas, on a shady terrace of the fortress and palace of Machaerus, was the Roman diplomat, Caius Clavius. Clavius was the key man between Antipas, Pilate and the Legate of Syria. Antipas found little in common with this diplomat, born in Rome and bred in Antioch. He was short, thin and whey-faced, with little hair and sunken, cowled eyes. He professed himself to be proselyte of the Jewish Faith, for reasons undoubtedly diplomatic. His voice, silky and insinuating, was less repellent to Antipas than those of his courtiers, since Clavius never indulged in flattery but spoke to the point, however indirectly. Moreover, the diplomat, while enshrouded in deceptive titles for unimportant or non-existent activities, was known by Antipas to have almost direct access to Caesar Tiberius.

Clavius had sought private audience with Antipas on a brief visit to Machaerus. First he went over the latest information from Rome about Antipas' profligate and spendthrift cousin Agrippa, currently at the Emperor's court. Antipas had other sources of information among the aristocrats of the Jewish community in Rome but he regarded the diplomat's more intimate reports as a favour, to be balanced against other sources of intelligence.

Clavius, as Antipas had long known, expected a favour for favour. The diplomat was quick to bring up another matter.

'Antipas . . .' said the diplomat abruptly, 'I am charged by the Procurator to broach another topic with you.'

'If it falls within my province . . .' Antipas replied graciously.

'Sources of information reaching the government suggest that there are signs of unrest, even rebellion of some kind . . . within your province.'

'Hmm. Bandits,' murmured Antipas.

'Not necessarily.'

'I am not slow to stamp on outright rebellion, Clavius, but there is none within my jurisdiction.'

'Nevertheless, this much is known: there are certain practices, certain "cults", preaching political upheaval couched in terms of religious change . . .'

'My dear Caius . . .'

'The situation is apparent. There are at least three militant groups carrying out acts of terrorism.'

'We have had to deal with some banditry, but I know nothing of this "terrorism".'

'In the last week,' said the diplomat carefully, 'three of our local officials have been murdered.'

90

'Where?'

'In Shiloh and Lydda.'

'Surely that is Pilate's business.'

'It is thought that the murderers came from your territories.'

'I shall do what I can,' said Antipas, trying to withdraw.

The diplomat remained firm. 'It is thought that these murderers are more than ordinary bandits or thieves. These are the first symptoms of rebellion. I know you would immediately put down rebellion, but there is none yet. There are, however, symptoms, Antipas, symptoms. One can easily sense the mood of the people. These new cults are stirring up revolution. Rebellion can, in certain cases, be contained within the state; revolution cannot. In this country both are intolerable. The political facts . . .'

'The people are not acquainted with your concept of politics, Clavius. They have only their religion. As for "cults"—your own life has not been without a change of sects.'

'In this province politics is religion—religion *is* politics. There is one movement whose adherents are stirring the old Zealot cause; and their philosophy, whether religious or political, is a threat to the security of the nation and the Empire.'

'Who are you meaning?'

'The followers of Yohanan called "the Baptist".'

'I have myself had observers make reports and find that the followers of this man's philosophy are looking for simplicity and waiting for spiritual deliverance.'

'*Spiritual* deliverance?'

'These men are guilty of no crimes. If there is unrest, Clavius, would you have me provoke the situation further?'

'We want the arrest of this man. Have him brought here. We will question him.'

'This man is more important to our people than the Roman idea of a "hero". This Yohanan is a poor man, a *holy* man. He is believed to be a prophet! . . . not that I, of course . . .'

'We know precisely,' said the diplomat.

'You are ill-advised,' said Antipas bitterly.

'It is believed that his followers are not numerous. If he is held, the following will fall away. In the body politic, as in the body religious, when the head is cut off the body dies. This thing will be stopped before it starts.'

'We do not do these things to our prophets!'

'You believe this man to be a prophet?' said the diplomat, icily.

'I *know*,' Antipas retorted, extricating himself, 'that the people believe the man is a prophet. There will be uproar.'

'We choose a minor uproar now rather than risk having to take more serious measures in the future. A calculated risk.'

'It is *my* risk!' Antipas protested in exasperation. 'It is in my province!'

'Exactly.'

'This interference is abhorrent and intolerable. It will damage confidence in my administration.'

'If the man is as innocent as you say, and as he pretends—we shall see. We do not have a policy of exterminating "prophets" or harmless lunatics.'

The diplomat bowed to Antipas and then gave him a stiff Imperial salute. Antipas waved a very rough approximation of this gesture of allegiance to the Emperor.

'You are most kind to accept our request,' the diplomat said formally. 'I know you will see to it that the matter is treated with urgency.'

The diplomat turned and walked away. Antipas seethed in frustration and anger. He took short paces up and down, up and down. Then he stormed away from the parapet and back into the palace. A Sadducean courtier with advance knowledge of the diplomat's request approached Antipas and asked if he could serve him in anything. Antipas composed himself.

'Yes,' he said, drifting back into his familiar dreamy, detached manner. 'You can take some instructions to the Captain of the Guard . . .' he said blankly.

esha and the brotherhood travelled down the road from Beth-Shean to Jericho. The group was split up into twos and threes since they did not want to be conspicuous as a large band on the highway. After Jericho Yesha planned to go on to Bethany where they could all stay on the farm of Eleazar before pressing on to Jerusalem for the feast of the Passover. Yesha had received news that the Baptist was not at his camp, but had been at the springs of Beth-Shean in advance of him. The Baptist left the message that he would contact him in Bethany. For this message Yesha had to go in the morning to Jaacov's well in Sichara and say the words 'I am thirsty', and he was informed of the Baptist's movements. Apart from this meeting at the well, Yesha pressed on quickly and spent no more time in Samaria.

There were many other pilgrims coming down the road to Jericho and Jerusalem in order to be sure of accommodation. Half a million people would eventually flood into the city for the feast.

Under the walls of Jericho, Yesha regrouped with his helpers. It was passably safe here as there was such a mass of people coming and going through the city gates.

Outside the city walls were the ragged tents and makeshift hovels of the cast-outs—the diseased, the leprous, the mad and the poor—who could not prove to the guards at the gates that they had sufficient means to keep themselves in Jericho or that they had relatives or friends to help them. When Yesha's band were a few hundred feet from the gates, they were beset by beggars. Yesha was able to distinguish, in the flock of beggars, a certain number who were not blind or crippled but hardened malingerers and parasitic idlers. Matthai and Shimon tried to brush aside the beggars but Yesha said to leave them. He would deal with this in his own way. Yesha picked out a strong little man, pushing his way from the back of the crowd, with his hand out for alms and crying 'Blind . . . blind . . . blind . . .' Tearing and elbowing people out of the way, he soon got to the front of the throng. Those furthest away dropped back to accost the next bunch of arrivals at the gates.

'Not here, Master!' the Rock urged. 'We should hurry through.'

'One moment,' said Yesha, purposefully. He reached out and grabbed the 'blind' man roughly by his clothes and pulled his face right up to his own.

'Blind . . . blind . . .'

Yesha spat in the man's left eye. The blind man's eyes sprang open in surprise. He tried to pull away but Yesha kept a firm grip on the fistful of clothes. Yesha spoke to him fiercely.

'Can you see better?'

The blind man was thrown into confusion but had to keep up his pretence.

'I can . . .' he gabbled, 'I can *almost* . . .'

Yesha spat in the man's open right eye and glared harshly into his face.

'Yes. Yes! I can see! Let me go!' the beggar howled. Yesha let him loose, and the man tried to flee but he was surrounded by many other outcasts who looked at his fearful rolling eyes and set up a clamour, shouting, 'He can see!' and 'That man cured him!' The crowd turned to find the face of the man who had done this miracle, running from stranger to stranger, tugging at sleeves and begging for the healer. Yesha was swept forward by the Rock and Matthai. The other helpers temporarily blocked the road and prevented anyone from following until Yesha was safely inside the city.

Several travellers who had seen the incident followed Yesha and his helpers into the city. An increasing number joined the parade. Mobs of the curious fell in as they moved briskly down the busy street. Rumours danced from ear to mouth.

'Where are we going?' asked Yohanan, close on Yesha's heels. 'Master, you must be careful.'

Yesha looked behind. There were perhaps a hundred people following them.

94

'We are a noisy crowd, aren't we, Rock?' Yesha grinned.

'A good noise, I'd say.'

'Master . . .' Yohanan blurted out, then caught himself and stopped bleating his worries and questions.

'I'm going to the synagogue,' said Yesha.

Yohanan could not restrain himself. 'They'll have us stoned!' he cried, very worried indeed.

'All of us?' Yesha said over his shoulder with an arched eyebrow.

The whole strange rabble followed Yesha, the Rock and Matthai into the splendid courtyard of the Jericho synagogue. The twelve brothers used their strength to keep the throng back and clear a space for the Master. Yesha clenched his fists and strode up and down. He ground his teeth and shouted wildly and incoherent names into the sky. Then he turned and harangued the crowd. The Priests were quickly on the scene of the disturbance, but such things were not uncommon and they watched carefully and noted everything Yesha said, down to its finest nuance.

'Clear the straight pathways to the Lord! Clear the way for the people to know and understand the living Light! Take the straight path with enthusiasm and the Lord will enter you without resistance! *Your* resistance! Your obstinacy and ignorance keeps him from your hearts! Clear out the unclean spirits! Clear the unclean spirits from their citadel! Clear and cleanse the land of the evil spirits which possess it! Let love unite us! Let our love of our Lord bind us together for this task! Let *love* enter our Temple! Let *love* sweep away the demons!'

Two Sadducees scrutinised the raving glaze-eyed madman in front of them. They did not recognise his face. He was not one of the usual old men who came and were possessed by the Almighty. He did not speak gibberish. His message was very clear and calculated and its meaning was having an effect on the crowd. The whole priesthood and staff of the temple had come from their divers offices, and the worshippers already there before Yesha's arrival now joined the large mob that had come with him. There were stirring cries from people in the audience. The temple guard stood ready but there was nothing here that caused them alarm. Many of the priests were as enthralled as the rest of the crowd. Only a small number of elderly priests were annoyed. Men speaking with tongues were one thing, but a poor dusty fellow making a good deal more than sense and working the crowd up was another. The two disapproving Sadducees were joined by others. Like sought out like.

'Arm your spirits! Arm them and re-arm them! Be ready for the wrath of God and be ready to march with his hosts when he comes to you! Be prepared to lay down everything when you are called, for the time is here! The word is the flesh of God and it is here! Search your hearts and examine your fears—the time is coming when the hosts of the Lord and legions of evil shall clash in a great war and the earth shall smoke and the heavens be torn apart! Know the truth of what I say. Be fearless *then*! Let your spirits be swords and let your hearts be your shields! The time is here—be ready when you are called!'

One of the Sadducees could stand this double-talk no longer. He pushed through the ranks around the speaker until he was near the front. The crowd parted for the Sadducee. They saw that he was angry and that there was sure to be a confrontation here.

'You! YOU . . . *YOU!*' yelled the Sadducee. Yesha turned and looked at the priest, his eyes flashing.

'Who gave you permission to speak here?' the Sadducee demanded.

'*Permission?*'

'Who gave you permission to speak here?'

'God,' said Yesha, blazing. He defied the Sadducee to contradict his statement. The Sadducee did not reply. Yesha turned to his audience and spoke personally to them. He stretched out his arms and implored the audience to hear his questions. 'Does a man need permission to pray in the house of his God? To pray for understanding?'

The Sadducee found his tongue. 'You are not praying, you are inciting a crowd!' he said.

'Inciting a crowd to what?'

'To violence.'

'I speak about peace and love and understanding. You are the one with violence on his lips.'

The Sadducee froze. 'Beware of blasphemy,' he hissed.

'What would the authorities have me do?' Yesha asked.

'Leave here. Take away these people that came with you.'

Yesha turned and raised his arms to the crowd. 'Our prayers are not wanted in this house of God!' he declaimed. Then he moved forward and made for the gate of the temple. The crowd clamoured and jostled around him. He sucked the whole throng with him as he walked, and he harangued them as he went. 'I can't pray in the temple, brothers; but I can pray in the streets!'

In a moment the whole temple was emptied. The Sadducee was joined by several others and a handful of Pharisees. They moved as a body to consult the Elders.

The angry Sadducee stepped aside and spoke to one of the young messengers of the temple guard. 'Go with that crowd,' he whispered. 'Listen to the wild man. Find out who he is. See what more subversive things he says outside these walls. Stay with him and see where he goes.'

The messenger hurried to catch up with the last of the crowd leaving the gate. The Sadducee rejoined his delegation of friends.

'That is the first time in my life,' he told them emotively, 'that I have faced a very, very dangerous man.'

Yesha was exhausted. He had spent the whole day preaching to the people in the streets, aware of the danger in doing this. He trusted in divine protection and the watchfulness of his helpers. None of them noticed the temple messenger at the back of the crowd wherever Yesha stopped to talk or rest.

'I don't think we should stay here, Master,' said the Rock, as the audience started to dwindle, seeing that the man had finished his preaching and was merely answering questions and expounding on the Law and the prophecies.

'We should go on to the farm,' Yohanan urged.

'Rock?'

'Yes, Master?'

'We will go to Bethany.'

Those few people remaining around Yesha were blessed and told that he was now proceding on his journey. The band set off down the street, which was busier now that the hottest part of the day had passed and breezes blew up the valley through the city.

Some yards behind Yesha and his companions the temple messenger followed. Several other people going in the same direction separated them, and numerous others brushed past going the opposite way. The messenger made sure that in spite of the other pedestrians and occasional mules he never lost sight of his charges. He had much to report to the Sadducee who had sent him on this errand. He had memorised most of the salient points of Yesha's speeches and discussions, though he had been able to discover nothing about the identity of the man or his followers. He spoke in the secular language with the accents of Galilee but there were no notable distinguishing features to the man except the authority of his voice and the mazed attraction of his eyes.

Close behind the temple guard was a small, slight, but extremely sinewy and tough man who pushed through the oncoming traffic. When he was right on the heels of the temple guard, he suddenly stepped to the side and into the path of a porter with a large sack. He bumped deliberately into the porter and at the same time drew a small curved dagger from the folds of his robe and pressed the point to the porter's stomach and grunted a curt menacing order.

'Run for your life!' he said. The porter needed no further convincing. He dropped his sack and ran. In an instant the man with the dagger stepped up behind the temple spy and in barging past him he thrust his dagger deep into the informer's side and with incredible strength tore the dagger sideways right round to the man's belly. The blade tore through cloth and flesh and guts. In scarcely a second the blade was withdrawn and had vanished. By the time the messenger had fallen in a bloody crumpled heap on the ground his assassin was several paces past him. As people rushed to the twitching corpse, the man turned and pointed after the porter running away down the street.

'He did it! There's the murderer! Get him!' he shouted.

A cry was set up along the street and the chase was on. The hapless porter was the quarry. The killer walked grimly on. He followed Yesha who had turned off into a cross street, missing the disturbance.

Night was coming on. Many of Yesha's helpers were too tired to walk further.

'We'll stop soon and sleep by the road,' Yesha told them.

'Master . . .' said Yohanan nervously, 'a man has been following us since we left the city . . .'

'I know,' said Yesha. He walked on a little further and stopped. 'We'll let him catch up.'

'He could be a bandit, Master. There's probably others with him hiding out of sight,' Yohanan fussed.

'Shut up,' rapped the Rock.

Yesha stood and waited as the man approached. His helpers stood watching carefully.

'You'll walk with us, brother?' Yesha asked as the man came close.

'Long road,' the man replied sombrely.

They kept walking for another hour until it was completely dark and they could walk no more. There was a grove of fig-trees. They settled themselves here and Andros took out the bag of provisions and handed round the first meal of the day. Nathaniel and Shimon built a small campfire to keep the chill of the night away long enough for them to get to sleep. After they had shared their food with the stranger, Yesha stood up and walked a few paces away. He stared up into the stars. The stranger got up and went over to Yesha, who led him a few yards towards the road as though to see the sky better away from the fruit trees. Both men gazed at the moon.

'Good to find you, Yesha.'

'I'm glad you've come, Judah,' said Yesha, earnestly. 'Have you a message?'

'Your brother sends no message but instructions to stay with you.'

'That is good.'

'Your men . . .' said Judah, 'two of them I know. The Baptist picked them?'

'They are good men. All are initiated. They couldn't be more passionate for the cause.'

'How much do they know?' Judah asked, very softly.

'Nothing,' said Yesha.

Eleazar's farm was outside Bethany and was surrounded by orchards. Two acres of fruit and vegetables and three acres for goats, a donkey and a cow, enough to keep the family in comfort, though it meant that Martha and Miriamne had to work as hard as Eleazar in the fields as well as seeing to their household duties.

The arrival of fourteen strong men on the farm meant that the girls now devoted most of their time to cooking, while the men took their places milking the goats and keeping the vegetables clear of weeds. Even so there were too many men for the jobs and so they created new jobs. They sawed logs, picked whatever fruit and berries ripened daily, cleaned out the stables and pens, fixed doors and weakening beams, mended parts of the roof, collected eggs from the nests of secretive hens and in a hundred other little ways made themselves welcome. Toma helped the girls with their cooking and delighted them by making little sweet things with honey and seeds, flour and eggs.

Eleazar swore his sisters to secrecy about their guests, and no word leaked into Bethany of the presence of Yesha and his men. It was a very safe place, though the four fishermen felt landlocked once they were no longer on the move.

In the evenings Shimon and Nathaniel would take their instruments and sing for everybody, sometimes traditional songs that they all loved and sometimes giving virtuoso performances of improvised and extempore chants in dithyrambic frenzy. The others clapped their hands and stamped their feet and let out shouts of the names of God when the spirit moved them. They would talk late into the night and Yesha would tell them of the things they were to do when they broke into smaller groups to preach the new word to all the country. Their task was not so much healing—though they were to apply what they learned from Yesha where possible—but to confirm initiates to their cause with baptism and the Light. Yesha told them stories and funny riddles to demonstrate points of the Law and the ways for men to combat the dark devils that plagued the coming of the new age. In the early hours they would go to their sleeping places around the farm buildings. Some allowed themselves the luxury of straw palliasses while the rest fell asleep wherever they were. Nathaniel and Shimon, who had spent most of their lives on the road, preferred to sleep outside under the stars.

The time grew close to when they should all go to Jerusalem for the days of the feast and offer their first fruits and bread of the Presence, sweet and dry cakes, to the Temple. The demons of disease had not taken the eldest children of Israel when they had been in Egypt because of the daubing of the blood of lambs on their doors and lintels. This sacrifice, the spring lamb, Yesha abhorred. The Baptist had taught him the true significance of the feast: returning the first fruits to God in return for the rape of the earth, its ploughing, the digging and burying of seed; a recompense for the pulling up of vegetables and the uprooting of God's sacred flesh embedded in the womb of the earth. Yesha told them that the sacrifice of the firstborn lamb was a misplaced ritual symbolising the firstborn of the Ram.

'When the last lamb is slaughtered in Jerusalem—that will be the sign of the New Age,' he told them.

It was the full moon of the month before the feast. Yesha planned with Eleazar for a communal sharing of the Light. Eleazar had often shared the vision of Yahweh with the Baptist, but the girls had never seen the Shining One. He knew how well his son had received the sacred thing and the boy was younger than his aunts.

'They are two young fishes,' said Yesha, concerning their birth into that age. 'They are floundering in the sea of unconsciousness and we must receive them with a drop of water from the fountain of the tree of life.'

'They are steady,' said Eleazar. 'I think they are too strong for demons to possess them.'

'Then we should let them join with us.'

After the sacrament, they prayed and meditated and called on their own sacred names of God. Eleazar, Miriamne, Martha and all their guests sat in a circle in the main room of the farm. Oil-lamps and candles burned. In a small bowl smoke rose from the softest essences of jasmin and sandalwood. The flames in the hearth flickered and glowed across the faces and mingled the bodies together. Soon there was silence in the room. Only the crackling, spluttering fire could be heard and it sounded like a heavy rain beating against the roof of the house. The melting faces changed shape. Some of them disappeared.

'It's wheels. It's *all* wheels. There's wheels inside wheels, and more wheels inside them—all whirling wheels . . .' cried a voice that might have been Yohanan or Chaim's.

'God . . . God . . . God . . . God . . .' muttered the Rock, swaying back and forth.

'Oh, oh!'

'Ha, ha!'

Ecstasy and awe were united in them. Those who attained the Light were seared by it, like moths dancing round a flame eager for their own deaths. The power coursed through their flesh, their blood, the tips of their toes and the roots of their hair.

Yesha became absorbed into the face of Miriamne. He saw that she, for her part, was looking at him, lost in him. There was no age to her. The fire that licked shadows on her face made her into all woman. She was a tiny child. She was a plump matron. She was the crone of winter—skeletal queen of ice. Images of ice and rock and fire and sea and heavens. The moon was beneath her feet and her head was crowned with stars. She was his mother, old and young, giving and devouring, taking away his pain and cares and enveloping him in her love. Like a child, he watched her immolating herself to protect and nourish him. The stars were charming him. Happiness was forced on him and everything but Miriamne vanished. He saw the secret conspiracy between them and how it spun and spun through all time that was now and forever. She spun illusions that set everything in motion. He was her son and her husband, sleeping, suckling, rolling together into one. And then the moving seasons shifted and she was his daughter. She was his sister and his beloved. Her motherhood dissolved, yet the love and loyalty she offered shone through. In a moment everything was different. She was someone he recognised—some*thing* rather. An opponent that could not have him. Her moon and stars fled away and she was clothed in black, gauzy layer on layer. Something that was deceiving his being into the lulled baby that was defenceless from the great powers of black and evil that he must fight in constant vigil. He was her father and he warned her of the demons that pursued her for, if she was not strong enough, they would seize him and crush him. Or was she that same demon band in herself?—made like the thing he loved and had chosen to lose—vengeful for his obedience and worship. He was helpless and lost in his need for her and frightened that she was not what she had made herself seem to be. He could recognise his mother, but he could not recognise this veiled one even when the veils were stripped away and the face he could recognise was there. Was the face another veil? Did face after face have to be ripped from her for him to know that this was the earth, his mother? Was Miriamne, this woman-faced, his bride? Who said that she was his soul? Was he himself the bride? Were they together the same thing—continually devoured and devouring, dying and being reborn in turns, in spins, and at the same time? They were one, two, three and the four in completeness and he knew that all were in him. How cunningly her images convinced him that he was not complete in himself and yet he could not trust it. Only together could they be divine and yet he shrugged off this divinity in fear of its wrongness—his wrongness. It shook him. It rocked him.

'Master . . . Master!' said a voice. The voice was shaking him. Only she was there. Only Miriamne could shake the earth under him.

'Master, *please* . . . we need help!'

Yesha was pulled out of his black fascination for Miriamne by the Rock. The room became one again.

'I was thinking,' said Yesha. He saw that everyone was gathered around someone stretched on the floor.

'Master,' said the Rock in panic, 'Eleazar is dead.'

'The vassal is the vessel,' Yesha said to himself, with regard to nothing that the Rock could understand. He had been trying to wake the Master for the best part of an hour. He did not dare pour water on him, though the humour of such a baptism of reality was not lost on the Rock. He shook his Master gently, then less and less gently to release him from his union with one of the uncountable millions of years of possible, impossibly possible paths to the understanding of the adventure of Yahweh.

'Eleazar is dead,' Yesha repeated. It seemed natural. It seemed perfect. How loving of death to release the ever-living soul to some clearly higher plane nearer his glory.

'The body is dead,' said Yesha solemnly, 'but I assure you that he is still alive.'

'Alive?' asked the Rock querulously.

'Somehow or other,' Yesha told him, still far far away.

'Lord, you must return to here and now,' said Judah, the voice of Judah.

Yesha tried to put the parts of his body together, to will himself to instantaneous reintegration, to remember.

'Is that you, Rock?' the Master asked.

'It's terrible and we're frightened,' the Rock affirmed.

'Please come, Master.'

'Help . . .'

'Master, you have the knowledge.'

'I don't know anything!' said Yesha with a big grin and then breaking into uproarious laughter.

Some shapes, familiar, unfamiliar, led him to the group around the figure of a man lying on the floor in a rigid and death-like tenseness. It was the body of Eleazar and he was definitely just a body; whether his spirit would ever return to it was another matter. Yesha began to find his feet on the ground and to establish the identities of those shifting flickering faces around him.

'It's obvious!' Yesha giggled. 'And I've forgotten what.'

'Eleazar, Master . . .'

'Eleazar?'

'He didn't say anything. He seemed in perfect contemplation, and then his expression was horror and he mouthed words that could not be heard by any of us. He was vomiting from his nose and mouth at the same time. We held him upright, those that could, and then he fell back dead, as though demons had attacked his beating heart.'

Yesha got on his knees and put his head to Eleazar's chest. He really had all the confidence that Eleazar was not dead. This form of entrancement by the Light looked very much like death but Yesha sensed the spark of life, though the heart did not appear to be beating.

With difficulty Yesha moved himself so that Eleazar's head was on his lap. He thought hard over his teaching. He had seen the Baptist deal with a similiar case long before.

'Rub his feet,' Yesha said. This was done. Yesha bent over Eleazar's face and pressed his mouth to the dead man's. He breathed in and out, rubbing the back of Eleazar's neck at the same time. After a few minutes he placed his hand on Eleazar's heart and felt a fluttering. One of the girls started to cry.

'He's not dead,' Yesha assured them all.

'Master . . .'

'He's sleeping now.'

'Master—what did you do?'

'I . . . breathed into him. Life is breath and I have breathed spirit back into him.'

'He's alive?'

'If one comes too close to the presence of God, it can cause a strain to the heart and mind. Only Lucifer has looked into the centre of the being of God and lived,' Yesha pronounced, slowly and with a slight slur to his words.

Yesha nursed Eleazar for another two hours and then saw his eyes open. Eleazar sat up slowly with Yesha's help and looked around him as though everything was new, as though seeing (as, indeed, he was seeing) somewhere else.

The girls wept and thanked Yesha and kissed him. All the brothers were amazed. It was not a vision they would forget.

By the time of the sun's rising, Eleazar was well enough to go outside with the others and offer prayers to the Light.

A troop of thirty men from the Herodian guard at Machaerus rode their horses into the middle of the Baptist's camp. A second detachment reined up outside the camp to give support should there be any trouble. The Captain had been told to bring back the Baptist alive, unless there was too strong resistance. It did not matter if others in the camp were dealt with harshly or killed. The Baptist was to be taken back alive. The fate of his followers was left to the discretion of the Captain.

The camp had grown to contain 185 members. Many of them—women and their children—were defenceless. All stood still, not knowing what was to happen to them.

The Captain trotted his horse a few paces ahead of his halted column. 'I have come for Yohanan, called "the Baptist". I have come with the authority of Herod Antipas to take this man with me to the Royal Palace.' He looked sternly around. 'Which of you is the Baptist?' he demanded.

There was no reply from the faces of the crowd.

'I have orders and authority to kill any man or cut down any rabble that hinders me,' the soldier warranted. 'I know this man is here among you. Let him come forward and I will see that no harm comes to your rotten skins!'

With a blood-curdling shriek, one of the men near the Captain drew a short dagger and brandished it above his head. He hurled himself at the horseman. Three arrows from ready-armed archers in the column swished into the attacker who fell dead in the dust. The Captain ignored the incident. The archers slipped new shafts to their bow strings.

'Please do not force me to reprisals,' the Captain snapped sharply.

The wild-looking Baptist stepped forward. There was a threatening rattle of weaponry from the Herodian troops.

'I am Yohanan bar Zachariah.'

'The "Baptist"?'

'Known by that name.'

The Captain made a signal to the column and two horsemen detached themselves, leading a riderless horse. A third man in desert robes that swathed and hid him rode up to the Captain.

'Is that the man?'

The informer nodded. The Captain indicated to his soldiers that they should take the spare horse to the Baptist.

'Come peacefully . . .' said the Captain.

Spontaneously, the hottest Zealots in the camp, fearlessly, foolishly, drew short swords and daggers and rushed at the column of heavily armed and armoured troops.

Four of the Herodian soldiers deployed and drew swords and lances. Archers urged their horses into the front and a volley of arrows was loosed. In a moment all those who were armed had been slain.

The Baptist roared out in terrible anger, an incoherent bellow of frenzy. He was quickly clubbed into silence by his mounted escort.

Some who had not rushed in to attack and who were weaponless were shot down by successive volleys from the archers. The lancers spurred into the throng and speared those who were running away.

A great ululation arose from the women. Many keened over the bodies of their slaughtered husbands.

Young Eleazar watched from a hiding-place under the folds of a tent laid out for repair at the edge of the camp. He saw the escorts dismount and tie up the unconcious Baptist. They heaved him onto the horse and laid him across the saddle. Eleazar prayed that he was alive.

The Captain re-formed his men around the Baptist and wheeled them around to leave. The screaming and wailing of the women and infants mingled with the clanking of spurs and armour and accoutrements.

The Baptist, across his horse, was flanked by guards. Blood poured from a wound on his forehead and splashed in small spots onto the stones.

Yaacov made an arrangement to see Yesha and Judah. His house was too exposed a meeting-place. It was the end of the days of the feast and the news had just arrived in Jerusalem of the capture of the Baptist. Yaacov wondered why Antipas had made such a mistake in arresting a man so widely considered a prophet at a time when the greater part of the nation was massed together in Jerusalem. The news spread so that in less than two hours a million people were aware of what had happened. Arrest, they knew, was rarely followed by anything but death. If this was a trick to lure sympathisers prematurely into open insurrection, it failed.

Yesha followed Judah and Yaacov down a crammed alleyway in despair. He prayed earnestly in his heart that this, finally, would bring the people to their senses and let them see that it was a return to the days when prophets were murdered, even at the sanctuary. He burned with rage that every stone of the Herodian fortress be torn to the ground. He called for all the plagues of demons and the hosts of angels to join forces and release the re-born Elijah so that he could lead his people to victory over all the filthy oppressors, the swine of collaborators, the destroyers of the Word that was Flesh, the fist of darkness ready to crush the tiny glimmer of the new-born Light. He was in an agony of anger. He could see no way around him that was not black and red. Anger and despair crushed his head until reason was gone. Voices crowded around him.

'Too many people know that the Baptist has already proclaimed his successor.'

'We were not prepared for this.'

'Everything changes.'

'This must mark the time. It could be the catalyst.'

'There is much more to do. There is much more we can do to help.'

'What, Mannasseh?'

'To fulfil the prophecies.'

'More have been fulfilled than you know.'

'It doesn't matter. It doesn't matter even if it is not done. It will be said to be done and believed to be done. Surely we can arrange that?'

'Every prophecy has been gleaned from the writings.'

'There are more. Popular superstitions . . . legends among the people.'

'It will soon be said that he is the anointed one named by Isaiah.'

'If things are to move this quickly, we will need more men who can fight.'

'You'll have them, Judah.'

'And die.'

'That, too, and willingly. We hope this can be bloodless.'

'We *know* it can't.'

Yesha was sunk in deep and terrible thoughts as the group of priests and patriots talked around him, deciding this, planning that, mulling over every jot and tittle of the Law and the prophecies and writings and folklore. Certain voices volunteered to draw up his family tree, relating him directly and by strong branches to the House of David. This would be widely circulated and would have its effect.

It did seem to matter that the 'anointed' saviour was not a term to be taken so openly. It could be misunderstood. It must be presumed that baptism was taken for anointing, and the Baptist's choice of the man should add to this conviction.

How dangerous it was to probe into the mysteries of 'anointment'. How easy it was for the Old Religion of the Kanaanites to manifest itself in the self-sacrificing spirits of the Kanaaim.

'You cannot present false appearances to God. He sees all and knows what we are doing and that it is for him.'

'If the Baptist is lost, we must see that their loss is increased a thousand times over.'

'If it is done with the utmost skill and care, it can be done!'

'How can we do something *now*?'

'We have to wait.'

'The Baptist may be saved . . .'

'No.'

'If he is killed, he is not dead. He lives.'

'What?'

'In Yesha.'

'How soon before Yesha is trapped and slaughtered?'

'I don't know.'

'What do you think, Yesha?'

'Yesha?'

'Yesh . . .!'

'I'm sorry . . .'

'How long do you feel you can act efficiently?'

'Efficiently?'

'Rousing without seeming to rouse . . . and staying . . . alive?'

'How long do the prophecies say?'

'It is the three and one-half year cycle.'

'Three and a half years, then.'

Yesha looked at this strange troop of learned men who thought they could do so much for him. He doubted if they would ever meet in another Passover feast.

'We shall have to plan for . . . emergencies.'

'If the Baptist dies,' said Yesha fiercely, his thoughts far away, 'plan for nothing but the immediate wrath of the Lord!'

The Baptist was tied to a chair. He had already been questioned and beaten up a number of times by inquisitors on behalf of Caius Clavius, the diplomat.

Antipas kept his nose out of the matter. He pretended to be unaware that the popular prophet was his prisoner.

Clavius himself had come from Jerusalem to conduct the examination personally. The arrest of the Baptist just before the

Passover was a ruthless move. The diplomat had discovered that there was, indeed, a great deal of feeling for this man, and that his fame far surpassed that of any of the other insurgents they had put down. But there had been no outbursts of temper from any radical groups, nor any official complaints received from any of the upper echelons. The diplomat deemed it safe to continue with his normal course of action. He had no doubts that the philosophies of this man had inspired many of the gangs of rebels and bandits causing unrest in the province.

The diplomat was let into the room where the Baptist was being held. Two mercenaries from Moab kept guard at the door. Herodian soldiers were not let near him for fear that they might aid the prisoner to escape. There was much more that the diplomat had to find out, and not very much time.

The inquisitor, who attended to the breaking of arms and crushing of legs, was a stocky brutal little Latin peasant who took a childlike delight in agony and never liked to hurry his workaday duties.

Brutality was abhorrent to the diplomat though he was able to bear all the necessary evil. He never stayed around to watch what happened—in this, at least, he had none of the Roman blood-lust.

When the Baptist saw Clavius enter the room, he turned his head away and spat on the floor.

The inquisitor raised his fist to slam it into the Baptist's face, but the diplomat restrained him.

'It's not possible to beat answers from you, is it, Yohanan?' he said coolly. The Baptist made no reply.

'I cannot imagine that plain old torture would do any better in unsealing your lips.'

'Sir . . .' said the inquisitor hungrily, 'in time I could . . .'

Clavius cut the peasant short. He tried a wily romantic approach on this great bear of a man. 'But, Yohanan . . . if you had a stretch of space . . . a view to that forever distant horizon . . . a sacred river and the smallest gathering of the sacred people . . . if then a man came to you and asked for the message that God had given to you, had *told* you to spread abroad and shout from the roof-tops—would you refuse?'

The Baptist looked at the diplomat. '*Roman*,' he clipped in disgust. Again the inquisitor had to be restrained from violence.

The diplomat carried on airily. 'Let me see now,' he said, and began quoting the Baptist's own lines. ' "I am a voice crying in wild places"—something like that, isn't it? "Prepare the way!"—things like that, am I right, Yohanan? You preach "love"—sorry, "Love" and "Freedom", don't you, Yohanan?'

The Baptist glared back wordlessly.

'Exactly what do you mean by freedom, Yohanan?'

No reply.

'Now correct me if I'm wrong—you preach about a "Saviour". A saviour? What could that mean? Is that a spiritual image you see or some kind of national leader? Or both?'

'I could knock it out of him!' the inquisitor insisted.

'I doubt it,' Clavius told the impatient torturer. He turned his attention fully to the Baptist. 'How many "Saviours" are there in your plans? How many do you think there are fit to rule this "Kingdom of God"? It is to be a kingdom on *earth*, isn't it? What with traditional priestly kings and councils of Elders and Imperial administrators and tribunals, I do see that it would be a great deal simpler for everybody if God *were* to come down, reinforced by legions of angels and cohorts of avenging spirits, and personally take over the Government. It would simplify matters no end, do you see? Our trade routes through this land would be secure, since God—on earth—would not deliberately hinder people going about their daily business. Of course, he would throw all profane temples and worshipped images out of the land, but so would I if I had the authority. How it would ease things! Of course, I have brought this up, but people, whoever they are, "chosen" or not, have their own beliefs and we try as little as possible to interfere with them.'

Clavius waited to see some impression on the Baptist's face from his words. He looked for an opening. There must be something that would make this man burst into a rage and start talking. From there with the correct goading, he might find out all he needed to know.

'Already your people are privileged,' the diplomat reasoned.

'Your young men are spared from service with our armies. No other land has this good fortune. When the Procurator was new to the territory, he brought the golden standards of the legions of Rome and placed them on the Temple. What a fuss, eh? The poor man was nearly removed from the post he had scarcely taken up. You see what high regard the Emperor holds for your priests . . . and your merchants? Taxes are lower here than in most other countries . . . they are even higher in *Rome*! Yet what a commotion there is here, what a grumbling, what a beating of chests and rending of clothes when money is parted with. Money for improved roads and aqueducts and public works to benefit all. How little genuine love for your fellow men! Far be it for me to even *think* what hypocrites inhabit this holy nation! What a drain on Royal and priestly funds there would be if you had to defend this country yourselves from bandits and the desert tribesmen who surround you and wait longingly for the day when there is no protection for your people. What new exile, new captivity would your people suffer without the shield of Rome resting over you?' The diplomat gave a sly hollow laugh. 'This land, this kingdom "given" to you by God has belonged to countless successions of tribes and nations and rulers before your people swept in from the desert and absorbed the native culture with the rich soil.' He began to speak sharply and more vehemently. 'Now it is a small, a minute and troublesome piece of land, a group of even smaller provinces that together make up a sub-province of Syria . . . and Syria, I may tell you, is *nothing* to the might of the Empire! It is a broken shard under the mastery of the Divine Caesar Tiberius!'

'Divine,' sneered the Baptist with the utmost contempt.

'Yes, yes. I know that there is only one God. Only *one* Lord. I sympathise with your contempt for the divinity of the Emperor, but more people believe in this divinity than a thousand of your nations put together. *That* is earthly power. It is a power that can see into the remotest places of the furthest deserts and find a man who would defy that power. Happily the Lord will grant your request to join with him in his Kingdom in Heaven, but he has lent his might on earth to Caesar Tiberius. That is a fact, do

you see? And do you know the interesting thing? In his omnisci-
ence he has picked on you—and he doesn't even know it.' Again
the diplomat grinned. 'Now it is me that is preaching. It must be
something of an experience for you to be at the mercy of a fellow
monologuist.

'There are simple people . . . simple-minded people who take
your talk of "freedom" and "saviours" and "a new kingdom" in
the wrong way, do you see?' He began to speak more abruptly.
'We will not have rebellion! We will not tolerate civil disorder!
When we see smoke, we stamp hard before a fire can break out.
When we see a cancer in a body, we cut it out! When we see the
symptoms of a malignant growth . . . a head with a rotten and
criminal body . . .'

'Let me! I'll . . .' the inquisitor was becoming impatient.

'No,' ordered the diplomat. He gathered his clothes around
him, indicating that he was leaving. 'First,' he told the inquisitor,
'I want him to think about it.'

Clavius walked to the door and then spoke calmly to the
Baptist.

'I want to avoid bloodshed. I want to know the leaders of your
movement. Their names. I earnestly hope that you will see that
it is God's will that your people do not destroy themselves. I
want you to consider the innocent. I want to remind you of the
thousands, the tens of thousands and hundreds of thousands that
may be slaughtered in an uprising. I want you to know that
sacrificing the names of a few will allow the many to continue
worshipping Yahweh in peace and dignity. I hope you will see
beyond your convictions, Yohanan. A few men for a nation. I
will be back here this night. Please consider my words.'

The diplomat left. The inquisitor punched the Baptist in the
body repeatedly until he was unconscious. It took a long time to
knock the Baptist out.

Nothing could persuade the Baptist away from his beliefs. He
had nothing to say to this Roman. There was so much he could
see that the diplomat could not. The Roman's presumption of the
ignorance of the 'wild man from the desert' he found amusing.
He knew the workings of Rome and the abominable forms of

worship practiced there. Borrowings and thefts from every pagan people had filled that city with temples. How could this proselyte, this Roman, whose true peasant Gods were just familiar spirits of hearth and home, ever understand the Light? How could he allow a vision to the children of Israel—a message which could not be understood by earthly powers?

The diplomat returned late at night. Extra lamps were brought to the room.

'What have you decided?'

'There's nothing I can say.'

'That's a pity.'

'The course is started. The wasps are in Jerusalem! Our priests push aside and falsely interpret our Law and nurse vipers!'

'Wasps, eh? Well, we shall have to stir the nest of hornets. Then they can be expected to show themselves. Let me assure you that I do understand your point of view. If your priests did not see the wisdom of Caesar's way, there would be no priests at all. As for your royal family—between these four walls—indeed, *Antipas'* four walls—they are as troublesome to us as they are despised by you. Herod Antipas is impossibly placed. I am sure that your death will cause him personal as well as political discomfort.'

The diplomat sighed and nodded painfully to the inquisitor.

'You're a dead man, prophet,' said the delighted inquisitor.

'A dead idea, one hopes,' said the diplomat briskly. 'I must return to Jerusalem. See that our messenger carries the news of this to Herod. See that my apologies are transmitted to him for my sudden departure, but urgent business calls me back at once. I'm sure he will understand.'

The inquisitor nodded. The diplomat looked into the Baptist's blazing eyes. Then he left the fortress.

The little inquisitor sat down for several moments grinning at the Baptist. Then he got up and garroted the bound prophet until he was only just alive; his eyes bulging open. The executioner sat around until the Baptist started to revive. Then the Latin peasant started to cut off the Baptist's head with a short blunt knife, hacking slowly through the sinews.

Yesha made sure that his men were now armed. He insisted that all of them, himself included, should carry a dagger or a shortsword. These were the best weapons they could hope to carry undetected at all times. When the band returned to Eleazar's farm after the feast, those unfamiliar with weapons were instructed by Judah.

Judah taught them how best to conceal their daggers and yet have them easy to reach and to slip away. He taught them how to grasp the handle firmly so that the blade pointed always upward. A stroke from an upraised dagger making a downthrust was both noticeable and easily parried. Judah's strongest point of teaching was not in how to defend, but how to attack. He explained how to use crowds to cover actions and how to stir false chases.

Yesha did not find it easy to think of his knife as anything but an implement for a last stand, should he be cornered with no way ahead except death. His attitude changed with the intensity of Judah's training so that his fury, his aching hatred for Herod Antipas and the Roman and priestly authorities burned and his message to 'gather together the people' took on a stronger meaning than ever before. The urgency of his mission blazed with every thrust he made. He saw himself cutting up the legions of black horrendous demons. He saw himself as the last custodian of the Light. He became, in those weeks at the farm, a wild thing. The Baptist lived in him. He had a mission to complete that was holy to himself and backed by all the agents of the Baptist. His was the inheritance and the task of carrying the Light into the Coming Age.

Judah and Yesha spent many evenings apart from the others going over their plans and considering the support they had been promised in Jerusalem.

'They want us to keep going—to gauge the size of our support.'

'They want us to wait and see,' said Judah.

'The Kingdom of God *cannot* wait. What do they expect us to do in the provinces?—sit and wait for a plague to come and strike down the persecutors?

'Now is the time to begin serious action. The people are united by the horror of the Baptist's death. We must act now. This minute!'

'Yohanan promised them that a man who was chosen by God would come after him. Many people already know that you are the man, Yesha.'

'The Baptist's plan will be executed.'

'It can be nothing short of a national uprising. We know that we can count on Galilee.'

'How many men in Jerusalem itself?'

'They have a man called Irijah. I know him. He has an organisation of about a hundred men inside the city.'

'A hundred?'

'All street-fighters. All men who know how to use their daggers and hold their tongues.'

'And what are we?—twenty?'

'Many, many more, Yesha. There are thousands waiting for you to declare yourself and lead them.'

'I don't know what more I can do.'

'You have a great following—use it! Yohanan promised them a *leader*!'

Yesha waved his arms in the air with exasperation. 'They expect a man who will change the course of the stars with a wave of his hand. They follow me waiting for miracles as though they dropped from my sleeves. The only miracle I have is the Light.'

'Yesha . . .' said Judah assertively, 'the means will be distasteful . . .'

'Dishonest.'

'There are no means. There is only an end. If you can sway the country as it is believed you can, then the end is certain.'

'Certain,' mumbled Yesha.

'If miracles are required, then make them. Move mountains. Part seas. You have already accomplished many miracles . . .'

'No.'

'In the eyes of the people you have. You know there are other agents proclaiming your deeds and many who have seen your healing for themselves and call it miraculous.'

'They don't know . . .'

'It doesn't matter. A miracle is a miracle. Invent them. Fake them. *Do* them!'

Yesha sighed. He sat thinking for a while and Judah did not interrupt him. Had the Baptist known he was going to die? There was no answer—no answers anywhere. He knew what he had to do, but could it not have been accomplished in some other way? Did God leave it to them at all times to scratch and kick and fight their way through existence? Yesha thought of the Baptist and the memories welled up—the patience of his teacher . . . the Baptist's own struggle with himself on this same matter. He thought of the Baptist's careful planning. Was it meant for this? It seemed that it was. He saw the end ahead as surely as the Baptist must have. He sighed again at the thought that, like Moses, he should lead the people, the children of God, on this perilous and bloody path and that he would see but not live in the Promised Land—the New Age. His blood raced at the pictures in his mind, the chaos and darkness that was in him and the people. Chaos and darkness were to be driven out by the Light. It was for this that the Light existed.

'We will strike with words, Judah,' said Yesha. 'And we will strike with swords and with knives and fire and stones at our enemies! There will be reprisals and we shall be quick and hard in avenging them! The peace of the Light must burst through this chaos!' He spoke wildly, staring into a world around him that no-one else could see. 'I see chaos as a great dark mountain, and then I see that the mountain is streaked with veins of gold. There are nuggets of gold and brilliant stones. I see those who have come to quarry the riches from the mountain buried under avalanches of rubble. I see myself as a pilgrim carrying the Light painfully up the side of the mountain to the very top where it can shine as a beacon over all the land!'

ouses burned. Bright flames licked the night. Arsonists struck through the town at the houses of tax-collectors, the villas of Captains of soldiers. One here—one there. Four soldiers hurried down a street, looking towards a blazing house. Two night shapes appeared from a doorway and drove knives into the unprotected body of the fourth soldier—the straggler. He fell, never catching a glimpse of his killers.

In Jerusalem the marauders were led by Irijah, the rebel leader in the city. He moved through the city with a group of six men. They reached a villa with high walls in a quiet street. Irijah threw up a rope and then climbed the wall, grasping the stones, using footholds that could not be seen, until he was at the top of the wall. He secured the rope and his companions scaled the wall with ease. Irijah pulled the rope up and coiled it at the top of the wall so that it could not be seen by passers-by.

They crossed a courtyard to the door of the villa. The door was forced quietly. Inside the house there were lamps burning in the hallway. From a room to the left of the hall they heard talking and laughing. Irijah looked around at his men. They were all ready and intent. They burst as one body through the inner door. A woman screamed. A fat merchant lurched to his feet in horror. Irijah looked around with disgust at the affected Roman fashions draped on their bodies. A servant rushed in, alarmed by the noise. He was struck down in the doorway.

'You know who we are,' Irijah said to the man.

The merchant looked at Irijah in terror. He cried out: 'I have money. Yes, yes. I have money here. I can give you everything . . . if me . . . my wife . . . I have it. *Please!*'

'Levi ben Arba!' Irijah called out icily. 'You do not know us but we know you. We are not robbers, but men zealous for the Lord who would rid this nation of all evil under his sight!'

'I'm a Jew! I give great amounts to the temple! *Countrymen* ...'

'You are guilty,' intoned Irijah, 'of collaborating with the Roman authorities. You are betraying your brothers. Your ships bring arms and armour here and take away men as prisoners and slaves—captives to serve as slaves to foreigners! And the arms you bring in—to be turned against your "countrymen". Let this charge burn into your spiritless body and know that this is the reason for your death!' Irijah turned to his men and indicated both the merchant and his wife to them with his knife. 'Both!' he said. The woman had no voice to scream. She puffed into a grovelling lump on the floor. The merchant shouted about money ... money. They were stabbed again and again. The bodies writhed, spurting fountains and spreading pools of blood. There was a lot of blood. Irijah walked to the blood and dipped his hand in it. He walked to the wall and drew a simple fish on it, so that it would be known that this was done not by robbers but by men of the New Age. He indicated to his men that they should now get away as soon as possible. He lingered for a moment to admire the big bloody fish on the wall.

There was a raid by soldiers in Caesarea. It was made in a swift house-to-house search. Informers had heard of a cache of arms. In the fourth house they found it buried under the floor. There were six swords, eighteen knives and daggers and one phial of poison. Three men were tried before the tribunal and were found guilty of conspiracy. One of the Zealots managed to hang himself in his cell. The two others were taken to a hill by a detail of soldiers. They carried their crosses and were tied to them. Four soldiers lifted each cross from the ground and slotted the base into the shaft to support it. The soldiers strained to push up the last cross, as though they were raising the standard on a long-beleaguered and hard-fought-for hill. There was a thud as the shaft of the cross hit the bottom of its slot. There was no sound from the crucified Zealots. Birds did not hover, for there was no smell of the fear of death in the air. After two days the men were burned alive by the sun. Their skin was parched and blistering. They were unconscious but still breathing shallowly with no strength to suck air into their chests. The soldiers got tired and broke the rebels' legs, so they could not push up with their feet to inhale.

Agents from Jerusalem, working alone, mingled with crowds in markets, spreading the rumour of the leader who was with them— who had come from the Baptist. They were careful with their information, never naming Yesha or any of his followers, but always using the prophetic titles from the Torah. They called the one who had come 'The Prince of Peace' and the 'Son of Man'. They equated his lineage with the royal house of David. They spoke of his miracles and the demons he had dispossessed. Of all these things they spoke to others as though they had just heard the news from someone else. Many who had seen and heard Yesha took up these words and embroidered on them and spread them secretly among their friends. When the Roman or Herodian troops captured or executed 'bandits' and 'brigands', the agents saw to it that the people knew that these were patriots, not thieves. They spread the smoke of rumour among the people so that for every Zealot patriot crucified, there were three who secretly armed themselves and got ready for the day when the leader would marshal his armies and array them in the Light for the day—the day of the End of the Days.

A Roman soldier, a mercenary Syrian in the Imperial forces, had the duty of seeing six heavy sacks of fine ground meal to the next post up the road. He had pressed some travellers to carry the sacks for a measured mile but released them from their obligatory burdens when he saw a group of poor pilgrims coming up the road behind him, fresh and ready to move the loads another mile. His mission was almost completed, and ahead of schedule. He hailed the pilgrims as they came up to him and demanded that they take up the sacks and carry them for the next mile. They cut his throat.

Twenty-seven soldiers were murdered in the three months after the Passover feast. Of the two hundred executed in reprisals, there were 180 who were both innocent and ignorant of any crime. Their families armed themselves and looked for the word of the new prophet.

An informer handed his information to the wrong man and died for the mistake. The job became so hazardous that few Jews were willing to serve further. Prices went up. Foreigners were unacceptable for the task. Information started to dry up. Certain merchants and shippers moved their entire households to Alexandria and Rome. Tax-collectors left their lucrative positions. For some it took no more than one or two threats to convince them to leave. Many of the collectors were so hardened to threats —even threats on their lives—that they ignored the warnings. They were very hard men. Their deaths kept up the flow of resignations—and disappearances.

At first Yesha and his followers stayed out of the way, keeping to caves in the rugged land as a band of robbers would. Judah made several journeys to Jerusalem and returned with messages and plans from the growing number of conspirators in the councils. Things were moving too fast, far too fast. Time was speeding up as the cycles of the Ages engaged. No time for waiting. No time. Yesha dispersed his followers. They were sitting in one large cave, as cool a cave as there was. He instructed them to establish contacts in the areas he had already appointed to them. He cautioned them to act as shadows when making contacts. He told them to seek out the poor in dark corners. He told them to spread the word of the Light of God which awaited them—to give the people the *good* news and to give it with authority and to answer questions as he had taught them.

'Every one of you has shown his love and devotion. Every one of you is prepared to give his life and commit his spirit.'

Yesha stretched out his hand. 'Give me your hand, Rock,' he said. Rock took Yesha's hand. His other hand Yesha gave to Judah. All of them joined hands in a circle. Yesha looked at them with fire in his eyes.

'You are the shepherds who will lead our stray lambs from the Age of the Ram into the New Kingdom, as once the Shepherd

Kings guided us into the last Age. You are shepherds and fishers of men and you are princes. Go now, and take the purity of this nation and restore it to the Lord!'

The men unclasped their hands and got to their feet. 'Return at the next new moon,' said Yesha.

Eleazar's son returned. Eleazar prayed in joy to the Master who had saved his son and his own life.

The Procurator of Judaea was in a foul mood. Somebody was going to suffer! He was overwrought with anxiety and tension. Muscular spasms pained his back between the shoulderblades. He was just about at the end of his tether.

In his main reception room at Caesarea there were a suitable number of guards and military personnel. There was a group of scribes ready at a moment's notice to take down whatever dictations or copyings they were given, in whatever language, and were able to translate them into the most concise Latin. Servants slipped in and out discreetly. Messengers arrived at almost every moment and their missives were directed to the proper secretariat. There were groups of Priests, Sadducees, Pharisees, waiting to be summoned to have the Procurator deal with their petitions and bargainings and favours. The assembly was subdued. They sensed and saw the edgy mood of the Procurator. Today did not seem all that good a day to ask for this or that little trifle.

With the Procurator was Caius Clavius. The diplomat knew that Palestine was no great reward for a Roman official, unless he was extremely ambitious and very young. Almost every Imperial regulation was lax here—unenforceable. Peaceful co-existence was well nigh impossible. Rome advocated a policy of religious tolerance; but the more these people used their religion as an excuse for disobedience, the more intolerant the Procurator became. Pilate showed no interest in receiving any of the emissaries or hearing anybody else's complaints. He was forty-five and tired of the heat and the flies, but he was the toughest Procurator that Rome could afford to give to this hell-hole. Rome was aware of his ruthlessness in his earlier career. They had supplied him with a number of interesting diplomats to keep him in check. He had to be very careful with these diplomats. Clavius, at least, he felt he could trust, to a degree, for support and for good reports to the higher echelons of the administration. Thus, he vented his frustration on the diplomat.

'Every intelligence report says something different! What's happening to the revenue? Who has the figures for the month? I do not know what is going on!' he complained in exasperation.

'One of man's great problems,' said the diplomat wistfully.

'What?!'

'To know what is going on.'

'I do not need your damned smart answers,' said Pilate, testily.

The diplomat murmured his apologies obliquely, 'I regret my inadequacy when faced with this situation . . .'

'My inadequacy!' snapped Pilate. '*My* inadequacy, you mean. Damn you, Caius, but the Legate of Syria will see this as my fault . . . directly—and only *my* fault! I can smell insurrection—that's what this is! There's murder. There is robbery. Arson!'

'Calmo, calmo, Procurator . . .'

'I could understand it if it was just attacks on my soldiers, or those of Antipas, but Jews are being killed . . . just as many . . . and *priests*, their own priests . . .'

An exceptionally brave band of merchants, carrying rolls and plans and slates of figures, approached the Procurator, seeking audience. The foremost and most audacious petitioner attempted to interrupt.

'Governor . . .' said the merchant, obsequiously.

Pilate burst into a rage. He shouted at his guards and called for his aides. As his adjutants ran to his side, he tried to regain his composure. Clavius sighed inwardly at this outburst of peasant breeding. Purse-lipped the Procurator spoke to his men.

'Get them out of here. Get them all *out*!'

The merchant and his group retired quickly. The aides instructed the guards and with efficiency and a minimum of upset, all visitors were discreetly swept from the hall. Pilate turned his back on the rest of his military personnel and walked to the fine open windows at the end of the room. The scribes were dismissed.

'I shall proclaim a state of emergency . . . and a curfew . . . and insist on reinforcements from Syria! If there is going to be trouble then the possibilities must be faced.'

'I would not advise that,' said the diplomat, carefully.

'I assure you it will be *totally* effective!'

'I do not doubt that, Pontio . . . but *I* wouldn't do it.'

'Why not?'

Pilate turned on his own aides. Some of them were pressing slowly closer to him, eager to serve and eager to listen to his conversation.

'Out!' shouted the Procurator angrily. '*All* of you out! Post the guards *outside*!' he cried and stood glowering until the last of the guards had retired. He turned to the diplomat and shook his head hopelessly.

'Why?' he asked, wearily.

The diplomat paused. 'The Legate of Syria, our dear friend Pomponius Flaccus, is new to the position. He is not at all like his venerable predecessor, Quirinius. He will decide that you have lost control of the situation. If he uses his troops here, the news will reach Rome . . .'

It was true. Old Quirinius had been the Legate for the first six years of his Procuratorship and he had always been calm and understanding, Pilate recalled. The old Legate had been the holder of the bounteous province for twenty-five years. He was mellow. Flaccus he had not met. This was his sub-province, already in rebellion. Pilate took the diplomat's point. He had forgotten Flaccus. He cursed. His hands were further tied. He walked across to a chair and sat down, exhausted but unable to relax. Sorrowfully, he recounted the complaints that tormented him.

'From the very first day I have been in this province I have had continual and unending aggravation. I came here proudly, prepared for the heat and the disorder and the squalor of this country. I, a Procurator, was to assume the power of a Governor. My orders were, and are, to be firm and to avoid offending their religious or cultural ways. It is *impossible* not to offend their religion! *Everything* offends it! You know, Caius . . .'

'I know,' said the diplomat, consolingly.

'Proudly I brought the standards of my Legions to Jerusalem; and before I had reached the city, there are complaints flying to Rome that I am desecrating their "holy" nation. When I placed the authority of Rome over their city, it was Rome that reprimanded me. *You* reprimanded me, Caius!'

'It was my duty, Pontio.'

'I plan good roads; it appears that I am defiling their sacred places. I plan an aqueduct to bring clean water to the poor in this sacred city of theirs and they accuse me of robbing the temple treasury. Naturally . . . why should people have water? The Temple has great water cisterns and springs for the *priesthood*. Why should the *people* have water? I have a programme of Public Works to complete . . .'

'I know,' commiserated Caius Clavius.

'The High Priests . . .' Pilate went on.

'You,' the diplomat stated, 'appointed the High Priests.'

'Two old men wise enough to play the game and always see to it that I play *their* way,' said Pilate bitterly. 'And if that was not enough, there's a King whom the people loathe. This unrest is *his* fault, you know.'

'Oh?'

'He killed some brigand and you see! . . . the people are already saying that it was a prophet he executed. Every thief we arrest is a martyr. Every bandit is a Holy man. You *see*? . . . It is quite clear to the meanest intelligence that this is a trap to have me removed!'

Pilate stood up angrily. Clavius listened carefully. The Procurator must be steered with caution.

'Execute some bandit . . .' spat Pilate, 'and you can be sure whole delegations will set sail for Rome to say that I have offended their religion by killing the holiest of their Holy men. On their way already, probably.'

'As you say . . . the fault is Antipas'. The incident was outside your jurisdiction.'

'Nonetheless it has spread to me. They'll do the same thing to me, you know. If they can . . .'

'Come, Pontio . . . don't worry. The Council knows which way to jump.'

Pilate was not easily conciliated. He slapped his thigh. He made rapid gestures with his hands in the Roman manner. 'It could be anarchy!' he asserted. 'It could be rebellion, or revolution. It could be civil war, for all I know. It could be *all* of these things, but it's going to *stop*!'

'Take action, by all means, Pontio. Continue with whatever punitive measures you like—but if you react too hard, there *will* be trouble,' said the diplomat with a touch of sternness. His tone changed. His tense changed to the future-oblique. 'It scarcely needs to be said that in such a case we both know whose head will be taken . . .'

Pilate grunted.

'You will be recalled,' said the diplomat. 'Even cashiered.'

'What is happening? Tell me what is happening, Caius,' Pilate begged.

'Unrest, Pontio—nothing more. You will lose soldiers and keep your temper. An uproar may be going on for a while about this Holy man, but he's dead. There is no movement. There are no leaders.'

'I *smell* something,' Pilate maintained tensely. 'Something serious. My long-experienced Procuratorial nose tells me.' He raised his fist and slammed it into the palm of his other hand. 'Oh my Gods!' he cried. 'How I hate these Jews!'

The brotherhood came together again for the new moon. They celebrated and sang together. All had made important contacts. Some had dared to speak and had been well received. The Rock claimed to have healed one or two people and seemed well pleased with himself. Everyone had dramatic exploits to recount. There had been some near misses with the authorities. Shimon the Zealot and Nathaniel had nearly been caught trying to break into a building where tax ledgers and files were to be found. Toma had done the most speaking, rousing his listeners with the doctrine that the poor shall be elevated above the rich in the New Kingdom. He spoke of the 'New Dispensation' that was the natural continuation of the Old Law. These things he had learned by rote from Yesha and he was very glad that his listeners were mainly poor and un-educated since they did not ask him complicated questions that he could not answer.

They celebrated in prayer and song and dance through the night and concluded the joy of their re-union with a solemn vigil at the rising of the sun. Later, as the sun grew hotter, they fell asleep, one by one, in the coolest cave. They had done much, travelled far and were exhausted by the celebrations.

In the evening, when they had woken to take a meal together, Yesha spoke to them.

'For every attack, from what you tell me, the reprisals are grow-ing ten times worse.'

All agreed from what they had seen and heard that this was true.

'Where I was, near Bethel,' said Philip, who rarely spoke, 'they cut down a group of pilgrims and executed twelve men.'

'*Twelve?*'

'That's what I was told.'

'You didn't see for yourself?'

'No.'

'What were they charged with?'

'The Romans claimed that they were bandits,' said Philip.

'How many will take up arms?' Judah asked.

'Those I met said they would rise when the leader marched on Jerusalem.'

All said that this was the general opinion. They would arm and prepare but would commit themselves to no action until it could be seen that the Leader had come with great armies to drive out the barbarians and establish a new priesthood. Some had been persuaded to form their own groups, others had already done so.

'We need *more* armed men. More committed men,' said Yesha.

'Who, Master?'

'Where, Master?'

Yesha looked to Judah who gave an almost unnoticeable nod of his head.

'Have you heard of Reuben bar Abbas?' Yesha asked them.

'Reuben bar Abbas?'

'The *outlaw*?' Yohanan exclaimed.

'Are we not all outlaws?' said Yesha.

They all laughed at Yohanan's jaw-dropped expression.

'I mean . . .' Yohanan stammered, 'I mean he's a bandit, a *real* bandit. He's a robber.'

'We shall enlighten him,' said Yesha, lightly.

'Do you know him? Do you know where to find him, Master?' the Rock asked.

'Not far from here,' Yesha replied and pointed out across the rough terrain towards Iturea.

'You wouldn't get near him, Master,' Yohanan pleaded. 'If you had anything of value, he'd slit your throat!'

'If I had nothing,' Yesha grinned, 'he'd slit it twice as fast.'

'Tell me where to go, Master. I'll see him.'

'No, Rock I'll leave tonight. By myself.'

'He'll have no respect for you, Master. He murders to amuse himself.'

'He has no God.'

Yesha grinned. He held up a little host from his neck-pouch, its white underside decorated with perfect lines radiating from the centre. Holding it still higher over his head he moved it from left to right around the circle so that all could see.

'I'll show him,' said Yesha.

Yesha wandered for days in the wild places where no wise traveller had any business to be. He travelled in the early morning and the later part of the day. It was the middle of the summer and there was little shelter from the awesome power of the sun. Where he could find no cave or crevice, he sought refuge from the heat in the ever-moving shadows of boulders and mountains. Soon he was out on a desert plain where there was no shelter at all. This border territory at the edge of the rugged land and the beginning of the desert was where the robber tribe of Reuben bar Abbas hid. No authority would waste time and energy crossing the hostile land. Even if they did, the bandits knew every mountain hiding-place, every defile, every natural fortress of rock.

Yesha began to lose his bearings. At night the stars looked different. Strange images, streets bustling with people, boats with full sails floated past his eyes while he was walking. The water was almost gone from his water-skin. Two more days he moved around in this area, making himself as conspicuous as possible. His white robe was heavy with dust. His feet blistered. His mind was lulled into visions. He could no longer tell day from night. Still he wandered, fearless of the wild animals, or the dangers of ravine and cliff and black bottomless abysses, shafts and craters that would carry him straight to the hellish depths of the earth. He could scarcely see where he was going—where his foot would step next. He knew that wherever he put his foot, it would be right. The moment he lost faith in his step, the moment he feared he would slip, he would fall. He kept going. He wandered in circles. His spirit tried to escape from the torture in his body but he held to it somehow. It was all there was.

Reuben bar Abbas had pitched his camp of fine white goatskin tents in a perfectly sited gulley with a way out onto the desert and plenty of fine vantage points for guards.

The robber chief had a big beard on a face that was scarred, broken-nosed, craggy and cured like leather. There was a twinkle in the Chief's eyes—a twinkle of cruelty or amusement. He watch-ed as one of his men came into the camp on a fine stallion, with someone or other slumped in front of him.

The horseman rode up and pushed the body onto the ground a few yards in front of the awning where the Chief reclined with two of his slave-women. The horseman dismounted. A boy led his horse away. Bar Abbas' man walked over to the crumpled body, without saying a word, and kicked it.

'Alive?' bar Abbas demanded. 'Explain this!'

'I found him,' said the horseman.

'Obviously. Where?'

'Near the pass. Alone. I was careful. The sun had got him and he couldn't see.'

'You should have killed him there.'

'He spoke to me, Chief. He kept saying your name.'

'Did he now?'

'He said he had a gift. He kept repeating your name and saying he had a gift for you.'

'You should have brought the gift and left the body, Lateef.'

'I searched him. I couldn't find a gift. He had nothing. I kicked him and called him a liar, Chief, but then he said his gift was good news. He said he had good news for you.'

'Aha!' said bar Abbas. 'You should have got the good news and then killed him!'

'He said it was a secret, Chief. I kicked him again and he was knocked out. I thought, well, better you get the secret. I think one more kick will kill him. So . . . there, Chief.'

Bar Abbas looked at the pitiable blind figure trying to struggle to his hands and knees. 'Fix him up. Bring him to me when he has his senses—then we'll see what we shall see . . .'

Some women changed Yesha's clothes in another tent. They poured water on him and fed whey into him. They bathed his eyes. Yesha woke. His vision was blurred. After a time he could see clearly again. A man holding a knife was sitting watching him.

'Can you walk?' said the man, bluntly.

Yesha recognised the voice of his captor. He flexed the muscles in his legs. He could feel them again. He nodded.

'Get up. Come.'

The man was at the opening of the tent in an instant. Yesha was unsteady but he got to his feet. Stumbling, he followed.

The Chief was in a very good mood. He had managed, in the hours Yesha was recovering, to become intrigued with the whole episode. What on earth, he wondered, could be good news? What was news at all? He saw Lateef standing by the campfire. The man was with him. Bar Abbas noted the proud way he stood—the composure in the way he looked at him. The Chief waved Lateef away and beckoned Yesha closer.

'I am Reuben bar Abbas,' said the Chief. 'Who are you?'

'One who would give a King another Kingdom,' said Yesha.

The robber Chief was forced to laugh. 'You do well to start with flattery, little lost one. Why, I can let a man flatter me for hours before I kill him. What do you want with me?'

'I have a Kingdom for you, Reuben bar Abbas. My gift is proof that I am not lying.'

'What is your gift?' the Chief said, laughing at this serious fellow.

Yesha untied the small leather pouch he wore round his neck. He reached into it and handed its contents to Bar Abbas.

'Eat it, Chief. It is . . . magic.'

Bar Abbas laughed even louder and grabbed pouch and gift with both hands. He divided it and put his arms behind his back.

'Which hand?' said the canny old warrior in child-like glee. Yesha pointed to the Chief's right.

Bar Abbas handed out his portion to Yesha.

'*You* eat!' he laughed. 'In *my* Kingdom we eat better,' he said and roared at his own joke.

Yesha swallowed what was given to him without qualm. 'There is great power in it. When the sun rises you will be . . .'

'A King?'

'A . . . God.'

Bar Abbas roared with delight. For the first time in weeks his eyes were wet with laughter. The idea! He laughed even more at the solemn, oh-so-serious young man.

'You're a magician!' the Chief hooted. His squeal of laughter brought two of his men running to him in alarm. He waved them away. They saw he was laughing and wondered what was going on with the stranger.

'A very far-wandering little magician. I should have realised you were a magician, or you would not live and breathe in front of me in *my* desert!' Bar Abbas declaimed. He looked at the magician's gift in his hand. 'A God, eh?' he said, looking intently at Yesha. 'Why not, magician? Why not?' he laughed and ate. 'Six *times* as much of the most terrible unknown poison would only give a belch to my tough old belly. My father reared me on

poison. I swear a snake would die if it bit me!' he guffawed. 'Sit
with me, magician. Sit down and watch your last sunrise.'

Yesha and Reuben bar Abbas sat absolutely still through the
night. The fire in front of the Chief's tent died down. A couple of
men kept watch over the Chief from a discreet distance. Once or
twice Yesha leaned over to the Chief and whispered in his ear for
several minutes. The Chief did not move or make any remark.
He sat spellbound. His face was lost in wonder. After Yesha
whispered to him, he seemed particularly elated. Light came
before dawn. The sky changed colour from the wan light of fresh
conquest over darkness, through heavy pinks of growing strength
to the first blood-orange tip of the glorious incredible sun.
Slowly the orb, the whole great disc was free of the earth.

Bar Abbas stared at the sun. Yesha prayed the morning prayer.

After a while the Chief spoke. His voice was very shaky and
he mouthed his words with difficulty. He tried to maintain dignity
when his pride, his very soul had merged with the One.

'Do . . . what? . . . You . . .' he started and then paused. He
pulled himself together and fixed his gaze, as best he could, on
Yesha. 'Do . . . you wish to join us?' he asked.

Yesha stared for a long time into the warrior bandit's eyes.
Then he spoke, slowly and with precision, to the very heart of
Reuben bar Abbas.

'I want you to join *me*,' he said.

Judah brought the news to Gur ben David and Yaacov in
Jerusalem. They were disturbed.

'Apart from being a bandit, he is a heathen,' said Yaacov.

'Now. Now,' said Judah. 'Whatever he was or wasn't before,
he is now a firm believer in Yahweh and the teachings of Yesha.'

'Things are moving too quickly,' Yaacov muttered.

'No,' Gur ben David pronounced. 'Perhaps this is as it was

meant to be. We expected to have to wait, as we have always had to wait. Perhaps we are expecting set-backs where there are none. It could be that the Almighty has chosen this time. His leader comes like thunder and lightning without warning after a hot day.'

'What shall I tell Yesha?' said Judah.

'Tell him that more and more of the Council are being swayed to us—secretly and slowly. The longer he waits, the stronger our position will be within the Council. The organisation of fighters under Irijah is very strong. He has a careful system working in the city. If Yesha has Reuben bar Abbas, that is the beginning of a real force in the country. I cannot try to prohibit this growing strength. Yes . . . tell Yesha to act as he must act.'

Judah spoke very precisely to Gur ben David. 'Yesha wants the whole plan moved forward.'

Gur ben David looked sharply at Judah. 'How much?'

'The next Passover.'

'The *next*?'

'This is what he told me to ask you.'

'It seems he is telling me.'

'What is happening is happening,' Judah replied. 'The longer the delay, the longer the Romans and our other enemies will have to break us.'

'He would be moving too soon,' Yaacov persisted. 'If there is too quick an attempt there is a strong chance of failure. Then we are back to nothing.'

Gur ben David paced up and down the room. It was a heavy problem. If the coup was an abortion, they would have revealed their hand. And yet, if Yesha were killed, would the movement die with him? Not necessarily. Not if it was played right. Something could be salvaged . . . He would have to consult the secret Head. There would be a myriad of details to settle. The Head would have to arrange things.

'Next Passover . . .' said Gur ben David affirmatively, 'in Jerusalem.'

Once again I am sending you all through the land. The people must know the time. They must know that they are to be armed. We have gathered the Light these weeks and you will spread it to those who will receive it. They must know that your words are not empty and they will believe. There may be those who hunt you down, who will slaughter you and crucify you. This is all they can do for they can never imprison your spirits. Seek friends and let your contacts know that all can be fulfilled—that the next months will be momentous. Death stalks you now, and there is no hiding-place. Work quickly and do not stay away too long. Return here if there are developments or pitfalls. Strike out from here and return to the safety of this fastness. I will move quicker than the quickest and I will strike harder than the hardest. There are six new moons to the time. I will be here at every new moon. Those who are returned then may wish to come with me if their tasks are completed. Eventually I will need you all to be with me. The Rock and Judah will stay with me now. The rest of you have your appointed errands. Go now, and the Lord will shield your spirits.'

Yesha and Judah met Reuben bar Abbas at the place and time that had been arranged. Bar Abbas had with him thirty of his men—those who had the finest horses. They camped at a place hidden just inside the folds of the mountains where there was an ancient and holy spring and pool, little known and seldom visited. It had been a place to which the Baptist made pilgrimages. Bar Abbas demanded that all his men be shown the Light as Yesha had promised. Yesha administered to each his portion, and when it was coming on them, he taught them how to pray. Many of them were tortured and punished by the Lord. They writhed on the ground and called for help. Yesha merely sat by and watched.

Those who felt the finger of God on their hearts saw the brightness around Yesha and appealed to him. He did not move.

A Roman stockade on the Damascus road had about 140 men, including non-combatant staff, under the command of a young Centurion appointed to the post by the Procurator. He had held the command for only two months and his men were not yet settled under him. There were only a handful of cavalrymen at this stockade and many of the soldiers were already out patrolling the road, seeing to the safe transportation of cargo, and checking on travellers. Under the new orders they were to check groups of Holy men to see if they were rebels. None of the soldiers could understand this order. They could see no connection between Holy old Jews and rebels. An appeal for clarification of the new orders had been sent to Caesarea. The messenger had not yet returned.

On a slope in the foothills above the stockade bar Abbas and two of his best men surveyed the garrison, still, baking in the sun. They watched a small patrol of four horsemen leave the gates.

'Have the fires lit,' said the Chief to his companions. The men rode down into the fold on the other side of the crest and rallied the rest of the band.

The war-party rode down on the fort, sleepy and unwary below. As the band got nearer the post, two horsemen galloped to the front of the other men. They carried braziers of flaming oil. The others attackers drew arrows and fitted them to their bows. The arrowheads, all but the tips, were bound in cloth soaked in oil. One by one they rode past the braziers, expertly lighting their arrows as they passed with a gracefully easy sweep.

The fire-tips struck the wooden fort. Its dry beams were tinder. The fire caught. Black pillars of smoke rose slowly. There was no wind to dispel it. The embers fell back on the inside of the stockade.

The fort blazed. Flames leapt thirty feet into the air. In panic and disarray soldiers poured from the gates and jumped from turrets and battlements. As they scrambled away from the fire,

136

bar Abbas' raiders cut through them. Horses imprisoned in their stalls screamed inside the fort. The stallions of bar Abbas' warriors held their nerve and were fearless even near the fire. The soldiers were hacked down with swords, shot down by the Chief's best archers, impaled on spears. The skirmishers whooped and hollered in the massacre. No survivors were found by bar Abbas' scouts. They gathered together and rode quickly back to the mountains and their far secret encampment before it was known who had struck. There was no reward to divide up—the fight had not been for booty. They would see the Light again and fight for it again.

During the rest of the day the patrols slowly made their way back to the destroyed garrison. They buried 104 bodies. The messenger returned from Caesarea to report to the Centurion. His body was not with the slain. He had died in the fire trying to free his mad horse.

Yesha and Judah and the Rock trekked over the roadless barren countryside through the remotest poorest villages in the north.

A meeting had broken up. Yesha had done what he could to help the sick, the aged and infirm. They were all attentive to his stories and delightful illustrations of the Law. They were moved by his stirring words against the authorities. Many went back to their herds. One or two lingered nearby, still watching.

'You are exhausting yourself, Master. You speak to twenty pig-farmers as though you were speaking to thousands.'

Yesha laughed. 'You sound like Yohanan, Rock. If I speak to any group . . . all are the same. You give all you can give or you are giving nothing.'

Judah sat down beside Yesha and talked to him very quietly and casually, as though about nothing in particular. 'Yesha . . . you see those men . . . those two there?'

'Yes,' said Yesha. He did not look up. He knew they were there.

'One of them was with the herdsmen in the crowd.'

'I saw him.'

'Did you see him in the last village? He wore a cloak . . . dark blue.'

Yesha shrugged.

'In the small town on the other side, his cloak was reversed. It is a motley patchwork on the inside.'

'I see,' Yesha nodded.

Judah stopped talking as the other of the two lingering men, a goat-herd, came nervously up to them.

'Have you questions, friend?' Yesha asked.

'I . . . believe. I believe you,' said the goatherd, emotively.

'What do you want?' Judah asked.

The goatherd gathered a certain peasant confidence. 'I'm the the richest one in this whole village. I have more goats than any three other men put together. I can afford the luxuries. You say that the rich will have to give away their wealth to come with you.'

'Yes.'

'Well . . . I'll come with you.'

'Is it the riches you are leaving or the nagging wife?' Judah grinned slyly.

'I'll do whatever you say, Master . . . Masters.'

'Were you born in this place?' Judah asked.

'I was, Master.'

'You know every man here today?'

'I'm the one that's come forward,' said the peasant, proudly.

'That man over there. Do you know him?'

'Oh, he's not from here, but I know him. He's come a way.'

'Who is he?'

'He's the servant of the Priest who owns all the land from that hill over there and three more hills beyond. His master as good as owns us, Master. If we wanted to breathe in his territory, he'd find a Law that said we couldn't.'

'And you want to join us?'

'Yes, Master,' the peasant bowed to Judah and Yesha.

'That man . . .' said Judah, and suddenly there was a knife in his hand. 'Kill him.'

The peasant trembled. His eyes popped. Then Judah laughed and tucked the knife out of sight. 'I was joking.' He smiled.

The goatherd sighed, relieved beyond measure. Yesha stood up and put his hand on the poor man's shoulder.

'Stay here, brother. Share your luck, the good fortune of your great wealth with the poorest among your fellows. The day is coming when you will be called again to use a weapon. Think on it, friend. Be ready.'

Yesha rested a little longer and then left for the next village with Judah and the Rock. After a half-mile or so Judah stopped.

'I have forgotten something, Master. I must go back.'

'We'll walk on slowly,' said Yesha.

Judah hurried back the way they had come. He returned to Yesha and the Rock before they had reached the next village.

'Did you find it . . . whatever?' the Rock asked.

'Yes,' Judah said.

In the village Yesha kept an eye open for the man who had been following them but he was not to be seen.

Matthai saw to it that seventy people got good weapons from his contact.

Philip and Toma travelled together. Toma would make speeches, hold discussions, in small farmhouses. He felt that his powers of public speaking were growing better every day. Philip arranged the meetings and acted as watchdog. Though Toma's message was a little too sugary, it visibly had the desired effect.

Nathaniel and Shimon went to the sea-ports on the coast and made arrangements with dealers in the backstreets around the water-fronts. Consignments of arms were to be smuggled to certain hiding-places. Small stores of daggers were bought in rolls of cloth from unknown patriots, somehow linked to Yesha. Eventually there would be secret stores of weapons throughout the whole country.

Matthai attached himself to three different rebel groups, making haphazard and mostly unsuccessful attacks. He distributed all the weapons that Nathaniel and Shimon could get to him. But none of these groups could agree about anything or live peaceably together. It was an almost impossible task to bring unity to these dissidents. He did not feel he was succeeding. At least they were properly armed for when the call came. He hoped that they did not cut each other up first.

Chaim, Yohanan and Andros travelled among the lake fishers.

The enthusiasm that greeted them wherever they went led them to believe that they had the complete and whole-hearted support of the people for Yesha.

Hashimoni worked quietly in a small house with two of his old friends, who had been copyists and scroll-makers. They drew up safe-conduct passes and other papers that would give the brotherhood good pretexts for travelling, should they be questioned by soldiers on the road or need the statements of payment of taxes which the authorities sometimes demanded in the cities. In his painstaking and meticulous work, he consoled himself with the thought that there would be no documents, forms, permissions or warrants, bills or receipts in the Kingdom of God.

Taddai, working alone with a donkey and cart supplied by his contact, took upon himself the task of transporting weapons gathered by Nathaniel and Shimon to partisans willing to use their fields, woods, barns as repositories for them. Hashimoni had just completed papers for him and was waiting for Taddai to come and pick them up. Taddai thought he would take the opportunity of his visit to Hashimoni to carry one more consignment. He was stopped by two soldiers on the road. They searched his waggonload of dried fish—considered a good deterrent. The soldiers casually tipped over the whole waggon. Knives and swords spilled out onto the ground with the dried fish. There was nobody near and Taddai hurled himself on the soldiers with his own knife.

The soldiers regretted having to kill their rebel before he could be brought to the tribunal. He would have been a valuable prize, worth, perhaps, a few days' furlough.

Irijah was under orders from ben David to make no attacks in the city. No suspicion was to be directed towards the Holy city. Irijah spent the time recruiting zealous men and training them. He knew that the time had been moved forward. It was to be all or nothing. He followed his orders and with great difficulty managed to restrain himself from killing at least fourteen collaborators marked on his list. Perhaps in the next few months—one at a time—looking like accidents . . .

    *   *   *

Yesha, Judah and the Rock were the first to return to the caves to welcome their followers before the new moon. They sat around a small fire at the mouth of the 'warm' cave.

The Rock stared into the sky, then gazed into the fire. He looked from Yesha to Judah; both were deep in thought or meditation. He poked the fire noisily with a stick and looked up to see Yesha smiling at him.

'Master?'

'Yes, Rock?'

The Rock had a sheepish look on his face. 'Master . . . I seem to have lost . . . or maybe *dropped* . . . I mean, Master, can I . . .'

'Of course, Rock,' said Yesha, reaching into the little bag around his neck.

Eleven of the twelve came back in time for the new moon. One by one they recounted their exploits to Yesha. He seemed well pleased with the feeling of the people. He was sure that the nation would rise when it was called. Now it was only a question of arms and numbers.

They waited for Taddai. He did not come. Only one thing could have happened. Judah was given his place in the zodion and Yesha had twelve again.

Judah left them after two days. Only Yesha knew his mission. The conspiracy of the members of the Sanhedrin itself could never be told to his followers. He felt sad that he could not share this with them for it would bring even more hope to them. They would realise that their cause was not just the mission to the people but was carefully planned, checked and affirmed with the help of the zealous among the highest priests. They knew of the existence of Irijah and his men; they knew they had the support of Reuben bar Abbas and many other groups. But of the high conspiracy in the Temple itself they knew nothing.

Yesha was not sure how far he could push the Jerusalem organisation to allow him complete freedom, while providing him with the information from the partisan merchants and sea captains. These captains and merchants would bring arms donated by foreign Jews who had never seen their country but believed, even financially, in the dream of its freedom. So far he had not been restrained. Judah had won from them the right to bring the plan to fruition two whole years before they (or the Baptist) had planned it.

They knew the Master's plan to take Jerusalem during the Passover; the disciples could not do their jobs efficiently without knowledge of the urgency of their movements. All of them believed implicitly that the whole people would rise up and drive out the Romans when the tax-files and census forms in the Temple were destroyed. Collaborators throughout the city would be killed by Irijah's band. The High Priests, Caiaphas and his ruthless old father, Annas, who held their office through the Roman Procurator, would be destroyed before the sight of God.

The power had grown so strong in Yesha that he knew he could lead the people and purify the Temple and the priesthood exactly as the Baptist had wished. The Baptist lived through Yesha.

It was possible that once the people had risen, the conspiracy within the Council would no longer have any need for Yesha. There was still so much he did not know himself. Had the Sanhedrin conspirators been recruited by the Baptist, or was it the other way round? Had they approached the Baptist for his support in *their* aims? Yesha was not unaware that he could be used—that they might be merely using him at this moment . . . or all along. He did not know if their plans might have radically changed since the death of the Baptist. These remained thoughts, merely thoughts, at the back of Yesha's mind. He never really doubted that he alone was the instrument of the Lord in this, his vengeance. The only thing that Yesha could not consider, that did not exist even as a most deeply hidden thought, was the possibility of his failure.

'When can we *do* something again, Master?' Yohanan asked.

'When Judah comes back we shall be together again. Then we'll see.'

In Jerusalem Judah met ben David, Mannasseh, Yaacov and Irijah. All were concerned that Yesha should now remain safe until the Passover.

'The Holiest of days comes in two months,' said Gur ben David, 'when the Passover falls on the Sabbath. Yesha must stay where he is, at least until two weeks before the feast. Then you should all go to Bethany, to Eleazar. We can make contact most easily there.'

'He's doing nothing he can get caught for,' Judah answered. 'He walks through the hills. Sometimes he goes to isolated villages. No attacks have been made for a long time.'

'You may think he is safe in these remote places, but I cannot see Yesha staying quiet for long,' Yaacov fussed. 'He'd preach a sermon to a goat if it cared to listen.'

'He prefers to think of his listeners as *sheep* . . . in accordance with the scriptures,' Judah responded, wrily.

'Return to him, Judah,' Gur ben David said. 'Tell him he is strongest where he is safest until he goes to Eleazar. See that he keeps the close support of Reuben bar Abbas. I will see that accomodation and all necessities are arranged for that here.'

'If just one tenth of those who come for the feast are ready when Yesha calls them to arms, we shall take the city!' said Irijah fiercely.

'And then?' Judah asked.

'Then God will return to his nation and it will be exalted above all others!' Irijah affirmed fervently.

When Judah returned to the cave, he told Yesha word-by-word all that had happened. Matthai was sent to bar Abbas to tell him to enter Jerusalem just before the Feast, when the last pilgrims were crowding in, and who to contact there. Matthai returned within a week to report that bar Abbas would do as Yesha had asked.

'Have we enough of the Light to spread in the city?' Judah asked.

'We have been seeing to that while you were gone. There is enough.'

'Then we should wait out the days until we go to Bethany.'

'No,' Yesha said firmly. 'The men are all tense. We will all go together through the country. It will be our last chance to walk among the people.'

'Gur ben David . . .'

'*I* must do this. Whatever they say. Those who want can stay here.'

'I'm with you,' said Judah. He shook his head and then broke into a big grin.

As one fearless group they travelled, sure of the Divine protection Yesha had promised them. They went to pray on a high mountain, a sacred place that none had visited before. There they found a pious community living on the mountainside. The children saw them coming and ran down to them, wanting to play. They rushed into the group and out, running in circles around them, laughing.

A little boy of about six tugged at the Rock's robe and ran away. When the Rock turned the other way, the boy nipped in and tugged his clothes again. The Rock turned quickly. He tried to grab the boy but was too slow. Suddenly all the children were with them, touching them and asking questions.

'I'll clear them off, Master,' said the Rock, ruefully.

Yesha was busy playing with two of the children. He did not hear what the Rock said. He was lost in the children's world. Ecstatically he looked up at the cloudy face of the Rock. 'Don't you wish you could play like that, Rock? Look at your sour face!' he laughed. 'They are free! Their imaginations are free! Their spirits are free! They are the inheritors of the Kingdom. Only when I am with the Light can I be as they are.'

A very old woman hobbled down the mountainside after the children. She could have been a hundred years old, so bent and frail and withered was she. The ancient lady had been given the task of watching the children and she feared for their safety with this strange band of travellers. When she reached the roadside, she beckoned the children to her without speaking. Obediently but reluctantly they gathered around her skirts, while she clucked and scolded them.

Yesha went over to her. 'Are they all your children?' he asked, smiling.

'Every one,' said the old lady.

'It's poor ground for a living you've got here, Mother,' the Rock said, relieved that the children had stopped pestering him.

'It's to go on living that we are here,' said the old lady. 'The end of the world is coming, you know.'

'Is it now,' said Yesha.

'We just stay and pray here.'

'Your prayers will be answered in Jerusalem,' Yesha told her.

'This is our sacred mountain; it is our Holy place. From here we pray and our prayers are heard.'

'You can't stop the end of the world from here,' said the Rock, gruffly.

'For twelve years we have,' the old lady said with a sharp look.

'We will pray here with you.'

'The world needs all the prayer it can get,' the old lady affirmed.

There were two days praying with the Light on the mountain-top. They were welcomed by the others on the sacred heights and joined in their rituals as well as teaching them their own. For a whole day before they left, Yesha told the children stories. By the evening everyone had gathered round to listen to the tales he told the children.

They dared, in broad daylight, to go into Kana. It was the safest of all the cities of Galilee and most of the populace had been out to hear Yesha speak before. They had lost many fighters to the Roman and Herodian soldiers. They were waiting for the leader and when he came the whole town came out to greet him. There was no fear of spies in Kana, nor were any of the town officials likely to cause trouble.

The news that Yesha and his whole party were on the road to the town arrived ahead of him and he was met on the outskirts by old friends and contacts and a few independent partisans. They ushered him into a market square where he would speak.

A woman broke from the doorway of her house and somehow managed to scramble through the bodyguards. Hands reached to pull her back, but before she could be properly grasped her extended fingers touched the hem of Yesha's robe.

Yesha stopped. He swirled around. His eyes were blazing. His face radiated a grim beauty.

'*Who touched me?*' he demanded, wild-eyed.

The bodyguard picked up the woman and she was brought forward to Yesha.

Yesha trembled as he glared at her. He breathed deeply. The woman fell on her knees before him. 'Master!' she cried. 'I have been bleeding for five years and I am dying, Master. There are devils in my womb!'

Yesha looked at her. He spoke sharply and in a loud voice, yet he was hardly aware that he was speaking. It was as though the voice of another was in him. 'The demons are gone, woman! They are banished! I call them out from you!'

The woman stayed on her knees weeping with hysterical joy. Townspeople gathered around her.

Yesha was charged with the force that made him shake. He started to pant as emotions flooded from him. He felt as if every pore in his skin was weeping. Distractedly, he turned to Judah. 'She touched me . . . I didn't feel it but I knew it. Such a *need* . . . I felt energy suddenly drain from me . . . I was angry, Judah. I felt that someone had *stolen* it from me.'

'Do you want to rest?' whispered Judah, in concern.

Yesha breathed deeply in and out several times before answering, 'It is coming back . . . It is back!' he said and sighed. 'I have never . . .'

'Don't talk,' said Judah.

Yesha sighed again and shook his head, not comprehending it all. Then he pulled back his shoulders and marched ahead. The gathering crowd thronged around him. The twelve, with the help of others, were forced to jostle them back. Women screamed to touch him.

After healing those that could be healed and helping the ones whose tormented spirits needed reassurance, he spoke to the whole town, passionate and inflamed. They left before the sun was down.

Yesha went up on the hillside to be with the Light. He told the others that he wanted to be alone and they respected his wishes. There was no-one who would disturb him when he made this private communion with the Lord.

It was many hours before Yesha came down. He saw that most of his helpers were asleep in the shade of a grove of trees. Some had gone off by themselves. Yesha too was tired. He lay down under the trees, beside his men. In the distance he could see Andros and the Rock collecting dry wood for the fire. Evening would soon bring the cold winds up the valley. He thought of all those he had cured of sicknesses, and the demons he had driven from countless others.

He remembered all the things Judah had told him that were arranged by the members of the priestly instructors. They called themselves 'the bridegrooms', he knew. Was he the bride? He knew that Israel itself was the wayward wife of Yahweh. It was said in the writings of Jeremiah the prophet. The Lord had said that Jerusalem would no longer be called 'desolate' nor 'forsaken' but 'the married and the delight of Yahweh shall be in her'. The words of the two prophets came into him. He was the bride, the soul of Israel. Israel a slave? A slave and a homeborn servant? Why is he become prey? The young lions are roaring upon him and the beating of the eagles' wings in his ears. This time of all times they will not lay waste to the land. They will not despoil the bride of Yahweh, for she is truly penitent. The Lord of Hosts has said, 'Hew down her trees cast up a mountain against Jerusalem: this is the city to be visited; there is only oppression in her midst.' Yaacov and the others were more than advisers; they were his grooms. Spirit and soul united in him for he was both the bride and his own bridegroom. They said he was the one who was anointed by the sacred seed of Yahweh, that all prophets were in him and that he was the Saviour of the nation. Sometimes he knew this, sometimes he was unsure and doubted, but always he was driven by relentless faith in the Light of Yahweh, in the Baptist, who was with him, in his vision of the Kingdom.

Who he really was, he did not know. The weakness of his body struggled against the God within him. They said that he was the son of God. Were they not all? They said that Yahweh was his Father. Was not Yahweh the Father of every man? He could not deny it but there were times when his body tormented him with it. He knew who his spirit was. Who then was his body? The thoughts turned over restlessly in his mind.

The Rock came back to the grove with a heavy load of brush-wood and good kindling. Yesha sat up. 'Who do you think I am?' he asked the Rock, abruptly.

The Rock was taken aback. Clearly the Master was still partly with the Lord and not entirely in his flesh. He threw his bundle to the ground.

'Some men say you are . . .' the Rock began.

'I know . . . I know what men say, Rock. What do *you* say?'

'I say that you are the spirit of the Lord and our saviour.'

'Do you believe that?'

'I *know* that!' said the Rock, grinning as he quoted the Master.

They went to two more settlements in Galilee and Yesha gave signs as he had been told by Judah. The signs came, and they came from him effortlessly, unexpectedly and without preparation. He gave the Light to those blind from birth and for the first time they saw the colours and shapes and symbols that were the manifestations of Yahweh. Still rumours spread that he had done more . . . that he had raised the dead from the ground, cured withered limbs, made handsome men of hideously disfigured lepers.

He made his last call to arms and then told all his men to disperse. They would not be together again until they met at Eleazar's farm at Bethany.

Yesha had done all he could do. Ahead was the Temple, and the Lord's victory.

The Procurator left Caesarea earlier than usual to establish his garrison in the Antonia fortress in Jerusalem. He disliked the annual movement. This year Caesarea kept only a skeleton garrison. The Procurator's duty was to keep the peace in Jerusalem at the time of their feast. It was a religious affair of some days' duration. The problem was to keep Roman order over the population of Jerusalem swollen by up to a million visitors who swarmed in from the rest of the country. Usually this trek, apart from its inconvenience, was a waste of the Procurator's time. The people were particularly quiet and pious. There were no crimes. His men got bored and even the Jerusalem whores were ludicrously unavailable. It even necessitated his making boring social calls on Antipas.

This time it was different, he was convinced. The destruction of a way-station and its inhabitants had caused a marked lowering of morale among the men. Clavius' advice was followed; he had not summoned supporting legions from Flaccus—not after the diplomat had let it drop that in Rome Flaccus had been a gay companion of Agrippa, Antipas' high-living cousin. But this Passover Pilate knew that something was going to happen. The men carried extra rations and extra weapons. They went prepared for a campaign.

When they took over the Antonia fortress, there was for once to be no relaxation of discipline. Pilate gave orders to his Captains to see that the men were kept extra fit and ready at a moment's notice for any disturbances.

Pilate's fortress was in perhaps the most advantageous position in Jerusalem. From his portico on the highest hill, he was able to look down directly on to the centre of activity, the courtyard of the Temple. Further on he could see the palace of Antipas, who came, like all dutiful Jews, to the Temple at this time, as his religion demanded of slave and King alike.

Pilate made the necessary arrangements for co-operation with the Temple guard, and then called for Caius Clavius to be with him while he saw the High Priests.

Caiaphas, the High Priest, together with his father Annas who had been High Priest before him, was ushered into the reception hall by a few hawklike elderly Sadducean Rabbis, a detail of the Temple guard and a formal Guard-of-Honour of the Procurator's men.

The various officials and guards deployed themselves in their proper stations in the hall. Caiaphas walked up to the Procurator at a slow and stately pace, mainly so that Annas could keep up with him.

'You were so good as to order us here instantly, Procurator,' said Caiaphas. His haughty tone and the polite sarcasm were not lost on Pilate.

'I will not mince words with you, Caiaphas, or beat around any bushes, burning or otherwise,' said Pilate, in like tone. 'I am taking extra disciplinary measures this year and I expect your people to be more than usually compliant with my wishes. It is quite apparent to me that an uprising—not a demonstration—a military uprising is being planned throughout the country. It would be the logical thing for any revolt to take place in this city during the week of your festivities.' He paused and relaxed again into cat-and-mouse politeness. 'Surely intelligence of this has reached my High Priests?'

'There is a certain turbulence in the people, Procurator. Popular superstition credits us with moving into the Age of Pisces. These things happen every few thousand years, Procurator, and should be kept in perspective,' Caiaphas replied coolly.

'High Priest . . . I am talking about an organised, political rebellion! In this city!'

Caiaphas turned to his father, who had been given a stool to sit on, since earlier complaints about the infirmity of his legs. 'Has anything of this reached your ears, my father?' It was well known that Annas was deaf as a stone.

'Eh?'

Pilate cut the farce short. 'There are a great number of people coming and camping around the city walls. More than we can properly survey . . .'

'It is our custom,' Caiaphas interrupted, piously.

Pilate sighed. 'I am perfectly aware, High Priest, that it is your custom. Thousands of my men who have marched here also know that it is your custom. Now listen to me! No doubt the majority are peaceful and law-abiding, but there is going to be a very strong radical element at work here. Some of these desperate bandits may try to create a disturbance and set off the whole population. I will see that anything like this is dealt with in the most severely effective manner.'

'I am speechless, Procurator.'

'These are my orders,' Pilate proclaimed. 'Every gate to the city will be closed *one hour* before sunset. There will be no meetings, rallies, speeches or demonstrations in any public place other than those at the Temple and family gatherings at private homes . . . as is your custom. You will see that the Temple is properly and fully kept in order by your Temple force. My troops will be ready to come to your aid . . . should that be necessary. Furthermore any Jew found in possession of a knife, sword, a stone or any kind of dangerous weapon in disobedience of my previous orders on this matter will be executed on the spot. I shall have two thousand of my troops dressed as pilgrims and mingling with the crowds around the city.'

'We appreciate the Procurator's concern,' said Caiaphas with a slight mock bow to Pilate. 'You may be assured of our co-operation and loyalty, however overworked your imagination.'

The diplomat saw the blood rush to the Procurator's face, and deftly stepped in front of him. 'My dear Caiaphas,' he said unctuously, 'the Procurator has very good grounds for what he says. If you are ignorant of this; if reports have not been reaching you from your provincial Justices, then so much the more serious is the threat. The Procurator, I am sure, overlooks your ignorance of this, as of so many other matters.'

'Who are these people you fear?' Caiaphas demanded.

'It is believed to be some kind of reawakening of the Zealot movement. Surely you remember their last outburst, Caiaphas? We were forced to execute two thousand in Galilee. This time it is possible that the movement may be disguised in the trappings of a religious sect. They may seek to protect themselves, when caught, by throwing themselves on the mercy of the Temple for protection and appeal.'

'We shall not reject righteous believers. We cannot deny them sanctuary,' Caiaphas said with deadpan smugness.

The diplomat took a few paces up and down in front of the High Priests. He stared at his toes for a moment. 'The last time the Zealots acted in the name of God, their first action was to murder what I believe they called "the foulest of Imperial hirelings". I seem to recall that they murdered the High Priests.'

Pilate had calmed down, and he was grateful that Clavius had stepped in before he had razed the city himself. He controlled his rage, but felt he deserved to stress his annoyance. 'You are not irreplaceable, High Priest. I will not even find it tedious to sign the scrap of paper . . .' he said in disgust.

'It is possible,' the diplomat went quickly on, 'that this news has been withheld from you.'

'That is impossible! You imply too much, Caius Clavius!' Caiaphas warned, but he realised at the same time that this could be true.

The diplomat continued cold-bloodedly. 'Such . . . *zealous* ignorance may cause my superiors to consider that the High Priests may be aiding and abetting their own overthrow.'

'That is preposterous!'

'For the ultimate good of their people, no doubt,' Pilate interjected.

'How dare . . .?' Caiaphas began.

'We dare!' snapped Pilate.

'The Temple is the nation's treasury, the bastion of the economy, the public purse,' said the diplomat soothingly to calm down the two men. 'Surely, my dear Caiaphas, you can see the greatest blow to us would be a blow against *you*.'

Annas had been deaf to the topic of conversation but he saw that it was heated and the occasional word reached him. His eyesight was not strong enough for him to lip-read. He could see, but only to read very close to his eyes. He decided to take advantage of his age to interrupt them with a matter that had recently been on his mind concerning the penning of the sacrificial cattle. 'The question of, er . . . the livestock, Procurator . . .' he said.

During the stay at Eleazar's farm a great many messages passed between Yesha and those in Jerusalem. Sometimes Judah would be in the city following developments and sometimes other messengers arrived, usually when there was more urgency. Yesha learnt of the increased security measures being taken by the Romans. The Procurator had imposed curfews, had brought his maximum number of troops to the Antonia fortress. Anyone looking the slightest bit suspicious was thoroughly searched at the gates for weapons, and it was being said that many thousands of people were leaving weapons outside the walls. It was hoped that they were hiding and not abandoning them.

Yesha seemed to recall the faces of one or two of these messengers but did not know where he could have seen them before. He had spoken to so many people and been in so many places that he could not always remember where he had seen them before, nor did he ask these men personal questions that might put them in jeopardy at some later time. They told him that the conspiracy in the Priesthood was suspected but not uncovered and that some of the conspirators in Jerusalem were being watched.

With each report the responsibility for the action in Jerusalem was being settled more squarely on Yesha's shoulders. The others at the farm saw the coming and going of these messengers and the many brief excursions of Judah but they did not intrude into the Master's business. Even the Rock and Yohanan, who were aching to find out what was going on, did not pry. If the Master had wanted them to know, he would have told them.

The last messenger to arrive, on the night before the group were to go to the city, brought a woman with him. The messenger told Yesha that he was expected in the city the next day and that everything was carefully planned and required the utmost precision in timing.

'Who is the woman?' Yesha asked.

'She is sent to you by the Baptist,' the messenger replied.

Yesha looked at the messenger for a moment. He understood that the woman was truly sent by the Baptist—something he had arranged for this time. He did not know for what purpose.

'That is all,' said the messenger and turned to go. Yesha went with him to the edge of the farmyard.

'God is with us,' said Yesha. The messenger nodded but said nothing in reply. He set off down the track to the road. Yesha walked back to the farm wondering about the woman and her role in his mission.

They ate in silence. Each had his own thoughts about the next days. The woman, Miriam of Magdala, sat with Martha and Miriamne. She was about twenty-nine years of age, but her face was untouched by time and, if there were one or two wrinkles of care, they seemed to add to her attraction. Her hair, dark and ruddy, had been freshly hennaed, the sign of a brazen prostitute. Many of the men considered this an ingenious device for a messenger . . . from Reuben bar Abbas, no doubt.

Her fine beauty was at the point when it was beginning to fade and where a woman can sometimes be more beautiful than ever. She did not seem to be like the many poor harlots who came to them to unburden their problems, when they were in the cities. Miriam of Magdala had a different, a radiant presence, that helped take their minds off the fighting to come.

After the meal was cleared, Miriam unwrapped a jar that she had brought with her, in a silk cloth. Calmly she walked over to

Yesha and knelt in front of him, placing the jar between them. Saying nothing she reached out and took off Yesha's sandals.

Yesha sat as though he were scarcely aware of her. His thoughts were changing images of the ancient, the pagan religion. The orderly woman, dressed as and playing the part of a sacred harlot. The marriage of the Kingdom and Gehenna . . . peace between the neighbouring kingdoms or a ritual devised by the Baptist for the one who emerged as the true leader? She poured oil, fragrant as late afternoon flowers that hung in bunches from the ancient walls. She warmed the oil in her hand and then started to rub it into Yesha's feet.

Yohanan was shocked, but it showed only in his face. He refrained from his usual complaints. Others took it as a bizarre ritual in some way connected to this Master who they considered a divine Prophet, and even more than that.

Andros, in charge of the provisions, donated by Yesha's grateful followers, regretted seeing such an amount of money, in the form of a very expensive oil in an even more expensive jar, being lavished on a Master who talked of the grace of purification by water: a great deal cheaper and no less spiritually valuable liquid. It rankled—though he only said so later, in private, to Yohanan— that such a thing should not be sold and the money used partly for their basic food supplies, meagre and frugal as they were, and the rest of the money given to the poor. The poor. He thought for a moment. What 'poor' would there be after the next days and the advent of the New Age and the riddance of the persecuting authorities? He smiled at his 'old way of thinking'. To live for a year on scraps of fruit, and donations of widow's mites which were precious, all the same, to those who had freely given when they could ill afford it. The hearts of both of the sisters of Eleazar were aching mixtures of admiration and jealousy. How arrogantly this henna harlot anointed his feet. And how at the same time they felt that they were doing this ceremony *through* her.

Yesha thought of the Magus. His face loomed over the jumbling pictures of the symbol of the sacred woman, the whore of God, who was represented by a white pyramid, a white cone, a virgin vulva. Sullied but ever renewing, this white angel in her ritual was imparting to Yesha something that the others would never understand. Not only the uniting of the Kingdom and Gehenna, he thought, amused with his pun, but a ritual of eternal life, eternal unification of the balance of the opposites, or rather the strong and the weak. Why the face of the Magus? Why that image from so many ages ago? She came from the Baptist. It was the Baptist's will that she was completing, and yet even the Baptist seemed overshadowed by the image of Helene, the Magus' common law consort, herself a redeemed soul, a fallen and raised woman. His 'moon-goddess', his 'Helen of Troy'. It was the image of the sky over the earth, the preparation of the bride, the All-Father and the All-Mother, the anointing of the King, the oiling of the dead body. It was all of these things.

Miriam's hair was long. She let it down, cascading to the floor, and used it instead of a towel or cloth to dry the Master's feet. Yohanan averted his eyes from what was, to his ascetic sensibilities, a shocking sight. He understood nothing of what Yesha saw.

Miriam murmured a little chant to herself, half-sung, half-whispered, like a small child. 'Master . . . Master . . . Master . . .' she repeated.

Yohanan could not restrain himself. 'Master . . .' he chimed in.

Yesha replied sharply. 'Keep your words to yourself, Yohanan. In the morning we go into Jerusalem and there may be death for us or there may be victory. Whatever is Yahweh's will.'

'Perhaps both,' said Judah solemnly.

'This oil is for my burial and my . . .' he hesitated, 'return to life.'

'What riddle is this, Master?' Yohanan asked.

Yesha did not reply for some moments. He was lost in the ecstasy of the ceremony that had been prepared for him, or another like him, by his long-dead teacher. Her hair on his feet was like the kisses of thousands of butterflies.

'We do a desperate thing, Yohanan, and we may all be killed. It is prophesied that the Deliverer will be taken and slaughtered.'

'Not you, Master!' the Rock exclaimed.

'Not if I can help it. Not if the Lord helps me,' said Yesha.

'You *can't* fail, Master!' the Rock pronounced.

156

'I know that,' said Yesha. 'This anointment confirms it.'

Miriam finished her drying and stayed on her knees, staring into the Master's eyes with a look of visionary adoration. Yesha smiled warmly and gently at her. The task was finished. Yesha picked up the jar to see if there was any ointment left in it. There was. He got up and knelt, in the same way as Miriam, in front of the Rock, and tried to take off his sandal. The Rock recoiled.

'Master! What are you doing?' he cried.

'Rock?' said Yesha with a note of disappointment.

'Never!' refused the Rock. 'I don't need my feet washed!'

Yesha laughed. The poor old Rock took everything at its face value.

'No-one with feet as clean as yours needs washing, Rock.'

'I can't let you, Master. Don't shame me!'

'Then you and I have nothing in common,' said Yesha harshly. 'Master and disciple are no longer one. I will anoint the feet of all of you, for on your feet you will carry the news to all the world. If you cannot understand this, then there is spirit in neither of us.'

The Rock's anguished face melted. There was a wrenching hard-breathing silence.

'Anoint me, Master . . . and my dull head and my rough heart as well!'

As many of the population of the nation of Israel as were able to walk, to be carried, to hobble, or to run, were on the road so as to be in Jerusalem for the Passover. The incoming people stretched for miles from every gate. Provincial scribes, Sadducees and Pharisees with their servants and households entered the city alongside swine-herds, beggars, the poorest of the poor. Some were singing and chanting prayers as they went, others walked in thoughtful silence.

Carefully spread out in the ever-changing landscape of groups of people were those who had come to Yesha's meetings and who had affiliated their own groups with his. A good distance from the gates word came back to the people that the Romans were detaining anyone they found with weapons. Not every single person could possibly be searched, so they were picking on any-one who looked like a possible trouble-maker. Many abandoned their weapons, others, more frantically dedicated to the Zealot cause, saw to it that their weapons were carefully hidden where children or friends' children could come out of the city and pick them up at a more convenient time. Old women became walking armouries; and they served proudly, for their husbands and lovers and sons had been murdered in the cause. Harmless-looking grandmothers, even great-grandmothers, had lost their men in the first rebellion years before and had also seen their grandsons butchered in the same cause in recent years. They were prepared to die for this cause that had already claimed so many of their menfolk.

Among them, some miles back on the rolling road over the sloping hills to Jerusalem, was Reuben bar Abbas. His men were well spread out among the pilgrims, from first to last, stretching over perhaps half a mile. No longer were they dressed in their rich desert finery, the booty of a thousand raids, nor did they dress as the poor, who were always suspect and the first to be pulled in when something went wrong. They wore clothes of respectable (usually dead) merchants. If the Romans had known exactly what they were looking for they would have been able to recognise the gleam of the Light in their eyes, in comparison with the normal proud and happy glow in the eyes of others. The Romans at the gates, however, were practical. Their orders were to look for 'rebels' and 'bandits' and 'terrorists' and even danger-ously large groups of men attached to 'Holy men'.

The children, the old women, the infirm were given no more than cursory glances. One old man who knew that he had but a few months to live was borne into the city on a stretcher with twenty-six knives, four swords, a bow and quiver of arrows under his blankets and bedding.

When word of the search reached bar Abbas, he already knew

what to do. Six of his men went as runners down the long line of pilgrims and collected the weapons of the rest. Under orders from the Chief they left the file on the road and cut across country to the camps outside the city walls. There they made contact with Simon the leper, a friend of Eleazar from Bethany, who was to be found in the safety of the great leper's camp. His tent, a veritable warehouse of scimitars, broadswords, rapiers and side-arms of every design, was identifiable to bar Abbas' runners by its position under the city walls and the distinguishing patchwork of black-and red-dyed skins. Each night these weapons were delivered into the city by every means—ropes and baskets, ancient underground ways, and ways through the wall known only to the leper and his closest followers. The dark period, the moonless nights, made these transfers possible, and until the Feast of the Passover, when the new moon shone again, they worked without stop.

Bar Abbas' runners completed their delivery and found out where they were to go to take delivery of their arms once inside. Then they joined the rest of their men as they came along the road.

Bar Abbas, looking incredibly devout and bellowing holy songs with the pilgrims around him, passed through the gate. He was cursorily searched but was found to carry no more than a prayer-roll and a respectable amount of money. As he was being searched, the Chief took note of the number of spies lingering inside the gate, watching for men they recognised or had clear descriptions of. One by one his men got safely into the city, some being searched, some ignored.

Irijah had got a room that looked down on the Dung gate, where Yesha was to enter. He too saw that there were numbers of soldiers dressed as pilgrims.

The Dung gate had been chosen so that Yesha and his men would have a chance to store their weapons with Simon the leper. Moreover, it was the gate furthest from the Antonia fortress. It would be impossible to arrange the carefully planned ceremonial entry of the Baptist's successor where it could be easily disrupted.

'Look at them. Just look at them!' Irijah muttered. The

soldiers in disguise were hard to detect for mostly Procurator's troops had been levied in Syria and other neighbouring territories under Roman rule. They were almost indistinguishable from their own people. 'It's their stench that gives them away,' Irijah said with disgust to the group of men packed in the room with him.

Irijah had taken over several houses near the Gate, donated by sympathisers and partisans to the cause. He had some forty men ready to create the necessary diversion at the gate when Yesha entered. He had a further 130 zealous men in other parts of the city. A messenger was to arrive ahead of Yesha, giving Irijah time to set up a diversionary action in the Upper City. This would draw off many of the troops at the Dung gate—the nearest to the confusion—while Yesha was welcomed by a crowd already assembled outside the gate.

'Everything is ready,' Irijah told his men.

Yesha and Judah walked together, in close conference, until they were less than a mile from the city. The rest of the band, which included Eleazar and his son, Martha and Miriamne and Miriam of Magdala, followed closely behind. None of them carried their weapons; the new ones were to be provided once they were in the city.

Yesha told his party to rest for a while by the side of the road. He took careful note of the position of the sun. They had made better time on the road than expected. For a while they sat and watched the hundreds of pilgrims pass them on the road. They were tense and excited, searching among the passers-by for those who would be their supporters when the city rose.

'Now the crowd must see a sign that will be talked of by everyone in Jerusalem,' Yesha said.

'It's arranged,' Judah nodded.

'Andros! Bar Talmai!' Yesha called to his two followers. They got up and hurried over to him.

'Go ahead of us into the next village,' Yesha told them. 'There's a white colt tied there. Bring it to me.'

'How will we know it, Master?' Bar Talmai asked.

'It is a very small village. How many white colts do you expect to see by the road?'

Bar Talmai blushed. It was odd to see embarrassment in so strong a man.

'If we're stopped . . .?' Andros asked.

'Tell them "the Master needs it",' Yesha said.

Andros looked puzzled but Yesha did not enlarge on his orders, and he set off down the road with bar Talmai.

'The people will see and hear that the prophecies are come true!' Yesha murmured stonily.

In a shady bower, secluded within the beautiful terraced gardens below his villa on the isle of Capraea, lay Tiberius Julius Caesar Augustus, Divine Emperor of Rome and the civilisable world.

The Emperor was stretched out, half asleep on a divan strewn with silks. Absently he fondled a boy of about fourteen. An exquisite golden-haired girl, perhaps ten or eleven years of age, sat naked on the end of the divan at the Emperor's feet. She smiled, when Tiberius lazily opened an eye, more libidinously than the most beautiful and accomplished courtesan in the Empire. Fondly she squeezed the Divine leg as the Emperor half-opened both eyes and brought his hand up to further shade them.

'Campi . . . where's Campi?' Tiberius asked languidly. 'Fetch Campi for me,' he told the boy, giving him a little pinch.

The boy ran off down an arboured avenue and appeared some moments later with the lean figure of Gratio Campi, for this month the Emperor's eyes and ears on the world.

'Divine Caesar,' said Campi with a low bow. His voice was nasal but musical—a combination the Emperor found rather funny.

'Ah . . . Campi . . .' the Emperor said lazily. 'Tell me something interesting. Give me some news.'

'Divine Caesar, your cousin . . .'

'*Not* family requests,' the Emperor sighed, interrupting Campi. 'Not one word about my relatives.'

'Divine Caesar. The name of that charioteer you . . .'

'*News*, Campi. Tell me about my outside world.'

Campi started out at a rattling pace. All the facts and figures raced past the tip of his tongue. 'Divine Caesar—in the day's trading the Egyptian corn imports were down by three points. Oil commodities took a tumble yesterday but are back to . . .'

'In brief.'

'The German situation looks bright. A report of some trouble in Palestine. Nothing confirmed. Negotiations with the West Gauls are breaking down . . .'

'Is there no *good* news?' huffed Tiberius.

'Divine Caesar . . .' said Campi, with a degree of uncertainty that added an amusing quaver to his voice. 'Things could not be better in the Empire as a whole.'

The Emperor flopped back, closed his eyes and with one splendid flourish of his hand dismissed Campi and beckoned the girl to come closer. 'That's all, Campi. That's all I wanted to hear. Everything in general and nothing in particular.'

Yesha approached the Dung gate riding on the colt, whiter than snow. Around him were his followers and the long column of families, the multitudes of the many classes of the populace, patricians and peasants, notables and nobodies.

'Make way! Clear the way! The Master is coming!' shouted the Rock.

Andros and bar Talmai went on ahead, running and shouting to all the people that the Master had come. When they were nearer the gate, they met with the crowds that were sitting and waiting for the warning. The advance alarm was passed to Irijah by one of those outside who opened a bolt of purple cloth and waved it, quickly rolling it up afterwards. Irijah set his plans into action.

At first those ahead of Yesha's band were annoyed that some rich person was trying to push through them until they saw that no attempt was being made to clear them out of the way so this personage could pass them. As thunder after lightning the rumour went back down the following crowds that 'He' had come. Those who knew of Yesha told those who did not that the man on the white colt was the Master that had been sent by the martyred prophet to save them. Excitedly they realised that they were in his presence—in his wake—and pressed forward until the road behind him was filled more with an army in close file than a slow-moving straggle of pilgrims. Even those ahead moved to the sides of the road in case the Master should wish to spur ahead and lead them as well.

When they got to the Dung gate, the soldiers inside had already been dispatched to deal with an 'incident', a diversion created by a crowd of unknown dissidents throwing stones at a small Roman force patrolling the area between the houses of the High Priests. For a short period the gate was almost completely unmanned.

Those who had waited all morning to make a demonstration of welcome—mixed with several of Irijah's men who would not be slow with their knives if there was anyone hindering Yesha's entry into the city—pressed in their hundreds to the wayside. Some found no place to stand aside to watch the spectacle (for all loved spectacles) and climbed into the trees in the roadside groves. They tore down the branches to see better. The fronds fell onto the crowds below who took them up and waved them, brandishing them above their heads like swords and crying joyously for the salvation of their spirits, their nation, their souls. They shouted for the word of God to be fulfilled—for the Word that was made of flesh and the Light. They threw their branches down into the road to make a carpet of the green fruits of the earth, that their long-awaited Deliverer would receive the honours of a king. The colt's hooves trod on the palm leaves and the stones on the road to the gate were not bruised.

As once before God had sent a man to lead his people out of captivity in Egypt and out of exile in so many lands, now he had come again! He had come to lead them out of the captivity of Rome and their exile from God. More leaves and branches were stripped from the trees and thrown onto the ground. In their exuberance the crowd even threw their cloaks onto the road.

Judah, flanked by the Rock and Matthai, went ahead of Yesha.

'He is come! Bear witness that the prophecies are come true! The time is come! The Light is come! The new kingdom is come! The saviour is come! The one who comes is come again! The son of the Father is come! The son of man is come!' Judah chanted, raising his voice louder than the whole assembly.

Overcome with emotion, women wept and threw themselves to their knees. One of Irijah's men in the crowd started to shout 'Osh-anna!', which is to say 'Free us!'. The cry was picked up by other Zealots throughout the crowd. In moments everyone was calling 'Free us! Free us! Free us, we beg you!' They cried it not as they would to Yahweh in the Temple to free them from their sins, but as a powerful prayer to Yesha.

From the tents and camps all around the gate hundreds more ran to see what the shouting was about. It was impossible to get near the road and all the trees were filled with people. Those who were able to push through the crowd or find a suitably high mound, even at a distance, saw a man clothed in the purest white, as a healer, and riding on a pure white colt of such shining perfection that it had no equal in the land. An unblemished white yearling was such a rarity that they could only wonder at the wealth of the man upon it. No riches could buy such a beast. They wondered at this for the communities of healers and saints had no treasures nor material goods. They heard the cries and chants and the proclamations of Judah, and suddenly they knew who this was! *He* had come.

Nathaniel and Shimon were at one side of Yesha and Chaim walked with Yohanan on the other. They, too, shouted to the crowd: 'Wake up, you sleepers! Rise out of your dead bodies!'

'Rise as the Light rises! Look on the brass serpent of Moses and live! Wake up! Rise up!'

Toma, Hashimoni, Philip, Andros and bar Talmai followed behind with Eleazar and his family and Miriam, all doing their best to act as a barricade against those behind, hundreds upon hundreds of them, trying to surge closer to the Master.

Yesha rode with his back straight, looking neither to left nor to right. His eyes were fixed on the gate. He could scarcely hear the paeans from his men or the clamour from the masses urging him on. He, Yesha, was not there. His spirit sang and danced with sun glinting from the golden crenellations of the Temple. The voices carried his spirit like a wind over the heights of Zion. The tension of the past months was gone. The hatred was gone—fled with the intensity of his purpose. Moving like the waters of his baptism, he felt his spirit flowing uninterrupted to its destination. He could feel its source. The water filled the abyss to the rim. The source of the water and the fiery rays of the head of the Temple were the same source. There were no more fears at every step, forward or backward. He had escaped. He was here and now.

There was chaos at the gate. One of the disguised soldiers hurried to the Captain of the Watch and told him what was happening. The Captain, knowing that his main body of soldiers were already quelling a disturbance, ordered the man to go to the garrison for reinforcements. The soldier ran to deliver the message. He was knocked unconscious by one of Irijah's men as soon as he was out of sight.

As Yesha, the crowd swelling around him, came up to the entrance, Irijah signalled for a group of his men to come out of three of the houses. Each soldier was closely marked and jostled out of the way without any apparent display of violence. One or two soldiers who received harder knocks pulled out their swords, only to be tripped up or suffer a disarming blow. These soldiers never saw their swords again, nor did others who had not unsheathed their blades. Irijah was an amazing pick-scabbard.

Yesha rode unimpeded into the city. Judah and the Rock helped him from the colt and covered his white robe by throwing a long dark cloak around him. Even the crowd lost sight of him, as though he were some magnificient apparition that had vanished.

The colt was taken by Andros who was joined by one of Irijah's band and the two men hurried around the first corner and led the animal into the second doorway. Two women were waiting there with pots of warm black dye. They poured the dye over the animal while the men held it steady. In a moment the white colt was no more.

Messages flew to the Antonia fortress and to the High Priests. Pilate was severe with his Captain of the Dung gate and had him flogged and thrown into a cell for two days of bread and water. The guards were doubled at all the gates but Pilate feared that the worst had already happened. A brigand with a huge following had got into the city. The Procurator questioned and re-examined the soldiers and spies who had been eye-witnesses to the event.

'He came riding in, bold as brass, on a white horse.'

'A horse?'

'A donkey.'

'A horse or a donkey?'

'It could have been an asses' colt, Procurator.'

'Can any of you tell me whether it was a horse, a donkey or an ass?'

'A donkey.'

'I thought it was a horse.'

'Who saw it?'

'Procurator . . . there were so many people crowded around . . .'

'Would you have known if it was an elephant?' Pilate asked sourly.

There was no reply. The witnesses had conflicting stories.

'Well,' Pilate sighed. 'It was white? Yes?'

'Yes, Procurator.'

'White, Procurator.'

'Not black, dun, piebald or bright red?'

'White, Procurator.'

'Yes, sir.'

'The man riding this white . . . animal—what did he look like?'

166

'A Jew, Procurator.'

'You don't say? I thought he might have been a pitch-black Nubian with a long scar on his right cheek and blonde hair . . . on a white elephant.'

'Procurator . . .'

'What did he look like, you wall-eyed, cockled-eared gowks!?'

'He was wearing a white robe . . .'

'He had a beard, Procurator. His hair was wild and hid his face.'

'Was he old or young?'

'Sort of . . . middle-aged.'

'Sure?'

'Perhaps he . . . I cannot report on that accurately, Procurator.'

'Is there no way we can recognise this man and lay hands on him?' Pilate shouted.

'It all seemed to happen at once, Procurator. It was impossible to get nearer,' one of the soldiers ventured timidly.

'Do you realise,' said Pilate bitterly, 'that this man is probably the leader of all the rebels? That he was able to ride into my city as though he were a king—defying my authority? Making asses . . . or donkeys out of my soldiers . . .'

Pilate was silent for a while.

'So,' he said at last, sourly, 'my soldiers are to be told to look for a Jew in a white robe, riding on a white donkey? Is that it? I suppose you think he's still riding around? *Idiots!* All *idiots!*'

'Procurator . . . we were not the only ones there . . .'

'How many got through the gate unchecked?'

'He had many with him.'

'He had many with him,' Pilate mimicked viciously. 'Let me tell you! More than six hundred people got through that gate! Your Captain, with whom I am slightly angry, sent three men to follow him. Have they returned? That is a rhetorical question . . . I doubt if we shall ever see *them* again!'

'There were men inside the gates . . .'

'I know. I know. All faceless and nameless. So you can see that I am delighted. There is a whole army in the city but nobody has seen them.'

'I don't think all that crowd were actually with him, Procurator. Many were people coming into the city anyway,' the soldier suggested hopefully.

'How many inside the city? How many people attacked the guards?'

'There were so many, Procurator . . .'

'Faceless, nameless and numberless!' Pilate spat. He waved to one of his adjutants standing by. 'Take these men and have them whipped,' he ordered sharply. The two soldiers were led away to join their Captain.

Pilate paced up and down. All his fears had been proven right, but that was no satisfaction. They had made their plans carefully, drawing the main body of guards away from the gate. All his diligent measures to prevent such an occurrence had failed. There were thousands of them, he thought. Thousands and thousands.

Three of the Council conspirators were placed under house arrest by Caiaphas without any specific charge against them. Five others were under surveillance, but knew it, and were thus rendered useless. Gur ben David was one of them. Yaacov, considered to be such a spineless and devout ascetic, was on no list of suspects. He was therefore the sole representative of the Priesthood at the meeting of the rebel leaders.

They met soon after darkness fell and while there were still many people on the streets. The gathering took place at the house of Yusef of Arimathea, a wealthy partisan too old to join in the fighting, but a devoted helper. He owned several houses in the city and other land in and outside the walls. It was Yusef who was in charge of seeing that all the men of Yesha and bar Abbas had places to stay and, if necessary, hide.

Irijah and two of his lieutenants were the first arrivals at Yusef's villa in the Upper City. Since all of Irijah's men lived in or close to Jerusalem, it was not necessary for Yusef to organise shelter for them. They waited for the others to arrive. Yesha and Judah came soon after Irijah, and Yaacov was with them only minutes later.

'Where is bar Abbas?' Irijah asked after the appointed time for the gathering was well passed.

'He has a desert sense of time,' Yesha replied. 'He'll come.'

'We should get on with it,' Irijah argued. 'We do not know if he has come at all.'

'I trust him,' said Yesha.

'Trust,' Irijah stated, 'is all very well, and I do not doubt you, Yesha, but the longer we are together in one place, the more danger.'

'We are all aware of the danger, Irijah,' Judah answered.

Irijah looked stonily at them. 'I have lost six men with eight more badly injured so you could get safely into the city,' he retorted. 'Any of them could have been identified and their families suffer the recriminations.'

'I am sorry,' Judah apologised.

Yaacov spoke up. 'We don't have all the night. The High Priests have imposed a curfew in the city. No one on the streets after the fourteenth hour.'

'The High Priests or the Roman masters?' jeered one of Irijah's companions.

'Soon it will not matter,' said Yesha.

One of Yusef's door-wards, like all the servants of the household a man zealous for his God, came into the room and announced Reuben bar Abbas. The converted outlaw came in grinning. He gave a laugh when he saw their serious faces.

'Such gloom!' he exclaimed. 'We are here, aren't we?'

'Irijah has had fourteen men killed or wounded,' said Yaacov gravely.

'Now let me see,' said bar Abbas. 'Four of my men were killed having a little fun with a gang of uppity Romans. Three were killed in some fuss at a goldsmith's. Eleven have been arrested for the most insignificant misdemeanours in various parts of the city. Oh, yes . . . two had a fight at an inn and cut each other up good . . . and sixteen have completely disappeared!' he said boastfully.

'That is terrible!' Yaacov fretted.

'There was to be no movement unplanned!' Irijah said angrily. 'There was to be nothing to alarm the authorities before we strike together. What a waste of men this is! What kind of support?'

'Alarm the authorities?!' Bar Abbas roared with laughter. 'Have you seen them . . . the soldiers in the streets? They are so jumpy they would kill a man for whispering in a corner. Do you think they can't see that something is going on here? Did you know that *oyur* Procurator has taken more than the usual handful from the Caesarea garrison? He's brought the whole lot! There is nothing those conscripted pigs of Syrians and Idumeans and the wanderers you call "Philistines" like better than killing Jews. How long have they had to stay their hands? Now they can freely do what they are trained and waiting to do. Before they had to make pigs of themselves by means of courts and tribunals and suchlike . . . now they can go the whole hog!' His laughing mood had become angry and serious. It startled them.

'This is no time to pretend that your enemies are unsuspecting little lambs. As you told me, Yesha, they are the last of the sturdy rams of the last age and they will go down fighting. Better that you should have waited a few more years and then they would have died, as all men die. Don't alarm them, you say, Irijah? Are you blind? Soldiers do not kill when they are all-powerful—they kill when they are alarmed, when there is fear in them because they are weaker,' he thundered. 'If the population rises with you, Yesha, it is not a question of their mighty forces overcoming a few bandits. The odds will be a few thousand against a *million*! They will come to the natural conclusion and capitulate at once!'

'The natural conclusion?' Yaacov inquired.

The Chief slapped his thigh and broke into a gurgle of laughter.

'Conclusion?' he hooted. 'The conclusion that they are out-numbered!'

'Tomorrow was to have been the day,' Irijah insisted.

'So it will be,' bar Abbas agreed. 'But I do not worry that my men are dead or taken or gone. They are their own warriors. It is a warrior's right to die when it is his hour. Nor could I order them to be quiet and go to bed when there is a city such as this to amaze them.'

'Perhaps,' said Judah thoughtfully, 'the incidents of the day may make them think that we have little strength and that it is not co-ordinated or aimed in any specific direction . . . that we *are* merely bandits and looters.'

There was a silence for a moment.

'How many men do we have to fight?' Yaacov asked. 'Not including partisans and believers and the whole of the people . . . how many? To fight?'

'More than one hundred and twenty,' said Irijah.

'Bar Abbas?'

'About one hundred . . . and forty-two,' bar Abbas replied, cagily.

'Including those taken?'

'Well,' bar Abbas grunted, 'maybe . . . maybe more than one hundred and twenty.'

'Maybe less?' Irijah suggested, with a taunting leer. 'We must know *exactly*.'

'I don't know,' bar Abbas admitted. 'At least a hundred.'

'Yesha?'

'One hundred and fifty-six promised. I can count myself for only twelve.'

'*Twelve?*'

Bar Abbas looked furious. 'Twelve? I thought . . .'

'There is good reason for that, bar Abbas,' Yaacov interrupted sharply.

'What? Tell me what?'

'Bar Abbas . . . Irijah . . . you are our strength of arms. Yesha is the spirit of the people. He has the million . . . the potential without which you will never see your "natural conclusion" . . . outnumbered Romans. You have said so yourself.'

Bar Abbas grumbled but made no more complaints. Irijah spoke to him.

'We are to use all our force to give Yesha cover. Once the rotten heart of the nation has been hacked out, when the tax-files have been burned, when the chain of command has been broken between the Romans and the Temple authorities, then there are thousands more who will run through the streets and to every hilltop and let the people know—they will rise up and show their strength. Already the word has spread that the saviour has arrived in the city and there is a feeling of wonder and excitement everywhere,' Irijah said.

'Where do we cover him, then?' bar Abbas asked.

'Where the crowds are thickest.'

'Where?'

'A diversion at Solomon's portico . . .'

'The *Temple*?'

'Yes.'

'Go on.'

'Then cover the Priests' Court and the Entrance to the Sanctuary.'

'And then?'

Yesha and Judah led the brotherhood among thousands of worshippers to the Temple on the Mount of Zion. The Temple had been erected by the old Herod on the site of the Temple built by Solomon and destroyed by Nebuchadnezzar when he took the aristocracy of the city to captivity in Babylon. Though all had seen the Temple before, it never ceased to astound those who approached it year by year. It reared up on massive masonry. At the Ophel corner the walls were 211 feet high and it was said that from its top an Arab with a spear looked like a flax-worm. They crossed the bridge over the valley of Cheesemakers, a wide and long way crowded with pilgrims.

Yesha stopped at the side of the bridge in the middle and looked down the great drop of hundreds of feet to the buildings below that housed the city archives. It was to be one of the main targets in the city after what was to be done to the Temple had been done.

172

'There is a disastrous abomination in the Temple,' said Yesha so that none but those around him could hear. 'We must strike at its heart though it may tear at our own. I prophesy this: not one stone of the Temple will stand on another—all shall be hurled to the ground and another shall rise in its place. A new Priesthood will be consecrated. The Holy place has already been polluted and it will not survive. This is *true*; everything will be destroyed.'

The faces of Yesha's band were grim. Heavy matters rested on their minds. They were fired with the Light and their wills were strong and fearless of death. Yesha steadied himself and led them on to the Temple.

'This must not fail!' Judah whispered urgently to Yesha.

'It can't,' Yesha replied.

A quarter of Irijah's men and part of bar Abbas' group entered the forecourt of the Temple by the Huldah gates through the Royal Portico. The rest of their men were joining with all the other armed groups who were under the direction of Simon the leper. They were to create disturbances through the whole of the Lower City in order, once again, to draw Roman troops. This time it was a greater disturbance that was planned—one that would draw a large detachment away from the Antonia, who were surveying the Temple for any signs of disorder.

There were thousands in the outer courts. Irijah waited tensely for word that the attacks in the Lower City had started. Yesha's men, together with those of bar Abbas and Irijah, spread along the vendors' stalls under the colonnades of Solomon's Portico. Here they busied themselves with buying oils, incenses and animals. Caged doves awaited sacrifice. Pens of sheep and oxen, an immense cattle-market with all the smells and lowings of frightened animals scenting the blood from the slaughter in the Inner Temple.

Bar Abbas' men lingered around the stalls of the money-changers where foreign Jews cashed their money into the appropriate currency to buy the things necessary to make their sacrifices.

Yesha and Judah went alone to the Beautiful Gate that led into the Inner Temple. They stood on the balustrade leading up to the rampart of Hel.

Suddenly Irijah saw activity on the watchtowers of the Roman fortress. Trumpets sounded. Soldiers previously mingling with the crowds or stationed with the Temple guards hurried across the Court of the Gentiles towards the stairs of the north portico that led into the fortress. The alarm was on. He waited until the Romans were gone. It was necessary to hold back for several more minutes while the soldiers were given orders in the fortress and sent out to quell the uproar in the city. Then, like a bolt from the sky, Irijah struck. He tore into a stall where doves were sold. Cages fell and burst on the marble paving. All at once there was chaos. Pens were attacked and crazed cattle stampeded into the crowd. Sheep ran bleating among the people. Bar Abbas and his men overturned the tables of the money-changers. Piles of coins cascaded everywhere. Treasure-chests crashed to the ground. Delightedly, bar Abbas' men helped themselves, pretending to join with the other pilgrims who were scrambling on their knees to gather up the gold and silver. The Temple guards ran from every part of the court. Guards rushed from the gates of the Inner Temple and even from the Priests' Court and the Sanctuary itself. In a few minutes all the raiders had melted into the crowds attempting to herd the cattle back to the broken pens. This caused pandemonium for they purposely tried to drive the oxen into other stalls that had so far escaped harm.

Yesha and Judah waited a moment and then hurried through the Beautiful Gate and across the Women's Court. Guards rushed past them towards the turmoil. The steps up to the Priests' Court and the great altars which poured with rivers of blood were unguarded. Yesha and Judah went unhindered through the gate.

Priests, barefooted so they would not slip in the torrents of blood, stood on the Great Altar of unhewn stone, hearing the cries of the people and animals, wondering what was happening. The Guards rushed from the Chambers of Hearth and Hewn Stone and the porch of the Sanctuary. No notice was taken of Yesha or Judah as they passed the three high altar-fires and the piles of salt, the marble tables for laying out flesh and fat and the low columns where rows of hooks and rings were fastened for hanging the dismembered parts. The Levites had all but abandoned

174

the great laver between the altar and the porch of the Sanctuary and the blood was beginning to overflow the drains. Sacrificial smoke billowed black and acrid. Purposefully, Yesha and Judah climbed the twelve steps to the portal, thirty-three feet in width and sixty-six feet high. Going through to the Inner Sanctuary, Judah noticed a priest nod to him—it was Mannasseh.

In the melée at the forecourt, Irijah and bar Abbas saw to it that their men were with the crowds who fled to the gates to leave the Temple. Their work there was done. A tremendous blow had been struck against the sacerdotal economy and authority. The rest was up to Yesha for it was up to the High Priest and leader of the New Age to deal with the High Priest of the Old. As surely as God was with them, so the mission would be executed. Outside the Temple walls, Irijah and bar Abbas joined forces to go down into the valley, unite the skirmishers and raid the city archives.

Judah, who had been given careful instructions, led the way to the office of Caiaphas. Side by side he and Yesha burst into the room. It was empty but for one Temple guard who had stayed at his station.

'What do you want? Who are you?' the guard demanded.

Judah kept his wits and spoke calmly but intently to the sentry. 'We have been sent to warn the High Priests.'

'Who gave you the right to come in here?' said the guard.

'The Captain of the Temple,' said Judah. 'We must warn the High Priests. Where are they?'

'They have already been warned and have taken refuge in the Antonia,' the guard replied, beginning to get suspicious.

'They have deserted the Sanctuary?' Yesha blurted out, appalled.

The guard drew his sword. 'Who are you?' he demanded again.

'The Captain told us . . .'

'The Captain escorted them to the fortress,' said the guard.

'Then . . . all is well,' said Judah. Yesha stood frozen. Judah nudged him. 'We shall go,' he said. Numbly Yesha turned to the door.

'Stop there!' cried the guard. He advanced on the two men with his sword.

Deftly, Judah stepped aside, drew his dagger and struck at the guard. The sword clattered to the floor. Judah stabbed twice more as the guard staggered. He was finished.

'We must go to the fortress,' said Yesha, with icy fanaticism.

'No,' said Judah firmly. 'We will fail the cause.'

'We *have* failed,' Yesha intoned. 'We will go to the Antonia and kill them. The people will rise!'

'We will join the others,' Judah insisted, roughly grabbing Yesha's arm. 'Something can be salvaged!'

'I have failed,' said Yesha, dully.

They left the Sanctuary unnoticed and skirted the place of slaughterings. The Temple guards and the Levites of the Nicanor Gate had resumed their posts on the steps. The Levites had started to sing and play again. None would think of stopping someone coming *out* of the Court of Israelites.

Yesha's followers, flushed with excitement, were grouped by the pillars outside the chamber of the Nazarites across the Women's Court. Yesha kept walking towards the Beautiful Gate. In twos and threes they followed him.

Some order had been established among the people in the forecourt but the damage had brought the commerce of worship to a standstill. The rumour was spreading among the crowd that the saviour had come and the children of Israel were to be freed. Many said it was the work of the Zealots; some knew it was. Others agreed that, whatever, it was an historic happening.

The Rock caught up with Yesha and Judah by the tomb of the Prophetess Huldah, beyond the gates.

'Master!' cried the Rock, and then with burning reverence he said, 'Lord!'

Judah pulled the Rock aside and spoke urgently. 'All of you! Rock . . . Andros . . . here . . .! Toma!' he called as the others arrived. 'The Romans will be on bar Abbas and the men of Irijah! Go through the city and spread the news! If there is any man who will fight for God, let him come now! Tell those

176

outside the gates and those newly arrived! We will fall as a great force on the Romans and destroy them! Spread out . . . go!' he commanded.

They ran through the poor quarter of Ophel calling for men to come out and fight for the promised Deliverer who was with them this minute. When they passed the wall into the Lower City, they fell silent. The streets were empty. Groups of soldiers stood at every corner. Everywhere they were questioned. They had been at the Temple, they explained, and were now returning home. They headed for the Gate of the Essenes to find Simon the leper.

Judah took Yesha to a house two streets past the Prophetess' tomb.

More than 150 men from Galilee who had weapons in the city joined the insurrection. Many came from Samaria—more than they knew. From the rest of the country the numbers were uncertain but there were well over 100 men. Thus, together with the warriors of bar Abbas and Irijah, there were at least 500 men in the fight to attack the city archives when they were surrounded by Roman soldiers from the Antonia.

The diplomat, Clavius, had persuaded the Procurator to take as few lives as possible in the streets. He asked Pilate to treat the matter as a mere exercise for the troops and dampen down the Captains and their blood-lust. There would be heavy criticism of wholesale slaughter in the streets if they were not careful; and it would not be forgotten in a hurry. The order was to take prisoners, except in impossible situations where killing the bandits could not be avoided.

Soldiers, both fully accoutred and those in ordinary clothes, who had been mingling with the population, fought a short sharp engagement. As soon as they arrived at the Archive building, the rebels split into their small units and spread out into the streets.

Of the Zealots who were inexperienced in warfare, especially street fighting, many simply took a stand and were, of necessity, eliminated by the soldiers with as little fuss as possible.

Bar Abbas and a group of his men, trying to make for a place where they had agreed to re-group, if all else failed, headed down what turned out to be a blind alley. A detachment of soldiers followed them.

The bandit Chief stepped out to the front of his men and drew his sword. His men held swords and daggers.

'Alive!' ordered the Roman Officer. 'If you have to kill some of them, do it—but I want that man in front! Whatever you do, I want the leader there *alive*!'

With a roar the soldiers charged on the rebels, whom they greatly outnumbered. Swords swung. Rebels fell wounded or dead. Four soldiers were killed trying to capture bar Abbas. Four more went in after him. Sixteen soldiers died in taking bar Abbas.

Irijah was caught crossing to the Upper City. He was badly wounded but they brought him back alive to the prison of the Antonia.

Yesha waited in the house where Judah had taken him. He was in the deepest despair. Over and over he mumbled that he must go out to his men and fight for them and die with them. In some way he had failed his God—some way that he did not understand. It did not occur to Yesha that it was his God that had failed him.

The house was empty. It was damp and seemed as though it had been unoccupied for a long time, which was unusual, for during the Feast there was no house that was not filled to bursting with relatives from the provinces or at least with paying guests.

After waiting for nearly two hours, someone knocked quietly at the door and Judah went to answer it. The caller was Yaacov. He was with another man that Judah had never seen before. Yesha gave no greeting to his brother, but Judah noted a strange flicker of recognition in his eyes as he looked at Yaacov's companion.

'What happened?' Judah asked, apprehensively. Yesha sat moribund, staring at the floor.

'Everything is lost,' said Yaacov.

'The people . . .?'

'They did not rise.'

'*Why?*' Judah asked, anguished.

'The Romans were ready. Too ready. Many came out to fight, but . . .' Yaacov broke off. It was difficult for him to overcome his emotions of defeat.

'Irijah?'

'Taken.'

'Bar Abbas?'

'Taken,' said Yaacov hollowly. 'Everything is dispersed.'

Yaacov looked with pity at Yesha on the floor. He saw that there was no use in comforting him. He understood how his brother felt . . . the cold demons of despair that strangle the heart when God has fled from it.

'How many died?' Judah asked.

'Three hundred. Two hundred were taken. Some . . . escaped.'

'What now?'

'Indeed, what now!' said the stranger. Judah looked at him. He was an old man, though it would have been hard to guess his age. Then Judah realised. Gur ben David was under surveillance, if not arrest. The other Priests were also in danger. This man, Judah felt, was the 'Secret Head', as he had heard two or three times the Council conspirators call him.

'The Procurator has withdrawn his troops to the Antonia, except for extra guards at the Temple and Caiaphas' Palace. He has sent criers through the streets announcing that a band of brigands, intent on looting the city, has been crushed. He has decreed that the leaders of these bandits will be executed tomorrow and the rest will either be imprisoned or executed after the Feast, if there is any more trouble.'

'Leaders?'

'Bar Abbas and Irijah,' Yaacov nodded.

The stranger walked across the room and squatted down beside Yesha, resting on his haunches. 'Remember yourself!' he said sharply.

Judah started, but Yaacov held out his hand and restrained him.

'Remember who you are! *Re-member!*'

Slowly Yesha raised his head and looked into the man's eyes. The man stood up and bent over, reaching out for Yesha's hands. 'Stand up, Master,' he said softly.

Yesha got to his feet.

'Come with me,' he said, and led Yesha into the next room, closing the door on Yaacov and Judah.

'You know what must be done now?'

'Yes,' said Yesha, numbly.

'What is the matter with you? Are you frightened of death?'

'No,' said Yesha.

'Where has your spirit gone, Master?'

'I failed,' said Yesha, and the old angry blazing look returned to his eyes. 'I failed!' he said, incredulously.

'Perhaps not yet.'

'What do you mean?'

'You failed? Yes, the city did not rise. It might have. It still may, though the damage will take a few years to repair. You are sworn to the cause, Master. You have not failed yet. If we complete the prophecies in the proper manner, we can create enough fuss in the Council to rally the people to a symbol. If this is handled correctly, we shall have the Procurator and some of his diplomats removed. A new Procurator may not be as competent as this man Pilate and the movement will flourish. Will you do as I say?'

'Who are you to tell me what to do, Magus?' said Yesha angrily.

'Why do you think the Baptist sent you to me?'

'I don't know,' Yesha replied bitterly. 'But it was a pitiable waste of time.'

The Magus grew black with anger. 'Time? You speak to me of time? I gave you your head with Time. You pushed beyond the limits of our planning and I let you! I let you because the Baptist sent you to me, because he believed you were divinely sent to deliver the nation. I examined you and prayed that you were the Man. I have searched . . . I thought I found him in my pupil but he broke with me and said he was not the one. Then he sent you to me and asked that I support you.'

180

'Your pupil? The Baptist?!' said Yesha, astounded.

'He failed me. You will carry us on and we will win!' said the Magus.

Yesha never believed he would hear such words from this man. There was no evasive humour about him now. He was a man talking politics and it was, Yesha remembered, the Magus who had told him about politics in the world and how they were to Rome as his belief in Yahweh was to Yesha. So—it was the old Magus who had chosen the Baptist and the Baptist had not been able to come to terms with it and then had finally understood his Master's purpose and chosen Yesha in his stead. Yesha was able to understand this without rancour. He had failed and he would die. That was certain. There would be no point in hiding and starting again. The organisation would have to be built afresh and there would be few who would follow him now.

'You think you really are the Man,' said the Magus.

'I *thought*,' said Yesha wearily. 'I prayed. I hoped.'

'I hoped, too,' said the Magus. 'We all did.' He paused. 'But you are not.'

Yesha did not reply. He sighed.

'You could do this your way or you could do it as we planned if the attempt failed. I'm sorry . . . I know you did not think once that it could fail. If you listen to me, we will achieve something out of this in the end. The Lord will choose his Time,' said the Magus and then he laughed. In the midst of so solemn and awesome and desperate a tragedy he laughed!

'You understand the importance of Time?' the Magus asked.

'Yes.'

'Then you understand its unimportance.'

'Yes.'

'And so with life and death.'

Yesha nodded.

'And means and ends . . . and . . .' He would have continued, but Yesha started to laugh. He saw the point of the joke . . . the great joke that lay ahead. Oh how poignant it was; how it brought tears to the eyes sweet as the dew on morning roses. How sad and funny. He laughed and cried at the same time and was aware of a great emotion that could not be described. A joke that lifted from him his greatest burden.

'Where are my men?' Yesha asked when he had calmed down. 'Are they safe?'

'They are with Simon the leper outside the city,' said the Magus. 'They are safe.'

'I wish them to be here with me in Jerusalem so that we may take the Passover meal together. I will not be here for the days of the Feast.'

'I will see that they are here an hour before sundown,' said the Magus.

'Tell me, Magus,' said Yesha intently, 'why does the Council listen to you? I know your wisdom and now I know about the Baptist, but is that all?'

'No,' the Magus nodded. 'You may believe this or not, as you choose. I had a son once. He was Judah of Galilee. He was considered to have failed, too, but *I* don't think he did. I see his spirit burning.'

Simon the leper directed the brotherhood to the house where Yesha was waiting. Judah let them in. Yaacov and the stranger had gone.

'There's a room upstairs. The Master is there,' Judah told them as they arrived one-by-one at the house. Each of them brought some part of the meal, as Simon the leper had told them to. It was a sorry procession. All were tense and aching with hostilities that should have been fought out in the day. They did not understand what had gone wrong. They knew of the men that had been lost and wished they had been there by their sides. They could hardly bear to face the Master.

Upstairs the room was without furnishings. They lit candles when it grew dark. The food was put down on cloths on the floor. No-one spoke.

They broke bread together and drank wine. Then Yesha

took his pouch from his neck and handed its contents to his men.

'When you eat this, think of me. This is my body,' said Yesha, intently.

They joined in the Light with Yesha.

Andros handed Yesha an earthenware jug which Simon the leper had said should be given to him when they had taken the sacrament. Yesha took it as though he were expecting it; he sat for a little while, cradling it in his arms. Deliberately, he took his knife from the floor and cut his arm. He let the blood pour into the liquid in the jug and then put it down and bound up his arm with a piece of cloth. The Rock helped him tie a sound knot. Yesha poured the contents of the jug into the wine-beakers circled around him. The drink was thicker than wine and only slightly red.

'This is my blood and the Light of my blood. Drink it and remember me.'

Each of them drank. This was a great mystery that the Master was unfolding to them. There were no qualms about drinking the Master's blood mixed with wine and an unknown, bitter, salty, sourish potion. The moment was too serious. Already they could feel the power of the Light coming on them. In seconds they seemed to be in the highest realms they had reached in any communions. In the potion there was milk, sourish milk which became sweeter as they drank.

The room became opaque and disappeared. They could hardly discern the shapes of their comrades around them. Yesha dropped the knife and wiped the blood from his hands onto his forehead and temples. It was the blood of the paschal lamb daubed on the lintels of his mind, protecting the God entering the courts of his temples and resting in his Sanctuary.

Matthai saw his Master and all those around him bathed in light and radiating blinding energy. Tongues of fire burst from their heads and great flames devoured them.

Then they were taken away. Their bodies became agitated, the muscles of their limbs were convulsed. Their bodies swelled and their faces distorted into terrific shapes. When the power of the

Lord touched a body, it rolled on the floor, foamed at the mouth
and vomited. The violent paroxysms gradually fell away as they
cried out and shrieked and spoke with tongues.

In this time the knowledge entered them: the knowledge of
their immortal spark and the Almighty's nurture of it, as the
Master taught.

Several hours later, they had all come back to their bodies, each
with a seed of knowledge illumined in him. They were able to
move about the room slowly and clear up the mess of the feast
and their unconscious convulsions. Still they did not speak,
though they were able enough. There was too much to think
about. Thought after thought entered and delighted the senses.
They were oblivious that their bodies had suffered any agonies.
Their thoughts were solely on their fearsome and unknowable
God and the joy and beauty of his creation.

Yesha stumbled slightly walking to Judah who was with the
Rock.

'Go…and do…what you have to,' said Yesha slowly to Judah.

'What do you mean . . . Master?' the Rock asked.

Yesha tried to explain to the Rock. 'Prophecies,' he said. He
could not explain more.

A thousand fears entered the Rock. Someone had gone. The
Master had prophesied something. So many things. All of them
made the Rock fearful for his Master's life and safety. Something
was wrong. Who had gone from them? Judah had gone. Where
to? Why? What had been said? Had Judah said something to the
Master? Had he cursed him? Or what? His love for his Master
was so great.

Yesha went to the window. It was still dark, but the blackness
was turning into the deepest of blues that came a while before
the first tints of dawn. 'Let us leave the city,' suggested Yesha.
'While the stars are shining.'

They left the house, getting used to walking in their bodies.
They breathed the air of the night city—from somewhere came
the scents of a baker's oven at work even at this early hour. The
dawn was the next day and the eve was the first night of the
Feast. They left the city gates unquestioned.

184

'I want to go to a garden . . . to Gethsemane,' said Yesha. 'The night flowers there are . . . everything.'

He walked down the dark road. The embers of thousands of fires at the encampments around the city were the perfect reflection of the stars in the heaven. It was though above and below were one great black globe with stars everywhere. This was the centre of the globe. The walk did not take long, or so it seemed. Yesha led them into a small walled garden where some people had set up their camps. They sat around a fire to which an old pilgrim beckoned them with a welcome.

Some fell on their backs and stared into the sky. Nathaniel and Shimon hummed a holy chant—they did not want to bring out their instruments for fear of waking people. Yesha stared into the fire. The old man had kept it glowing gently by feeding it with small twigs and stems. The Rock sat alert beside Yesha, as though keeping guard.

A few hours later Yesha heard the sounds of a body of people coming towards the garden. Judah had done his work. How Yesha had had to beg Judah to go! In the end, Judah understood that it had to be. He understood what could come of it. He had wept when the Magus explained it to him as Yesha looked on. Now it was done. Yesha turned to the Rock and spoke urgently.

'Rock, are you armed?'

'Yes,' said the Rock.

'Please, now . . . use it only in self-defence.'

'What?'

'Rock . . . if they say they saw you with me, you are to say you have never seen me before! Do you understand me?'

'What, Master?' the Rock cried in consternation.

'Deny that you've ever seen me. Keep the teachings alive, Rock. There are those that will help you.'

'Master, I would die rather than deny knowing you.'

'Do as I say!' said Yesha authoritatively. It was a command.

Then Rock heard them. A squad of Temple guards and perhaps forty soldiers coming up to Gethsemane. He jumped to his feet and ran through the garden alarming those who were sleeping and calling the brotherhood to action.

The soldiers were upon them. Rock saw Judah walking towards Yesha, standing still beside the fire. Judah . . . between two of the guards! Judah walked up to Yesha and embraced him. He said nothing, but hugged his Master intensely for a moment and then stepped aside. The guards stepped up to Yesha and took hold of him.

The Rock went blind with rage. He waved his sword as though he were crazy . . . possessed with the power. In a downward swing, he cut into the helmet of one of the guards. The blow only grazed the guard, slicing into his cheek and taking the lobe from his ear.

There was confusion throughout the garden. Too dark to see, the Rock charged forward and fell over a stone. The guards lost sight of him. He crawled over to the wall. Yesha and a number of others—Shimon, Nathaniel, bar Talmai—were being led from the garden by troops. Then he saw Judah, standing free! The soldiers were passing him by! He had betrayed them!

The Rock stood up and ran across the garden. He drove his sword into Judah and hacked at his body. 'Traitor!' he screamed. 'TRAITOR!'

He was seized by the last guards leaving the garden. They beat him brutally in a cell. They asked him with their fists whether he knew this bandit. He told them he had never seen him before. They kicked him in the head and used a stick on his feet, but he did as his Master had told him and said he did not know the man. The soldiers did not recognise him as the dark figure who had wounded one of them. They knew that he had killed one of the bandits . . . the one who had led them there. The Rock said he had attacked the man with a sword he had found on the ground because the man had a knife and was going to kill the last of the guards from behind. It sounded plausible enough, but was worth a nasty beating.

'You sure?' said a blurry figure. A block of wood crashed into the Rock's jaw.

'I never saw him before.'

It was dawn. Judah's body was buried by the pilgrims in Gethsemane.

186

The Procurator was not delighted to be woken up at dawn, on a public holiday, having just successfully quelled a riot. It was as bad as being woken by his wife and he thought ruefully that he might as well have brought her with him. Usually he left her in Caesarea so that he had a few weeks every year where he was not kept awake by her fits and starts and bad dreams.

'What is it?' said Pilate, wearily, from his bed.

'Procurator . . . the leader of the bandits has been captured!'

Pilate was out of bed in an instant. He splashed his face with water and dressed quickly. 'The one who caused the disturbance at the gate?' he called out.

'We believe so,' said the aide outside the door.

'Where is he?'

'Caiaphas is holding him.'

'What?' Pilate exclaimed. 'Get Clavius up. See that he meets me immediately in my office. Get some breakfast brought there.'

'Yes, sir,' said the aide and hurried off to carry out the orders

Pilate was beginning to remember the events of the day before, and though it was excellent news that the bandit had been captured, it did not sound so fortuitous that he had been taken by the High Priest. That impossible man was bound to be stirring up some kind of trouble for him.

He met the diplomat and several of his officers in his office.

'Where is this man? I want him here! I want him executed with the others this morning!' Pilate stormed.

'The representatives of the High Priest are outside.'

'Send them in.'

Clavius went up to Pilate. 'I have a feeling this is going to need very careful handling,' the diplomat cautioned.

'What are they up to?'

'I don't know yet. We shall see,' said Clavius.

The representatives of the High Priest were admitted and came straight to the Procurator.

'You have taken the rebel leader,' said Pilate. 'I congratulate you. Send him to me and I will deal with him.'

'Procurator . . .' began one of the Priests. 'When we arrested this man we did not know who he was.'

'What do you mean?'

'This is not a rebel or a bandit,' said the Priest. 'He is known throughout the land as a healer and a Holy man.'

'Oh, no. Oh, no,' Pilate sighed. The same old story again. How could they dare after the events of yesterday! 'You try me too much!'

'Why then did you arrest him?' the diplomat asked the Priests.

'We thought that this was the man who had desecrated the Sanctuary, but we have found no proof. No witness can say it was him. None who saw the disruption at the Temple can say for sure that they have ever seen him before. There seems to be little more we can do.'

'There is no question!' the Procurator posited imperiously. 'I want him executed.'

'We have no authority to execute him,' said a Priest.

'Of course you have. What authority did you have to arrest him?'

'It is as has been said, Procurator. This man carried no weapons. He was not even *in* the city—he was arrested outside the walls. Some treacherous fellow—probably a *real* brigand—informed us that this man was the leader of the bandits who caused havoc in the Temple. We see clearly now that this was a lie. It was an attempt to discredit the authority of the Priesthood. There would be a great deal of sympathy for this man if he were treated unjustly.'

'It is a little late to tell me this now. If you are squeamish, send him to me.'

Clavius murmured in Pilate's ear. 'Perhaps it would be best if we did not handle this one,' he said. 'Let us see to it that the Jewish courts condemn him. Let them murder their own Holy men.'

Pilate nodded. 'Tell Caiaphas that he is to give this man whatever fair trial is necessary and then execute him.'

'Our courts can only accuse a man of blasphemy. If a man is guilty of that, we can have him stoned to death. That is all we can do, Procurator, as you know.'

'Then that is what you *will* do. He will be condemned for blasphemy or devil-worship or practising magic . . . whatever you like; then stone him.'

'It is the first day of the feast,' said an old Sadducee.

'Not until sunset, it isn't,' Pilate said sharply. 'Do not assume me ignorant of your customs.'

'Procurator . . .'

'Whether you have him stoned or whether I hang him up with his fellows is no matter to me. However, as it is, the arresting party should be his executioners.'

'We do not execute our Holy men and Prophets!' a haughty Priest declared.

'So now he is a Prophet?' sniped Pilate. 'Next thing he will be the High Priest himself.'

There was an outburst of protest from the Priests. The High Priest would hear of this effrontery, they swore.

Pilate shouted at them. 'You will try him as I say! Tell Caiaphas that this is an order! The man who informed on him will be your witness.'

'The man is dead, Procurator.'

'How is that?'

'He was killed by a valiant free citizen who saw that desperate fellow about to attack our men.'

'A "free citizen"? What man has the right to hold a weapon in the city?'

'It was outside the city, as I believe I have said,' a Priest stated.

'Where is that "valiant citizen" now?'

'He has been questioned and released,' the Priest replied.

'Can you not see,' said the Procurator, as though addressing a class of simpletons, 'that your informer was right? He was murdered before he could talk further, and now you have had the stupidity to release the very bandit who prevented this from happening. Tell Caiaphas my orders. He has bungled and he has amends to make!'

'The High Priest will receive your request,' said the leading Priest, demurringly. The delegation withdrew.

Pilate paced up and down puzzling over what schemes these villainous Priests were preparing. If they had found a man they thought had led the uprising in the Temple and then found that he was innocent, why had they come to tell him? For no other reason than to make a fuss since he had not sent soldiers from the Antonia into the Temple. How could he? They were busy protecting the city from rioters. No doubt if he sent soldiers to their aid, they would have complained the next day that he had interfered in a matter that their own guards could handle—or so they would swear. One thing was clear. The man, whoever he was, however Holy, had been informed on and the informer had been killed. It was a certain indication of the fellow's guilt. Clavius was quite right. Let *them* kill him.

Walking back with the guards, as the sun rose, Yesha took what was left in his neck-pouch and swallowed it. The guards did not notice.

When they got to Caiaphas' Palace, they struck him in the face a few times, asking him who he was. When he told them that he was Yesha the Nazarene, a poor man and a healer, the guards jumped back from him in consternation. They had heard his name. Rumours about the holiness of this man had reached their ears. One of the men hastily told his Captain, who was horrified. The man they held had a huge following among the people. He could not have done what he was accused of or the whole city would know of it. He was a Holy man, a friend and follower of the murdered Prophet Yohanan.

'*Yesha the Nazarene?*' said Caiaphas in alarm when the news was brought to him. 'The informer said . . .' The High Priest felt he had been trapped. The rebels had deceived him into taking the famous Nazarene. It was yet another way of attacking his prestige and his most precarious position. If Pilate were a reasonable man, this whole incident could be hushed up. Caiaphas sighed. The Procurator was not a reasonable man.

The returning emissaries made it clear that the Procurator was not only unreasonable but spoiling for a fight. Caiaphas drew himself up stiffly. Very well—as the Procurator ordered—there would be a trial. He had already questioned the healer and there was no doubt that he was innocent of any blasphemy. Whatever the Procurator ordered, Caiaphas had no intention of killing this man. The whole Council would be summoned. Even at this early hour, they were to be brought to the Palace. Every man in the Sanhedrin would see that justice was done.

Yesha was brought before the assembled Council.

'You have been accused of the crime of blasphemy. You can be stoned to death if you are guilty,' said Caiaphas, formally indicting Yesha. 'Answer if this is true.'

Before Yesha could reply a member of the Council, it was Mannasseh, jumped to his feet crying, 'Who has brought this charge?'

'The charge has been made by . . . the Procurator.'

There was a gasp through the council chamber. Blasphemy there was, but on the part of the Procurator. Who was he to set himself above them on matters concerning their own God?

'It is not true,' said Yesha evenly, when the uproar abated. 'I preach the word of God. You have no complaint with me.'

Another member of the Sanhedrin stood up. He addressed Yesha.

'It has been rumoured that you have been acclaimed by many people as the Deliverer. Do you claim this?'

'If it is said, it is said by the people—not by me.'

This reply was met by a murmur of approval from the assembly.

Another council member stood up. 'It has been said that you heal people by calling for the help of demons,' he said. This was truly a serious accusation. The Council turned to Yesha to see how he would reply.

'Demons do not drive out demons,' said Yesha. 'It is God's love that heals. I have called the names of demons but always to call them from the body and banish them in eternal darkness. I do this as one whom the true God has blessed with the power of healing. You yourselves follow this practice.'

Again the answer met with approval. Caiaphas looked around the room for any more accusations. There were none. Caiaphas rose to his feet. 'I find no blasphemy in this man and cannot condemn him,' he pronounced and the assembly made clear their acclamation. The decision was affirmed in an unanimous vote.

A new group of emissaries came to the Procurator. They were admitted.

'Well?'

'The High Priest sends you his greetings, Procurator . . .'

'What?' Pilate bellowed. 'What is this?'

'The High Priest begs to inform you that the man has been tried and no fault can be found with him on any charges that can be ministered by the Sanhedrin.'

Furious, Pilate turned on Clavius. He spoke low and witheringly to the diplomat. 'Your idea! I am openly defied! I wanted to make an example of this man and by Hell I *will*!'

'Procurator . . .' the diplomat said warningly. There was still time for some last-ditch diplomacy. 'The Court of Herod. The man is from his province . . .'

'No more outcries from him! This city is not under his jurisdiction. Of course, he will refuse to have anything to do with this . . .'

'Pontio, for your sake . . .'

'This is my decision—on my head be it,' he said and then turned to his aides and the emissaries from the High Priest. 'If there is no law and order in the courts then *I* must enforce it,' he spoke sharply. 'Send the man to me.'

'What is the charge?' protested the leader of the emissaries.

'Sedition!' snapped the Procurator. 'I charge the man with attempting to overthrow, with violence, the Government of Imperial Rome and the Divine Emperor. Captain! I want a detachment of men to see that he is handed over! Immediately!'

Yesha stood before the Procurator.

'What have you to say for yourself?'

No reply.

'Get him out of here,' said Pilate with a contemptuous sweep of his hand. 'Crucify him with the others. I want them all dead by mid-day. Take this one and beat him.'

Yesha looked at the strange vermilion creature with no shape and wondered if it had spoken.

Yesha was whipped. Three soldiers kicked him and smashed him in the face. Then he was taken to join Irijah and bar Abbas, who had already been savaged by the soldiers when they were captured. Yesha was very weak and could scarcely register what was going on. The three men were taken to a store-room in the Antonia. The door was unlocked and a Captain flung it open. The room was full of wooden crosses stacked one on another.

'There you are!' said the Captain, cheerily. 'Take your pick.'

They took their crosses from the store-room and lifted the heavy wood onto their shoulders.

A squad of soldiers on execution duty and a further number of legionaries stood by to act as an escort in case there were any further riots or attempts to rescue the bandit leaders on their way to the place of execution.

They were led out of the city by the Tadi gate, for to go through the city markets, on this, the busiest of days, before the Feast started at sunset, would have alarmed any lingering sympathisers. It was a long walk around the North wall to the hill of Goath, the traditional Roman execution-place. The cranium-like shape of the hill was plainly visible from the Upper City, especially the Palace of Caiaphas. It was a hill of no great height or importance, but it presented a slight bump of a silhouette on the skyline. It served its purpose.

The procession moved towards the hill. The path was almost

empty, except for those who had chosen to camp there. No crowds came thronging from the city. They did not yet know what was happening. Others stayed away for fear that they might be arrested as bandits for their curiosity.

Yesha stumbled several times. The beatings had snapped much of his strength and the Light was growing more and more powerful in him so that he could not feel the muscles in his arms and legs. After the soldiers had hauled him to his feet a number of times, they assumed that he had been beaten too hard to carry the cross any further. A detail of soldiers went to the nearest camp, found a stout Greek proselyte and ordered him to come and carry the cross of the weak-kneed criminal. The man had no choice but to comply. As soon as he had deposited his burden at the baleful place, he made off as quickly as he could.

The crosses were laid on the ground and the three men were held down. A big soldier gripped Yesha's arm and held it to the cross with his knees. Another soldier held the wrist down with his foot and tight bonds were tied around so that the arm could not be moved. This process was repeated with the other arm. Then the soldiers turned their attention to Yesha's legs. They lifted the bottom of the cross while other hands crossed Yesha's feet and bound them fast to the wooden stake. This done, they dropped the cross to the ground, leaving Yesha unable to move anything but his head. He lay on his back and stared at the sky. Irijah and bar Abbas were bound in the same way.

The soldiers returned to Yesha and stood over him. One of them carried some thick iron nails. He squatted down and placed the nail over the centre of Yesha's palm. The nail was not sharp. It had been used and pulled out from many crosses.

'Careful . . .' said the soldier holding the nail. 'Don't flatten my fingers.'

There was a clang of metal striking metal and the tearing sound of flesh and small bones as the nail entered the palm. There was a bright spark from the iron as the second hammer-blow fell. The soldier let go of the nail and the one with the hammer brought the hefty instrument down again. After six good blows, the nail was driven well into the wood.

194

'Not a sound out of him,' said a soldier.

'His eyes are open—he's not unconscious.'

'Other hand . . .'

The soldiers moved to the other side of the cross. The nail was driven through Yesha's other hand, deep into the wood. One nail, thicker than the rest, the width of a miller's flat thumb, was driven through his feet just below the ankles. This took many more blows for the thickness of the bone and the strength of the sinews did not yield easily to the large iron peg. Once the point touched the wood, it was banged home easily.

The soldiers stood around for a moment and admired their handiwork. There was not much blood from the wounds, though little red rivulets began to pour and drip onto the ground where it was sopped up in the dust.

'Are you awake?' a soldier asked. Usually the shock rendered their victims unconscious by this time.

'Yes,' said Yesha.

'How do you feel now, then?'

'Feel?'

'Well!' said the soldier to his fellows. 'Here's a cool one!'

The soldiers moved away from Yesha to continue with the ritual, first with Irijah and then bar Abbas. Irijah gave a few sharp cries and then was silent.

'See?' said the soldier's voice. '*He's* out. That's more like it.'

Bar Abbas neither cried out nor was he by any means silent. He cursed his executioners in five different tongues. He swore at them with every obscenity that he had ever learned since he was weaned from his mother's poisoned milk.

'The tough one,' said a voice. There was a crack as the soldier with the hammer, having driven in the last nail, struck bar Abbas on the head to shut him up. Some of the Chief's Syrian curses had themselves struck home.

One by one the crosses were raised and dropped into their slots. The tallest of the soldiers went around with a sharp knife and cut the thongs that had bound the Zealots while the nails were being knocked in. The full weight of their bodies fell on the three nails that supported them. Cartilages cracked, ligaments were torn with a wrench and sinews strained in their sockets.

Yesha did not feel the chafing of his wounds as he arched his back to breathe. He did not hear the bones in his feet shatter as he pushed up for air. Later he did not see the departure of the escort of legionaries with the Chief Executioner. He did not see the small groups who had gathered at the foot of the rise. He saw the Light. In his heart he laughed. He saw the spark of the Light of his life; its travels through uncountable bodies in uncountable cycles of ages. How long he had been growing up . . . growing to be fit to rest in the sight of his father. For how many years, as a man knows years, had his spark of Light been lost from the love, the eternal embrace of his father. His real Father. Had he been lost all this time, or had he lost them as a naughty child? Yesha saw the thousand ages of his childhood and the infinitely loving way his young Light had been nurtured through bodies of aeons of bodies. He wept with joy. Now he was ready! Now he was welcomed! Now he was wrapped in the heart of the Allfather—*his* father. Never again would his Light be moved to make breath for another infant, boy, man—moved and moved again. This time he was home. His father told him that he was home. Whatever it was he had done; however he had got lost, he was welcome!

The soldiers sat around in the heat. Once in a while they looked up to see how the bandits were cooking. They were pouring with sweat. Their robes were soaked. The decurion in charge got up and went from bandit to bandit. He slit their robes with his sword and ripped them off. The sun fell on their naked flesh.

'There!' said the decurion boastfully to his soldiers. 'Who said I have no compassion?'

'Let's see about that,' said one of the soldiers, pointing out to the decurion a man coming up the hill. It was an old Rabbi, a poor one. Even when new his threadbare clothes were poor things.

'Makes yer big heart melt, don't it?' taunted the soldier.

'Well? You, Rabbi?' he called. 'What do you want?'

'I have come to give comfort to these men,' said the old man.

196

The soldiers laughed. 'What is comfort to them?' the decurion asked.

'A little water from a Holy fountain. It will comfort their spirits.'

'Water?' he snorted. 'I'll be breaking their legs in a minute and they'll be dead. If you want to give them water . . .' he looked around at his men with a grin and then turned to the old man. 'Go on. You have permission.'

As the old man climbed up towards Yesha, the decurion made a sign to the soldier with the hammer, who went up and examined Irijah, poking at him to see if there was any life in him. Some lasted days, some were dead in minutes. Irijah was alive. The soldier swung his hammer several times until the bones in the bandit's legs were completely smashed and limp. Now he had no leverage. Suffocation would take his life quickly.

The old Rabbi took out a sponge and poured some liquid from a water-skin onto it. He held it up to Yesha's lips. 'Suck!' he said urgently. 'Drink this!'

Uncomprehendingly, Yesha sucked at the cold wet sponge. In his mind he saw his father giving him water and he was so thirsty. The water tasted bitter. Suddenly the great Light started to fade. Blackness closed in all around. Darkness took away his father! His own Light was being taken. 'Elohim! Elohim! Don't leave me!' he screamed. His head slumped on his shoulder. The soldier with the hammer had just started smashing bar Abbas' legs.

'Clear off, Rabbi,' said the decurion. 'There's no point carrying on.'

The old Magus looked at Irijah and bar Abbas. He nodded to the decurion and ambled slowly down to the bottom of the hill, where others stood.

The soldier with the iron hammer took a last hefty smash at bar Abbas' knees. He looked up. Bar Abbas no longer had the breath to curse. The soldier looked satisfied. Swinging his heavy mallet jauntily, he walked over to Yesha. It looked like blood was trickling from his mouth. The soldier shook the body. He peered into the face. Already there was a tinge of blue in the bandit's lips.

'Hey!' he shouted. 'This one's dead!'

'Is it the one they beat this morning?' the decurion asked.

'Yes,' the bone-breaker called back.

'Leave it, then,' the decurion told him.

At mid-day the decurion inspected the bodies. His instructions were to see that they were all dead by this hour. They were. He had no orders what to do then. He waited, but no-one came to relieve him or give him any new orders. He sweated out in the sun until the middle of the afternoon, then decided to take his men back to the garrison. Usually they gave the bodies of criminals to relatives or, if there was no mother or wife, to anyone who asked.

'Anyone want these bodies?' he yelled.

Eleazar, Miriam and Yohanan came up the hill.

'Which one?' said one of the soldiers, getting ready to decamp. Yohanan pointed to Yesha. Another group came to claim the body of Irijah.

'This one?' the soldier asked, pointing to Yesha with his spear. 'Yes.'

'You're sure it's *this* one?' said the soldier, meanly sticking his spear into Yesha. He laughed uproariously and walked away to form up with his squad.

With the greatest care, Eleazar, Yohanan and Miriam took Yesha down from the cross. They were horrified at the wound in his side. They wrapped the body in a white shroud. Blood pumped slowly from the wound into the sheet. Miriam moved around to hide it.

Those who took down the body of Irijah then took down the body of bar Abbas. The decurion and his men waited.

The soldiers lifted the crosses from their slots. Three men carried each cross down the hill on their shoulders. The decurion led the way. The last soldier, unburdened by virtue of having won at dice, brought up the rear. They carried the crosses back to the store-room.

# Epilogue

Thirty-three years later the Zealots were so strong throughout the land that they seized Jerusalem. The people rose and the Romans were driven from the Antonia and every one of them was massacred. The High Priest and his brother were murdered.

The Zealot leaders were Eleazar, who was a captain of the Temple guard and the son of a former High Priest, Ananias, and Manahem, a son of Judah of Galilee. Manahem declared himself to be the Saviour and put on the sacred Robes-of-State as King and High Priest in the Sanctuary of the Temple. He was driven out by a rival group of Zealots through the Huldah gates into the Ophel quarter where he was tortured and torn to pieces.

Three years later the Romans came back in force. They killed a million and a half Jews. The Temple was burnt to the ground and razed until not one stone stood on another.

The Zealots retreated to the fortress of Masada where they were beseiged for three and a half years by the Romans. Finally, the Tenth Legion under Flavius Silva, with thousands of prisoners, built a ramp up to the impregnable mountain stronghold. Nine hundred and sixty men, women and children chose death rather than surrender on the night before the Legion took the fortress and appointed ten men to kill them all. From the ten one was chosen to kill the remaining nine. This man set fire to the food-stores and the palace and fell on his sword beside his sacrificed family.

When the Romans marched in the next morning, they had a shocked and hollow victory.

Meanwhile, on the road to Damascus . . .